Handsome and the Yeti

Genderbent Fairytales Collection

By KuroKoneko Kamen

Copyright © 2018 by KuroKoneko Kamen

Cover Design by Leah Keeler

ISBN-13: 978-1717046352
ISBN-10: 1717046355

All rights reserved. No part of this book may be used or reproduced in any manner whatsoever without written permission except in the case of brief quotations embodied in critical articles or reviews.

This is a work of fiction. All characters are invented. Any resemblance to persons living or dead is purely coincidental.

Other works by the author:

<u>Genderbent Fairytales Collection</u>
Handsome and the Yeti
Handsome and the Yeti audiobook coming soon!
More genderbent fairytales coming soon!

Rockstar Ghost
Rockstar Ghost audiobook coming soon!
Rockstar Ghost Resurrection
His Heavy Metal Heart
Rockstar Ghost: Wedding Night

Wicked Bartender
Wicked Bartender audiobook coming soon!
Wicked Bartender Redemption

Incubus Chocolatier
Incubus Chocolatier audiobook coming soon!
Incubus Chocolatier Retribution

Hollywood Merman
Hollywood Merman audiobook now available!
Hollywood Merman Revelations

Druid Vampire
Druid Vampire audiobook now available!
Druid Vampire Requiem
Druid Vampire: Wedding Night

Vampire Punk

Twilight Gigolo

Galactic Goth
Galactic Goth audiobook coming soon!

Highlander Hellcat
Highlander Hellcat audiobook now available!

Highlander Hellcat Revolution

Bitch Heiress X Samurai Butler
Bitch Heiress X2 Samurai Butler

<u>Samurai Superheroes Saga:</u>
Cowboy Samurai X Badass Android
Geisha Assassin X Smartass Hacker
Foxy Yokai X Punkass Cyborg

Sir Genkaku Host Club
(Books 1, 2, 3, and 4)

Sanky Panky Pirate
Sanky Panky Pirate Part II

This book is dedicated to-
Ely Fanconi
&
Auntie Maritza Rodriguez

Chapter 1:

Bellamy DeWinter lived in a small town in northern Alaska named Yeti Town. The town got its namesake from the Nepal folklore legend of the yeti, also known as the Abominable Snowman. A yeti was an ape-like creature, taller than an average man and covered in snowy, white fur. Apparently there'd been sightings of such a creature in the nearby forests by the Hunters that lived in town and the town's name had been changed shortly thereafter.

The majority of the people that lived in Yeti Town were either Hunters or furriers. This was mostly due to the sudden increase in predators - bears, polar bears, lynxes and wolves - that started appearing around the town. This abrupt influx of predators in the area put not only the human towns that were in close proximity to the creatures in danger, but also the farms and cattle ranches, which had livestock to worry about protecting.

In recent years and in this modern era, the hunting of animals for their furs had become controversial, but due to the fact that this increase in predators in the area was *not* natural, but unexplainable the Hunters of Yeti Town were able to make a living hunting, and killing these predators and selling their meat and fur. Since they were providing a service to the ranchers and farmers the controversial aspect was entirely overlooked, and the Hunters were looked upon as heroes.

Eighteen-year-old Bellamy and his mother, Doris, had moved to the isolated town because Bellamy was *cursed*. If a female saw Bellamy without his round, nerdy glasses on his face she would instantly fall in love with him.

Bellamy had been aware of this strange curse since he could form rational thought, and his mother had taught him how to stop the effects of the curse by always wearing a pair of nonprescription glasses. Sunglasses would also have the same affect, and could nullify the effects of the curse.

When Bellamy became a senior in high school his luck finally ran out. Due to his nerdy appearance he'd been targeted by a group of bullies, taken to the men's room, and beaten up. His glasses had been punched off his face and then stepped on.

Bellamy left the bathroom while trying to keep his head lowered, but it was inevitable that he had to look up to see where he was going. Unfortunately, at that very moment lunch had ended and the hall was flooded with students. When Bellamy looked up a large number of female students saw Bellamy's handsome face and instantly fell in love with him.

At the time, Bellamy was living with his sickly mother, Doris, in their tiny apartment. The place was so small there was no escape from the phone that started ringing off the hook from Bellamy's fan girls that began calling. Bellamy's fax machine also started spitting out love letters from his new stalkers.

At first it was almost funny, but then the content of the love letters started to become more and more desperate as time passed. Other handwritten letters that were delivered by the mailman started to include photos of the girls, locks of their hair, fingernail clippings, and some letters were even written in blood. It was downright creepy.

Bellamy's mother, Doris, already had a weak constitution and could barely handle the added stress of the unsettling love letters, the phone ringing off the hook, the girls that stood on the sidewalk outside of their apartment building demanding to see Bellamy, and later the kidnapping attempts on her son. It all just became too much for Doris to handle.

Even the therapy sessions Doris had been going to no longer gave her peace of mind. After the most recent kidnapping attempt on Bellamy, Doris decided that she had to protect her son somehow. Doris was also filled with an overwhelming sense of guilt. It was *her* fault that her son Bellamy was cursed after all. Doris had suffered from the curse herself before Bellamy had been born, and the curse had been passed onto him.

After one of Bellamy's babysitters had tried to kidnap him, Doris decided she had to find a way to stop the curse from activating and had started covering Bellamy's face with a scarf to see if that would work. When it did, Doris tried covering Bellamy's face with just a mask where his eyes were barely visible, and this worked too. Next Doris tried sunglasses and when those worked she lastly tried nonprescription glasses.

Doris had the feeling that the reason the nonprescription glasses worked to stop the effects of the curse had something to do with the old mythos that 'the eyes are the windows to the soul'. As long as females didn't make direct eye contact with Bellamy he was safe from the effects of the curse.

Wearing glasses had become a simple solution to stop the curse, and Doris and Bellamy had been able to live in peace for many years. Doris reprimanded herself that perhaps she should have warned Bellamy to be more careful at school, or provided him with an extra pair of glasses, but it was too late now. Bellamy's female classmates had already fallen crazily in love with him.

It was also around this time that Doris learned of the death of her parents. They'd been Hunters living in Yeti Town and had been overwhelmed by a pack of vicious wolves during one of their usual hunting expeditions. The hunting cabin that used to belong to her parents now belonged to her. Doris instantly decided to take Bellamy to live there. There in the isolated town Bellamy would be *safe*.

Unfortunately, Bellamy wouldn't be able to graduate from high school, and it would be difficult for him to get into a college without a high school diploma, when and if they found a way to break the curse. But that's why Doris was determined to support her son financially.

This is how Bellamy DeWinter found himself living in the small Alaskan town with his sickly mother. To make a living Doris made woodcarvings of various animals that lived in the Brooks Range area of Alaska: brown and black bears, polar bears, moose, goats, foxes, coyotes, ravens, lynxes, and wolves.

For hours and hours Doris would sit in her comfy armchair by the fireplace in the living room, and carve little wooden figurines of animals until the calluses on her fingers popped and bled. She was highly skilled at woodcarvings.

Sometimes Bellamy would help his mother by making woodcarvings of his own, but usually Doris insisted that Bellamy didn't need to do anything to help out with the household finances, and that he should instead continue to concentrate on his self-study.

Bellamy knew his mother felt guilty and blamed herself for their current situation because of the curse. But Bellamy didn't see it that way. He saw it as *his* fault that they had to live here in the middle of nowhere now. If only he'd been braver and fought back against those bullies. If only he hadn't let them break his glasses, none of this would have happened.

Because of him, his mother had gone through a lot, and her already poor health had declined from all the stress. That's why he never complained to his mom about living there in Yeti Town. There were only a few young single women his age in the town that might have showed an interest in him, and he made sure to avoid them as much as possible.

Most days, Bellamy had his nose stuck in a book in self-study. He was determined to go back to school one day, and get a college degree. He wanted to get a high-paying job so that he'd be able to support his mother financially, and give her the easy life she deserved after everything that had happened.

Bellamy had to admit to himself that it could get rather boring though living there when compared to how his life used to be back in New York. There wasn't much to do for fun in Yeti Town. The town's inhabitants were mostly Hunters, and Bellamy had no interested in learning that particular trade. The other people that lived there were either a part of the Hunters' families, jewelry makers, or woodcarvers like his mother.

There was a mine close to Yeti Town that contained several types of semi-precious stones that the townspeople made jewelry out of. Alaska was known for its jade, quartzes and even diamonds, but this particular mine contained other semi-precious stones that were normally found in South America.

Bellamy had become fascinated by all the different types of semi-precious stones the jewelers worked with - agate, quartz, rose quartz, onyx, obsidian, jade, jasper, red jasper, tiger's eye, turquoise, lapis lazuli, and more.

The semi-precious stones may not have been as valuable as diamonds, rubies and emeralds, but Bellamy thought that they were uniquely beautiful in their own way.

To stave off his boredom, Bellamy started going to the small local library and checked out all the books that were available on gemstones, and gemology. Bellamy had his nose buried in a book about stones more often than not.

Bellamy didn't care about his lack of a social life since all he wanted was to protect the peaceful life he and his mother were currently enjoying in Yeti Town. His books became his only friends. It was lonesome without any friends his age, but peaceful. And Bellamy just wanted to keep it that way.

However, peace and quiet never lasts forever. The Hunters had become curious about their new neighbors and had confronted Doris about Bellamy. After they'd discovered that Bellamy was so young they instantly decided that he must be lonely, and should make some friends his own age. The Hunters immediately told their children that were around the same age as Bellamy all about him, and of his 'plight'.

This meddling resulted in someone knocking on Bellamy's front door one Saturday night. It was eight o'clock at night. Doris was in her usual spot, seated on the plush armchair by the fire in the living room and carving a small piece of wood into the shape of what Bellamy thought looked like a dancing monkey. *Oookay.*

Bellamy was seated in the armchair across from his mother, nose in a book about Alaskan jade. He frowned and looked up from his book at the door, wondering who would be coming to visit them at this late hour.

A secretive smile curled Doris's lips when she heard the knock at the front door. "Could you be a dear and get the door, Bellamy?"

Bellamy frowned and his brow furrowed slightly. His mother was acting different from usual. "Are you expecting someone, Mom?" he questioned as he stood up, and approached the front door with his now closed book still in hand.

"I'm not," she began softly. "But you are."

"Huh?" Bellamy said as he opened the door to see who it was. Staring back at him with wide, mischievous grins on their faces were two young men around Bellamy's age. Because of their flashy fur coats Bellamy deduced they were the sons of Hunters right off the bat.

One of the young men had sandy-blonde hair, pale skin, and honey-brown eyes. The other was an African-American teen with short black hair, brown eyes, and super white teeth. They were both wearing friendly, amiable expressions on their faces, but this didn't make Bellamy any less nervous about what their intentions were. He already had a bad feeling about this.

They looked past Bellamy and smiled at Doris. "Good evening Mrs. DeWinter. We're here to pick up Bellamy."

Doris nodded knowingly. "You boys have fun!"

"Thanks, Mrs. DeWinter!" The African-American teen crowed as he and his friend latched onto Bellamy's arms and began to drag him out the door.

"Huh? Wait, what?" Bellamy sputtered, giving his mother a look of sheer disbelief. Why had his mother o-kayed this? Didn't she realize how dangerous it was for Bellamy to hang out with people his own age?

When his mother just waved him off, Bellamy let out a resigned sigh. *My life officially sucks.* He thought morosely as the sandy-haired teen shut the door.

Bellamy glowered at the two young men that had interrupted his precious reading time. "Who the hell are you guys?"

The two teens chuckled in amusement at Bellamy's surly attitude. "I'm Crispin," the sandy-haired boy started and jerked his thumb at the African-American teen. "And he's Oscar."

"And we're here to rescue you, Belle." Oscar flashed his gleaming white teeth in a teasing grin.

A muscle beneath Bellamy's eye ticked in irritation. "Rescue?"

"Yeah, our parents told us all about you," Crispin began to explain. "Like about how you didn't get to graduate from high school due to your mother's health, and more importantly how you have no friends."

Oscar slung an arm around Bellamy's shoulders amiably. "But fear not. Now, you have *us*."

"Wonderful." Bellamy's tone was sarcastic.

"We're going to introduce you to the other people in this town that are our age, so you can make even *more* friends," Crispin said excitedly.

Bellamy felt his temples beginning to throb. Just how important did these guys think having a social life was? He was already feeling exhausted.

"And more importantly we're going to introduce you to the fine, single ladies in this town." Oscar waggled his eyebrows at Bellamy in a playful manner.

"And this is what I was afraid of," Bellamy muttered darkly to himself in a voice so low that the other teens didn't hear him. A chill of fear crawled up his spine, and he had to suppress a groan of despair. Young men his age had a one-track mind. This was nothing new. All they ever thought about was girls and sex.

The last thing Bellamy wanted right now was to be introduced to girls though. If something happened, and they saw his face - they'd fall madly in love with him. And go slightly crazy. Their 'love' would quickly turned into lustful desperation. *And those girls can become freakin scary.* He shuddered as he remembered how his old female classmates had finally formed an alliance and had tried to kidnap him.

What had his mother been *thinking* letting him go out with these guys? Sure, *they* were guys, and thankfully the curse didn't affect them, but guys his age were *always* on the prowl for chicks.

Bellamy felt like hitting his head against the wall repeatedly. *Why me?* He inwardly moaned. Before Bellamy had even realized it, his two new 'friends' had dragged him down the main street in town and had stopped in front of some kind of bar or tavern.

Like most of the rustic buildings in Yeti Town it was made out of logs and had a sloping roof. Swinging over the front door from two chains was a hand-painted, wooden sign shaped like the head of a polar bear. The polar bear's mouth was wide open and clenched between its sharp teeth was the establishment's name: *Polar Bear Pub*.

Crispin puffed up his chest proudly and waved his hand at the pub in a dramatic fashion. "And this, my new friend, Belle, is the *Polar Bear Pub*. It's the best bar in town!"

"It's the *only* bar in town," Oscar added dryly.

"My older brother, Wren, is one of the two bartenders working here, so we'll be able to get a couple of beers!" Crispin bragged, since technically they were still underage.

"Great," Bellamy droned as he was dragged into the pub. He couldn't help but glance around at the interior décor curiously. Most of the long tables and chairs were made out of solid pinewood. An enormous stone fireplace took up most of the back wall and several comfy looking chairs had been situated in front of it.

Animal head and antler hunting trophies covered the walls. Though Bellamy wasn't too surprised by this since pretty much all of the men drinking in the pub were Hunters. Bellamy was able to recognize them as Hunters due to the outfits they were wearing: white or gray fur coats, winter camouflage, and heavy boots. The rifles and shotguns leaning against their chairs were also a dead giveaway.

There were two bars inside of the *Polar Bear Pub* - the largest that took up most of the right hand side of the pub was exclusively for the adults. A shorter bar on the left was for the teenagers that were around Bellamy's age. Really, the teens should have only been allowed to order nonalcoholic drinks but the adults seemed to turn a blind eye if their children wanted to have a few beers on the weekends since they were being supervised anyways.

Crispin and Oscar led Bellamy over to a small group of teens that were surrounding the bar on the left. "Hey, everyone," Crispin began in a loud voice to get everyone's attention, "I want you to meet the new guy in town - Bellamy DeWinter."

The group of teens' focus was suddenly on Bellamy and he could tell that they appeared to be excited about a newcomer to their small town. Bellamy raised his hand in an awkward greeting. "Hi."

Almost instantly, Bellamy was surrounded by a mob of teens that were bombarding him with a ton of invasive, and personal questions. "Where are you from?"

"New York," Bellamy replied.

"Ooo he's a city boy," a girl cooed.

"Why did you move *here*?" one of the boys asked in an incredulous tone.

"My mother's health-" Bellamy started to explain, but was rudely cut off by one of the girls.

"Is it true you didn't get to graduate from high school?"

A scowl formed on Bellamy's face. "Yeah."

"Home schooling rules!" a random boy shouted and fist pumped the air.

"Are you single, or do you have a girlfriend?" a girl asked boldly with a glint in her green eyes.

"I, er, I'm single," Bellamy reluctantly answered after a long stretch of silence had passed as the teens awaited his response.

"Eeee!" the girls squealed loudly. Bellamy was forced to plug his ears with his index fingers in order to drown them out.

Just how desperate were these Alaskan girls? Bellamy wondered worriedly. They hadn't even seen him without his glasses yet and they were already acting ridiculous. He supposed their behavior had a lot to do with the fact that it was slim pickings for a boyfriend when you lived pretty much in the middle of nowhere.

Bellamy mused for a moment about what things might be like if his circumstances had been different, and if he weren't cursed. Perhaps, he would have been happy to be surrounded by a bunch of desperate, pretty girls. As things were, however, he remembered just how crazy girls who thought they were in love could be and shuddered.

Crispin grabbed three beers from his bro at the bar, and quickly distributed them. Crispin and Oscar held up their beer bottles in Bellamy's direction. "To new friends!"

"Yeah." Bellamy could barely keep the skepticism out of his tone as he clinked his bottle against theirs. He bitterly remembered what had happened to his high school friends once their girlfriends had inexplicably turned their sights on Bellamy, and how they'd given Bellamy the cold shoulder after that.

As oftentimes happens with groups of teenagers, the group split in two - girls and boys. Bellamy was actually glad for the girls' sudden apparent shyness. He could breathe easier without them being in such close proximity.

An hour ticked by without incident, and Bellamy was beginning to feel hopeful that perhaps nothing bad would happen to him this evening. Letting his guard down a little, Bellamy glanced around the pub and couldn't help but notice an incredibly attractive young woman that was seated at a table, surrounded by a group of fawning guys.

Bellamy's eyebrows rose to his hairline as he took in her flashy appearance. She was wearing a tight, v-neck, red dress along with a floor-length white and black fur coat. The corner of Bellamy's lip twitched in amusement since the coat was definitely necessary to provide her with warmth when wearing such a skimpy dress. Her thick, black hair cascaded down around her shoulders in waves, and sultry lashes accentuated her intelligent, dark brown eyes.

Bellamy took a sip of his beer as he let his gaze travel over her curves appreciatively. He was a little buzzed. He pointed his beer in her direction. "What's the deal with Cruella de Vil over there?"

"Isn't she beautiful? Her name's Astonia Sharpe," Oscar began, a dreamy expression on his face. "She's French. And she's awesome. She's also my future wife. She just doesn't know it yet."

"Uh huh," Bellamy agreed dryly.

Crispin draped his arm around Bellamy's shoulders conspiratorially, a rueful smirk playing on his lips. "You'll have to get in line." He nodded his head in the direction of the guys surrounding Astonia with hearts in their eyes. "All those guys over there are in love with her. It's like she has her own personal reverse harem."

Bellamy had been in the middle of taking a sip from his beer and promptly began to choke at Crispin's words. "Harem?" He arched an eyebrow. "You don't mean she's sleeping with all of them?"

A flash of anger crossed Oscar's face at Bellamy's careless words. "Hey! Don't talk about Astonia like that! She's *not* that kind of girl!"

Bellamy quickly put his hands up before him in a surrendering gesture. "Whoa, sorry man. I didn't mean anything by it."

"She's just a big flirt," Crispin began to explain. "It's pretty obvious she just likes the male attention. Apparently, no one in this town has even managed to *kiss* Astonia yet."

That dreamy, lovesick puppy look was back on Oscar's face again. "There's nothing I wouldn't do to get a kiss from Astonia." He released a wistful sigh of longing.

"Yeah, good luck with that," Bellamy said as he took another sip of his beer to hide his unease. Crispin and Oscar's obsessive behavior with Astonia was a little too similar to how the girls who saw Bellamy's face without his glasses acted.

"It sucks that *everyone's* in love with her," Oscar muttered darkly. "But how could they not be? She's smoking hot."

"In love?" Bellamy arched an eyebrow at Oscar. "In *lust* maybe," he murmured to himself. Those guys over there were just in love with Astonia's outer appearance. There was no telling what kind of person she was on the inside, but as Bellamy watched Astonia preening under the boys' attention he began to get an idea of how narcissistic she was, and shook his head disappointedly.

Astonia was just playing with those guys. But playing with people's *emotions* was dangerous. Love was dangerous. Bellamy knew this from firsthand experience. He grew bored of observing Astonia and remembered that luckily he still had his book with him. He opened it up and began to continue his reading about Alaskan jade, and how the term was really referring to two minerals - Jadeite and Nephrite.

Astonia surreptitiously glanced over at Bellamy DeWinter - the 'new guy in town'. She was sure that he was probably gawking at her stupidly just like all the other guys in the pub, but she was in for an unpleasant surprise when she saw that he'd actually taken out a book and had started to read at his own 'welcome to the town' party.

Astonia's jaw slowly dropped open as she gawked at the bookworm. He was completely ignoring her presence! It was like she didn't even matter. And after she'd done him the honor of gracing his party with her presence. Astonia Sharpe did not like to be ignored - *would* not be ignored! *How dare that nerd ignore me! Just who the hell does he think he is? Hah?* She thought venomously.

"Would you look at that? That nerd is actually reading a book in the middle of this party. How pathetic," Astonia sneered loudly, and her boy toys laughed in a jeering fashion as if on cue.

Bellamy just sighed, ignored Astonia's immature outburst, and continued to read. He was used to people making fun of him and bullying him due to his nerdy appearance.

A muscle beneath Astonia's eye ticked in irritation as Bellamy continued to ignore her. "I mean, how *uncool* is that? Maybe he moved here because he's mentally disabled or something." She cackled and again her boy toys joined in.

Finally, Bellamy shut his book with a loud snap. He turned and glared at Astonia. "You like making fun of *disabled* people?" He narrowed his eyes at her critically.

Astonia flinched guiltily. "What? No. It's just you're so...*weird*." She waved her hand through the air as she tried to search for a better word. "So...different from the rest of us."

"Well, excuse me for being weird." Bellamy slid off the barstool, book in hand. "It's become much too noisy in here to continue reading my book." He turned to give Crispin and Oscar an apologetic look. "Sorry, guys, I'm gonna call it a night." He started to head for the front door.

Astonia fumed as she watched Bellamy. She hadn't even dismissed him yet! *He* was dismissing *her*. *I'll show him.* Just as Bellamy passed by her chair she stuck her foot out and tripped him.

Bellamy fell flat on his face, and his glasses flew off his face, skidding across the floor. His eyes widened in panic as soon as he realized what had just happened. *My glasses! Shit!* He inwardly swore. Bellamy frantically scrambled across the floor, reaching out for his glasses, but someone beat him to it.

"Oops, sorry." Bellamy heard Astonia's voice as he watched a delicate hand with red-painted fingernails reach out and pick up his glasses. "I have such long legs that it's hard for me to keep them under the table."

Bellamy swallowed nervously and stood up as slowly as possible. He tried to keep his head lowered and his face shielded by his bangs. "Give me back my glasses, Astonia," Bellamy demanded as he reached his trembling hand out to her. *Shit, shit, shit. Just don't make eye contact. Don't make eye contact.*

A wolfish smile curled Astonia's red lips. "What's the magic word?"

"Please," Bellamy said through gritted teeth.

"Alright, fine. Here you go, *nerd*." Astonia laughed as she handed Bellamy his glasses.

Bellamy let out a sigh of relief, grabbed his glasses, and quickly raised his face so he could put his glasses back on.

Suddenly, it was eerily quiet inside of the pub and Bellamy realized that Astonia had stopped laughing. With his glasses now on his face, Bellamy risked looking up at her.

There was a look of astonishment on Astonia's face, her brown eyes wide. "You…you're so *handsome* without your glasses. How is that even possible?"

"Shit!" Bellamy swore in her face realizing it had only taken a second - just *one* measly second - for the curse to activate. "Sorry…I gotta go!" He turned and bolted out the front door.

Less than a minute later, however, the pub door opened, and Astonia emerged chasing after Bellamy. "Hey, Belle, wait!"

Bellamy grit his teeth and didn't slow down. That's when a gunshot split through the night and a mound of snow that was directly next to Bellamy exploded. He decided he'd better stop unless he wanted to end up full of holes.

"I said 'stop'," Astonia called out in a strangely calm tone. "Turn around."

Bellamy gulped, raised his hands in a surrendering gesture, and turned around slowly to face Astonia. His eyes widened when he noticed that Astonia was holding an old-fashioned double-barrel shotgun in her hands. Most of the Hunters these days used semi-automatic rifles or pump-action shotguns.

Astonia approached Bellamy with a smile curling her scarlet lips. She stopped only when the gun barrel was pressed against Bellamy's chest. Bellamy knew that she had one shot left in the shotgun. "You ran away from me." There was an incredulous note to her voice. "That wasn't very nice. Now, take off your glasses. I want to see your face again."

Bellamy hesitated, but he had no choice - this lovesick biatch was crazy enough to blow a hole in his chest if he refused. He removed his glasses and glared at Astonia. "Happy?"

Astonia gasped, blushed, and lowered her gun. "I didn't imagine it then. You really are drop-dead handsome. Do you know what this means?" she asked Bellamy in a giddy manner.

"No. Not really," Bellamy replied warily.

"I finally have a boyfriend!" The Huntress exclaimed happily.

"And *who* would that be exactly?" Bellamy's brow furrowed in confusion.

"You, silly." Astonia shoved his shoulder playfully. "You're the most handsome guy in Yeti Town. And that makes you the best. And I deserve the best."

Bellamy swallowed thickly, and wiped his hands on his pants to try and hide his nervousness. "And if I *refuse*?"

Astonia raised her gun at Bellamy and pointed it at his heart. "I'm known for my bullets never missing their mark. Especially, if it's the heart of a handsome young man. There is *no* escape. You are mine, Bellamy DeWinter."

Bellamy's head was throbbing; he could feel a headache coming on. He rubbed at his temples with his index fingers. *Shit, shit, shit.* Bellamy had no choice but to agree to this ridiculousness. For now. He couldn't cause his mother any more problems and stress. "Fine. But I really need to get going now. It's getting late and my mom waits up for me." He turned to go.

There was a soft clicking sound as Astonia began to playfully pull down on the trigger. "Aren't you forgetting something?"

Bellamy turned back around, and raised his eyebrow at the Huntress. "What?"

Astonia offered him an innocent smile. "Where's my goodnight kiss, Belle?"

A muscle in Bellamy's jaw ticked. "Think you could at least lower your gun first? It's kind of a mood killer."

Astonia laughed loudly and lowered her shotgun. "Of course, darling."

Bellamy stepped forward reluctantly until he was standing directly in front of her. He tilted his head sideways and leaned forward for a kiss. He intended for it to be a quick peck on the lips, but as Bellamy tried to pull back Astonia wrapped her arms around Bellamy's neck and kissed him fervently.

Then Astonia started to try to get her tongue into his mouth in a desperate manner. Bellamy stubbornly refused her entrance, and kept his lips pressed together.

Once Astonia finally pulled away so they could breathe again, they were met with boisterous cheers, catcalls, and whistles. "Whoo! Yeah!" "Way to go, city boy!"

Bellamy groaned and looked past Astonia to see that a crowd of people had gathered in front of the *Polar Bear Pub*. The pub's patrons had become curious due to the gunshot going off outside, and had all exited the pub to see what Astonia had done now.

Bellamy spotted Oscar's betrayed expression in the crowd, and felt his stomach twist itself into knots. *Great, just great. More icing on the shitty cake.* "Now, I really gotta go. See-ya." He sped off down the snowy sidewalk and did not look back.

Astonia smiled and waved. "So long, honey!"

When Bellamy reached his home he opened the door as quietly as possible and entered. Thankfully his mother was fast asleep in her chair by the fireplace, and didn't hear Bellamy as he rushed into the bathroom, sunk to his knees in front of the toilet, and proceeded to puke his guts out. *That crazy bitch...*

He felt...violated.

Was it normal for a guy to feel that way when a hot girl kissed him? He wondered ruefully. Still, that kiss had been *against* his will - even if she *was* attractive. Other guys would have probably done anything to be in his shoes. But not Bellamy.

He was feeling overwhelmed as his body was wracked by dry heaves. There was only acid left inside of his stomach at this point. Suddenly, it was all just too much. All the stolen kisses he'd experienced throughout his life, all the unwanted groping. He'd been treated like an object. He supposed he knew what a lot of women must feel like - being treated like sex objects.

I'm being retarded. I'm a guy. What does a stolen kiss matter? Bellamy scolded himself as he straightened and made his way over to the sink. He brushed his teeth and rinsed his mouth out with *Listerine*.

After that he splashed water on his face and looked at his haggard expression in the bathroom mirror. His already pale skin was even paler than usual, his deep blue eyes were sunken, and his long dark brown hair, which he wore pulled back into a ponytail, looked limp and lifeless. Everything that had happened tonight was because of his handsome face. He was almost tempted to just pour acid on his face, but...

That would just make his mother cry, and then she'd probably blame herself for his rash actions. Bellamy decided that he had to deal with the 'Astonia problem' some other way, and without his mother finding out about all this.

Bellamy began to pace across the tiled floor as he thought about his options. He wondered if just giving in to what Astonia wanted might lessen the effects the curse had on her. Maybe after she'd slept with him she'd leave him blessedly alone. It was his only hope.

He was going to have to get his mother out of the house in order to put his plan into action. Bellamy knew that his mother was planning to travel to the next town over to sell her accumulated woodcarvings to a gift shop there in just a few days. That's when he'd put his plan into action, he decided.

Bellamy quickly wrote a letter to Astonia, and set up a date with her to make sure she wouldn't show up while his mother was still at home. The night of his mother's departure, he and Astonia would dine together, and then…he shuddered. He'd give himself to Astonia. Bellamy only hoped Astonia would be patient and wouldn't show up randomly to do something stupid while his mother was still at home.

***

Doris DeWinter knew something was bothering her son Bellamy. Over the following days, Bellamy helped her to finish her woodcarvings until a nice sizable collection was ready for her to take to the next town over where she sold them to a gift shop that specialized in having souvenirs for tourists visiting Alaska.

A couple of the carvings she was going to sell were of a yeti. Or at least, what Doris thought a yeti probably looked like. She pictured him as being a tall, monkey-like creature with fluffy fur covering his entire body except for his face. She'd come up with the idea to carve the yeti due to the town's popular urban legend that an actual yeti, or Abominable Snowman, had been spotted in the forest nearby.

All of the Hunters in Yeti Town wanted to kill the yeti and get famous. Doris shook her head ruefully. She had the feeling that her yeti woodcarvings were going to be a hit.

Despite appreciating her son's help with the woodcarvings, Doris couldn't help but notice that ever since the party he'd gone to with the Hunters' teenaged boys he'd become awfully quiet and withdrawn. She began to worry that perhaps *something* had happened at the party, which Bellamy hadn't told her about.

She'd just wanted Bellamy to have the chance to make some friends his own age, but maybe she shouldn't have meddled. It had been selfish of her to force Bellamy to go to that party when the reason she wanted him to go was to relieve her own guilt over the fact her son hadn't been able to finish high school and currently didn't have any friends.

Doris still felt responsible for the curse that her son now suffered from and for him having to live out there in the middle of nowhere with her.

When the day of Doris's trip to the next town arrived, Bellamy helped her to pack all of the woodcarvings into a large burlap sack which he then secured to the back of the dogsled. A team of five huge Huskies was already attached to the sled. The dogs were incredibly intelligent and would be able to get Doris to the next town even through a snowstorm.

Doris was dressed in a gray fur-lined coat that had pretty, white fur trim on the hood, a pair of winter camo pants, gloves, a scarf, and heavy boots. "Thank you, Bellamy," Doris said as she mounted the sled, and picked up the long, brown leather reins.

"Don't mention it, Mom," Bellamy said. He rubbed the back of his neck uncomfortably. "You sure you're going to be okay on your own out there?"

Doris offered Bellamy a reassuring smile. "I'll be just fine. I've made the run on my own before and the dogs know the way. What would you like me to bring you from Coldfoot? A new jacket? A new book?"

Bellamy thought for a moment. He didn't want to trouble his mother with buying him anything. But there *was* something he wanted. He was missing a rose quartz for his stone collection. Surely, it wouldn't pose too much trouble for his mother to find him a small rose quartz at the gift shop. "Can you bring me back a small rose quartz for my stone collection?"

Doris raised an eyebrow at the humble request. Most teens his age would probably have asked for the latest smart phone. "A rock? That's all. *Bellamy…*"

Bellamy took his mother's hands in his and squeezed them tight. "Yes, mother - a rock. You know I love stones. And it's the only one missing from my collection."

Doris gave Bellamy a searching look, but then let out a resigned sigh. "Oh, alright. If that's *really* what you want. I'll bring you back the prettiest rose quartz I can find."

"Thanks, Mom." Bellamy leaned over and placed a kiss on his mother's cold cheek, momentarily warming it against the frigid Alaskan air.

There was a haunting sadness in Bellamy's blue eyes, and Doris wanted to do something to erase it. All they had was each other.

"Be safe," Bellamy added when his mother didn't get the sled underway immediately.

Doris smiled thinly, and snapped the reins. "Mush!" The dogs barked and shot off down the snow-covered road. As soon as Bellamy was out of sight, she frowned. Her son was hiding *something*. But she'd have to wait until she got back to find out what it was.

Driving a dogsled was easier than it looked since the dogs did most of the work. Or at least, this is how Doris felt about it. She barely had to guide their movements with the reins since the dogs confidently knew where they needed to be going, having done this run with Doris before. Doris also felt safe and protected having five huge dogs with her and probably would have been scared if she'd been out there alone on a snowmobile.

It wasn't long before they were winding their way through the forest with tall pine trees on either side of the narrow path. A wolf's howl echoed through the forest making Doris swallow nervously. She wasn't a Hunter like her parents had been and never carried a gun with her. Her dogs were her only protection against predators. So far she'd never had a problem on this road between the two towns. But she was feeling slightly paranoid for some reason. That howl had sounded a bit...unusual. "It couldn't be...the yeti?" Doris mused aloud with a nervous tremor to her voice.

Abruptly, from out of the trees a gigantic, white polar bear emerged onto the road right behind Doris, thudding loudly behind the sled. It opened its maw wide, and roared at Doris loudly, showing off its sharp teeth.

"Oh my God, a polar bear!" Doris's eyes flared in alarm. She snapped the reins. "Mush! Hurry! Go faster!"

The team of dogs broke into a faster run, and continued their way swiftly down the main snowy road with pine trees blurring past them on either side.

Just up ahead, Doris saw that a tree had fallen onto the main road, blocking their path. "Oh no!" There was nowhere else to go. "Wait..." She spotted another road to her right and steered the dogs to head in that direction instead.

Doris and the dogs flew down the narrow path and just a few minutes later exited the edge of the forest, emerging onto an expansive frozen lake. Doris squinted as she tried to see the other side of the lake but it was so far away it wasn't visible yet.

Even though it was unsettling how large the lake was, Doris didn't hesitate in snapping her reins again. "Mush!" Her sled flew over the thick ice of the lake smoothly.

The polar bear burst out from the tree line a few minutes behind Doris and her dogs, and charged after the sled. The ice started to crack due to the polar bear's tremendous weight. "We're not going to make it," Doris moaned, but then she miraculously reached the other side of the lake. The sled shot down a narrow path, which ended at a black wrought-iron gate that was a part of a towering stone wall that enclosed a large estate.

For a moment, Doris wondered if she'd have to get off the sled and try to figure out how to open the gate - when the gate opened of its own accord. Doris briefly pondered if the gate was electric, but snapped the reins and drove the sled through the open gate.

Doris glanced over shoulder, her mousy brown hair whipping in front of her face, and obscuring her vision slightly, expecting to see the polar bear following her through the gate, but watched as the polar bear skidded to a halt at the open gate entrance. It opened its maw and roared angrily, and appeared to be frustrated that its prey had escaped.

Doris frowned, wondering why the polar bear hadn't followed her inside, and watched as the wrought-iron gate slowly closed behind her on creaking, rusty hinges. When Doris turned her attention to what was in front of her, she gasped in astonishment.

Doris and the dogs were approaching a Tudor-style mansion that looked like it'd fallen right out of a fairytale storybook. The mansion was made up of several different wings with triangular-shaped roofs. The dogs guided the sled right up to the sweeping staircase that led to the front door.

Doris hopped off the sled and approached the mansion warily. She put her foot down on the first step, and looked down due to the clicking sound of her booted heel hitting the surface of the step.

The steps looked like they were made out of blue ice. Doris removed of her glove before reaching down and touching the step. She'd expected it to be freezing cold, but she realized it wasn't ice. It was a blue quartz crystal.

Doris laughed at her own foolishness. Apparently, she'd watched the movie *Frozen* one too many times. This wasn't a palace made of ice, but it was still incredibly impressive. It must have cost a fortune to build the mansion entirely out of blue quartz like this. Doris mused about the possibility of an eccentric billionaire living there.

She carefully made her way up the slippery stairs, and arrived at the front door. Her dull brown eyes were immediately drawn to the beautiful doorknocker. It was made out of a dark blue lapis lazuli and had been carved to resemble the face of a yeti with a large metal ring in its mouth. Doris reached out and stroked the doorknocker. "What incredible craftsmanship." She took a deep breath to steel her nerves, grabbed the metal ring, and knocked. The door opened and she stepped inside.

To be continued in…Chapter 2:

Chapter 2:

"Oh, thank you. I seem to have lost my way-" Doris rambled as she entered the mansion, and the door was shut behind her. But when Doris turned around to see who'd opened the door for her - there was no one there. She frowned. "That's funny, I could have sworn I heard *someone*."

Standing next to the door was a six-foot tall statue of a male butler with a stern expression on his face. The statue had been carved out of a gigantic piece of gleaming, polished onyx. Doris's eyes widened at the sight of the statue, and she approached in order to get a closer look.

She reached out and touched the groves of its intricately carved suit. "Extraordinary. Whoever carved this statue was a master sculptor. There's so much detail. Even the checkered pattern of the butler's tie has been carved into the stone." She stared into the butler's face for a moment. "He almost looks...*alive*."

That's when Doris heard the sound of retreating footsteps. "Hello?" She called out, glancing around the impressive foyer. The floor of the foyer was checkered stone in different colors - blue lapis lazuli, blue-green turquoise, brown tiger's eye, orange jasper, and green Jade.

"Bellamy would *love* this place," Doris mused aloud as she walked over the stunning floor and entered the living room. A large, crackling fire was blazing inside of the marble and brick fireplace. An armchair that appeared to be upholstered with a dark green material sat directly in front of the fireplace.

Doris walked over and took a seat. "Ow." She hadn't expected the chair to be so…hard. At first, she'd thought the chair had been upholstered with a velvet material, perhaps satin, but now…Doris ran her hand over the green arm of the chair. "Jade. This chair is made of solid jade." Her voice was tinged with awe. She'd never seen a piece of furniture quite like it before.

Out of the corner of Doris's eyes she caught sight of a female silhouette. "Ah, finally, another person." But when Doris turned her full attention upon the figure she discovered that it was a statue carved into the likeness of a maid, and made entirely out of lapis lazuli. Doris's eyes widened as she took in the detail of the maid's outfit - her frilly little hat, apron, and heels. She also looked incredibly lifelike.

Those statues were beginning to give her the creeps. Just where was everyone? Doris wondered fretfully. *Someone* had to have opened the front door for her, and *someone* had to have lit the fire.

Doris shrugged her shoulders and allowed herself the luxury of warming herself by the fire for twenty minutes. That's when the clinking sound of cutlery reached her ears. "Hello?" Doris stood up and headed in the direction she'd heard the noise come from.

She entered a spacious dining room. The twenty-foot long dining table was made out of a solid piece of obsidian and was surrounded by eighteen armchairs that were made of different semi-precious stones for a very colorful effect.

At the head of the table on the other side of the room a place setting had been arranged with a plate of food and a full crystal goblet of red wine. Also, standing on the other side of the room was another stone statue. *Oookay.*

This statue was made out of translucent blue quartz and had been carved to resemble a little girl that reminded Doris of Shirley Temple with her head of ringlets and cute, frilly dress with puffed sleeves and *Mary Jane* style shoes.

Doris warily approached the head of the table and took a seat on the hard chair. She was famished, and salivated as she looked down at the plate of food sitting in front of her. It could only be described as gourmet cuisine: stuffed quails, *au gratin* potatoes, steamed green beans drizzled with garlic butter, and a slice of freshly baked bread.

Unable to hold back her ravenous appetite any longer Doris dug in. "Oh my God, this is so delicious." Doris moaned as the tiny bite of quail she'd plopped into her mouth practically melted on her tongue. She'd never eaten anything so decadent before in her entire life.

She picked up the crystal goblet next, took a sip of the wine, and when she discovered it was sweet she chugged it back. The wine warmed her belly pleasantly. She set the now empty goblet back down on the stone table and would have felt embarrassed by her behavior if she hadn't been alone.

"Would you like some more wine?" a small, childish voice asked.

"Oh, yes, thank you," Doris absentmindedly replied.

Someone began to refill Doris's goblet. Doris's eyes widened slightly as she watched the red wine being poured into her goblet and turned to see who was doing that. She gawked at the sight of the statue of the little girl refilling her goblet. A scream slipped past Doris's lips, and she scrambled out of her chair as she immediately tried to put as much distance between herself and the statue as possible.

"Oh drat, Daddy told me I wasn't supposed to move," the little girl lamented. "I forgot."

"G-G-Ghost!" Doris exclaimed as she ran out of the dining room. This mansion...was *haunted*. The stone statues were...*alive*!

Doris exited the mansion, ran down the front steps as quickly as she could without breaking her neck, hopped onto her sled, grabbed the reins, and snapped them. "Mush!" She commanded her dogs and they obediently took off, heading for the front gate.

Doris had almost reached the gate when the garden suddenly captured her attention. All of the plants were made of stone. The bushes were stone clusters that resembled crystalline sea anemones that had burst out of the ground.

One such cluster was made entirely out of rose quartz. *Bellamy.* Doris thought, abruptly remembering her son's request for a small stone. Doris pulled back on the reins, halted the sled, and hopped off before approaching the odd rock formation. "How beautiful. Surely, one little stone would not be missed?" She reached out and broke off a piece of rose quartz. However-

An angry roar boomed all around her and emerging from behind a stone tree was-

Doris gasped and dropped the piece of quartz from her limp fingers. "The yeti."

The yeti was...*real*. The urban legend was true! The six-foot tall yeti had a somewhat slim figure that was covered in fluffy, white fur. Doris frowned when she noted that the yeti appeared to be female due to its womanly curves, and slender waist. The yeti's midriff had been shaved to reveal the creature's blue skin and bellybutton.

The yeti's monkey-like face had sky-blue skin, and her otherworldly eyes were solid silver. The yeti had long, messy white hair, and a pair of small black horns curled out of the top of her head, making Doris gulp at their *demonic* appearance.

The yeti girl was furious. "Ungrateful thief! Was my gracious hospitality really that lacking?" she demanded with her hands on her hips.

"I-I'm sorry. I did not mean to...I...it's just a stone," Doris finished lamely.

"*Just a stone?*" The yeti echoed with a dark edge to her voice. "That's what I thought once upon a time, but no longer! I was cursed to look like this because of one tiny stone! Come with me!" The yeti grabbed Doris's arm and began to drag her along while heading back towards the mansion.

"W-Where are you taking me?" Doris asked breathlessly, her entire body trembling in fear.

The yeti arched a fluffy white eyebrow at her. "The dungeons. Where else?" A cruel smile curled the yeti's dark blue lips, revealing her pointed fangs.

"D-Dungeons?" Doris stammered, right before she fainted.

***

As soon as his mother's dogsled was out of sight, Bellamy called Astonia and told her to come over for dinner at seven. Bellamy felt nauseous as he thought about what he planned to do with Astonia that night. He was going to give her his virginity. After that, hopefully she'd leave him and his mother alone so they could just live in relative peace and quiet.

I'm a guy...it shouldn't really matter who I give my virginity to. I'm not some innocent maiden. I shouldn't even be bothered by this. Bellamy told himself firmly.

Keep telling yourself that, Bellamy. A skeptical sounding voice piped up in his mind.

Bellamy ignored his reservations and cooked Astonia dinner. He'd decided to make a simple chicken potpie. Just when he was taking it out of the oven - the doorbell rang.

"Coming!" Bellamy called out, setting the potpie down on the kitchen counter. He approached the front door, and opened it to reveal Astonia.

"Hello, darling. Did you miss me?" Astonia questioned with a sly smile playing on her lips, but continued speaking before Bellamy could even respond. "Because *I* missed you."

"Yeah, sure," Bellamy replied evasively as he dodged a kiss and ushered Astonia inside.

Astonia was wearing a floor-length, orange, fox fur coat that had a large hood that she lowered as she made her way inside Bellamy's home. When Astonia removed her coat to hang it on a peg by the door it revealed what she was wearing underneath - a knee-length, black dress with an orange belt, and thigh-high black leather boots with pointed toes.

"Mmm, something smells good," Astonia commented appreciatively as she sniffed the air. "What did you make?"

"Chicken potpie," Bellamy replied in a droning tone.

"Well, I'm starving. Let's eat!" Astonia declared happily.

"Sure," Bellamy agreed.

Astonia watched Bellamy like a hawk while he served two plates with generous slices of chicken potpie, and carried them over to the small, round dining table where Astonia was already seated.

Astonia glanced around the interior of the kitchen with a scrutinizing look on her face. "Your home is so *small*." She scrunched up her nose in a snooty manner. "Your entire house could easily fit inside of my living room."

A muscle in Bellamy's jaw ticked in irritation at Astonia's condescending attitude. What the hell was he supposed to say to a rude comment like that anyways? "That so?"

"Oh, yes, my family owns an enormous mansion. It's the biggest in Yeti Town," Astonia bragged. But then a thoughtful frown formed on her face. "Well, *second* biggest. There used to be a mansion near here that was even larger than our own. That's funny…I can't remember what happened to it." She shrugged carelessly. "Whatever. It's not important. After I manage to track down and kill the yeti - I'll be rich and famous. Then I'll have a mansion built that's even bigger than my parent's."

Bellamy arched an eyebrow at Astonia's bold and slightly crazy declaration. "Don't tell me you actually *believe* in that silly urban legend?"

Astonia's expression turned serious. "Oh, I do. It's not just a legend. The yeti exists. And I will hunt it down and kill it. I'm sure its white fur will make me a nice coat." Her red-painted lips curled into a wicked smile at the thought. "I'll probably have enough fur to make a matching hat and muffler."

Bellamy swallowed nervously at the fierce, somewhat murderous expression on Astonia's face. He was beginning to feel sorry for the yeti. He knew what it felt like to be in Astonia's sights. And what it felt like to be prey that had no escape. "I don't doubt it."

Throughout dinner, Bellamy could scarcely eat a bite of his potpie. His stomach was tying itself up into knots and he felt nauseous. He couldn't wait for this to all just be over. *I'm doing this for my mother and for her peace of mind,* Bellamy reminded himself.

Astonia asked for some wine and after Bellamy managed to find her a bottle she pretty much ended up drinking the entire bottle by herself. She was such a boozehound.

Bellamy regretted he hadn't drunk more - it may have helped with his nerves.

Dinner was over far too quickly, and Astonia chugged back the last of her wine. A predatory glint came to her brown eyes as she set the empty wineglass down on the dining table, and licked her lips. "That was delicious, Bellamy. Thank you. I think it's time for *dessert*." She stood up from her seat, sashayed over to Bellamy, grabbed his arm, and forcibly hoisted him out of his chair.

With a morose expression on his face, Bellamy looked down at his untouched plate of food. Astonia hardly noticed his unease, and started to bodily drag Bellamy up the stairs to the second floor. She impatiently looked down the hall, and nibbled on her lower lip. "Which one is your room?"

"Second door on your left," Bellamy informed her.

Astonia dragged Bellamy over to his bedroom, opened the door, and shoved him inside before flicking on a light switch that illuminated the room. Astonia took a moment to critically inspect Bellamy's room. To the left was a single bookcase filled with books on woodcarving, carpentry, and gemology. To the right was a desk and chair. The desk's surface was covered in books that were either piled up or open. Scattered along the desktop was a colorful collection of semi-precious stones.

A small frown formed on Astonia's face as she took in the amount of books that were in this room. "That's...a lot of books. And is that a rock collection? You really are such a *nerd*. If you weren't so good looking without your glasses I would *never* go out with someone like you."

Bellamy remained silent.

Astonia shrugged and her attention turned to Bellamy's bed. At least it was king-sized and was covered by a cushy patchwork quilt. Astonia supposed that Doris had probably made Bellamy that quilt. She felt a flash of jealousy since her parents would *never* make her such a sentimental gift.

Bellamy flinched slightly at the sound of Astonia closing and locking the door. The Huntress grabbed Bellamy's hand and led him over to the bed before shoving him down onto it. Astonia smiled devilishly at Bellamy as she began to perform a sensual striptease for him.

First, she removed her boots one by one. Then she unbuckled her orange belt, twirled it in the air like a lasso, and tossed it aside. She probably thought that was sexy but Bellamy just cringed at the display. Astonia reached behind her and started to unzip her dress. She slid out of the dress to reveal her lingerie: a black silk bra trimmed with orange fox fur and matching silk panties.

Bellamy raised an eyebrow at the lingerie that looked a little Halloweeny - but of course he wouldn't dare to say that out loud. "Is that...fox fur?" Bellamy questioned instead, and swallowed, his throat felt dry.

"Why, yes, it is. Isn't it beautiful?" Astonia grabbed Bellamy's left hand and placed it directly over her right breast. "Isn't it so soft? I *love* furs."

"I hadn't noticed, *Cruella*," Bellamy said sarcastically.

Astonia only looked mildly irritated by the comment. She sauntered closer and straddled Bellamy's prone body. Astonia reached out and removed Bellamy's glasses before setting them down on the nightstand.

When Bellamy's handsome face was finally revealed Astonia let out a little squeal. "Eeee! Oh, Belle, you really are so handsome!" Unable to hold back her sudden burning desire for him she leaned over and smashed her lips against Bellamy's.

Bellamy didn't reciprocate the desperate almost bruising kiss. He just lay there, and let Astonia do whatever she wanted. The Huntress continued to kiss Bellamy as deft fingers began to undo the buttons of his shirt. She started to have trouble with one of the buttons, however, and growing impatient decided to simply rip Bellamy's shirt open, sending buttons flying through the room.

Bellamy's eyebrows rose at the action while Astonia just smirked against his lips and kissed a trail of hot, wet kisses down to his collarbone where she nibbled at his flesh there. Bellamy had the sinking feeling that Astonia was trying to give him a hickey, and was already worrying about how he'd hide it from his mother.

Astonia pulled back and admired her handiwork for a moment before resuming her ministrations and kissing her way down Bellamy's bare chest. Bellamy turned his head to the side as he tried to ignore what was happening and where Astonia was most likely headed.

Astonia kissed her way down Bellamy's lean, muscular chest until she reached his bellybutton. She decided to lick his bellybutton teasingly before laving her tongue down his happy trail to the waistband of his pants. "Let's see if little Belle wants to come out and play. Shall we?" The Huntress started to undo the top button of his pants.

Bellamy gulped, and the sound of his zipper being pulled down seemed strangely loud in his ears.

At that very moment the sound of dogs barking and howling from right outside the house reached their ears. Bellamy's brow furrowed in confusion as he wondered how his mother could possibly be back already. He realized that something must have happened and unceremoniously shoved Astonia off of him before running over to the window and moving the curtain aside so he could look outside.

Bellamy looked down and saw his mother's dogsled, but...there was no sign of his mother. The burlap sack filled with the woodcarvings was still attached to the back of the sled. A chill of unease crawled up his spine at the sight. "Mother!" He snatched his glasses off the nightstand, put them on, and ran for the door.

Astonia was shocked by Bellamy's sudden behavior. "Bellamy? What's going on? Hey!"

Bellamy ignored her as he exited the bedroom, flew down the hall, ran down the stairs, and headed for the front door. He spotted Astonia's old-fashioned double-barrel shotgun sitting next to the door and picked it up. On an afterthought, he decided to grab Astonia's leather knapsack that was most likely filled with cartridges for the shotgun.

Astonia's indignant shriek came from the top of the stairs. "Bellamy DeWinter, don't you *dare* walk out that door!"

Bellamy glanced over his shoulder up at Astonia, who'd hurriedly wrapped the bed sheet around her body. He held up her shotgun and smirked. "I'll be borrowing this, babe. Thanks!" Bellamy opened the front door, exited, and slammed the door shut behind him.

"Bellamy! You get your ass back here, right now! Argh!" Astonia's outraged scream could be heard through the door.

Bellamy continued to ignore the Huntress, and rushed over to the sled. "Hey, boys, what happened? Where's Mother?" He pet and soothed the whining dogs. Bellamy walked around the sled and examined the burlap sack filled with woodcarvings. Three slashes had been ripped into the fabric.

Those slashes looked like...claw marks. *Mother!* Bellamy thought worriedly. Not even bothering to get his winter coat, he hopped onto the sled, grabbed the reins, and leaned forward to speak to the dogs. "Take me to Mother, boys. Mush!" He snapped the reins, and off they went.

The dogs unerringly took Bellamy through the forest until they reached a fork in the road. A fallen tree barred the left path, but the dogs didn't even pause and took the right fork, heading down this side path until the sled exited the edge of the forest to reveal an enormous frozen lake.

Again, the dogs didn't hesitate as they shot out running across the frozen lake's surface. Bellamy heard the sound of the ice cracking beneath them, and gulped. He looked over the side of the sled, but the ice appeared to be holding their weight. For now.

Up ahead was a thick cloud of mist that Bellamy wasn't able to see through. The dogs didn't seem to be bothered by the mist though and as soon as they'd successfully crossed the lake they entered the mist and continued their way until they came to a towering, black wrought-iron gate that was a part of a stone wall that encompassed a large estate.

The way the gate opened on its own made Bellamy wonder if it were electric. As soon as they were able the dogs shot forward pulling the sled inside and past the outer wall. The dogs led Bellamy past the gardens. Out of the corner of his eye, Bellamy noticed that all of the plants, trees, bushes and flowers all appeared to be made out of different color quartz stones.

The stone garden was amazing, but Bellamy barely noticed its splendor due to his worry about his mother. Any other time, he would have definitely stopped the sled, whipped out his magnifying glass which he always kept handy in his back pocket, and studied the stones to his heart's content.

Bellamy's blue eyes flared as the Tudor-style mansion came into view, and then towered over him impressively. It appeared to be made out of ice. No...a blue quartz stone, perhaps?

It was stunning, but Bellamy was *still* more concerned about his mother than anything else. As soon as the sled stopped in front of the staircase that led to the mansion's front door, Bellamy hopped off the sled, and ran up the slippery stairs.

He didn't bother knocking, just grabbed the doorknob, turned it, and opened the door before letting himself inside. "Mother? Mother! Where are you?" Bellamy called out as he made his way into the foyer.

Bellamy started when he caught sight of a figure out of the corner of his eye. He spun and saw a statue made of onyx that looked like a butler. *Oookay.*

He chose to ignore the statue for the moment, and continued his way further into the mansion, while continuing to call out for his mother.

"Bellamy?" a raspy voice reached his ears.

Bellamy narrowed his eyes at the door the voice appeared to have come through and opened it. He ran down the steep stone steps and entered what could only be described as a medieval dungeon - a long corridor with cells on either side. He swallowed and called out again, "Mother?"

"Bellamy, I'm over here," Doris called out weakly.

Bellamy followed the sound of his mother's voice until he found the cell that she was in. He set the shotgun and leather pouch down on the floor before grabbing the cold, metal bars with his hands, and peering inside of the cell. The cell was incredibly primitive, and looked like it had simply been carved out of the rock and then enclosed with a barred door.

Bellamy frowned when he noted that there didn't even appear to be a bed for his mother to lie on. "Mother!" He called out to her, spotting her seated on the floor towards the back of the cell with her back against the hard, cold stone.

Doris forced herself to stand even though her back ached and walked over to the barred cell door. "Bellamy, what are you doing here?" She shook her head. "It's too dangerous for you to be here. You need to leave this place before *she* comes back."

"She?" Bellamy shook his head; there was no time for that now. He had to get his mother out of there as quickly as possible! He looked around wildly for something he could use to break the padlock on the door. *Shit.* He was beginning to feel helpless when his eyes landed on the shotgun he'd borrowed from Astonia. He decided the butt of the shotgun would have to do.

Bellamy picked up the shotgun and slammed its butt end into the padlock until the lock broke. "Yes!" He flung the cell door open. The barred door protested against its rusty hinges and creaked loudly. Bellamy rushed inside and immediately wrapped his mother up in a protective hug. "Mom. Don't worry. I'm getting you the hell out of here."

Doris hugged Bellamy back, but a frown formed on her face. "But, she-"

"Shhh. Come on, let's go." Bellamy picked up the shotgun along with the leather pouch before placing an arm around his mother's waist in order to support her so that they could begin their escape. In this manner, they began to climb the stairs that led to the first floor of the mansion.

As Bellamy helped to keep her standing, Doris admired her brave, strong son for a moment, and couldn't help but notice that the front of his shirt appeared to have been ripped open. "Bellamy, what happened to your shirt?"

"It's a long story, Mom," Bellamy replied evasively, and decided to quickly change the subject. "Who the hell has an actual dungeon in their home these days, huh?"

Doris eyed Bellamy suspiciously for a moment before letting out a resigned sigh. She'd make Bellamy tell her all about it later. "It's like something right out of a horror movie."

They exited the door at the top of the stairs, and made their way into the foyer with its magnificent, checkered, rainbow-colored stone floor. "We're almost there," Bellamy said softly as they headed for the front door.

"Halt right there!" a growling female voice called out in an imperious tone.

Shit. Bellamy turned to face the voice, and gawked at the sight before him. "The yeti?" A creature with a feminine appearance was descending the curving grand staircase, which led to the second floor landing. The yeti was covered in fluffy, white fur all over except for its face and midriff where it had blue skin. The creature's eyes were a solid silver color with long, dark lashes. Bellamy's eyes darted up to the tiny horns on the beast's head. "It's real?" He raised the shotgun in his hands and pointed it right at the yeti. "Stay back you…*monster*!"

The yeti's eyes flashed with anger and she let out an enraged roar before running the rest of the way down the stairs. Bellamy hesitated since he wasn't a hunter or killer, but then pulled down on the trigger anyways. His hesitation cost him though, and the yeti nimbly dodged the shot.

"Shit!" Bellamy swore, realizing he didn't have time to reload the shotgun before the creature would be upon him. The yeti grabbed the shotgun right out of his hand and proceeded to crumple the gun into a ball with its bare hands. "Holy crap!"

Bellamy blurted as he took in the creature's show of superhuman strength.

Doris was looking at Bellamy with a shocked expression on her face. "Bellamy, where did you get a shotgun?"

The yeti opened its mouth and roared loudly into Bellamy's face. "You…you tried to shoot me! You…you're a *hunter*, aren't you?" she demanded in a scathing tone.

Bellamy was surprised by how feminine the yeti's voice sounded, and he also couldn't help but notice that the yeti appeared to be wearing dark blue lipstick. *Okay, that's weird.* He thought. "I…I'm not a hunter. I just came here to get my mother."

"Ah, yes, your mother," the yeti sneered, her expression darkening. "She will not be leaving here any time soon. She is a thief and must pay for her crimes."

"My mother is *no* thief!" Bellamy objected, his anger beginning to overshadow his fear of the yeti. "What do you *claim* that she stole?"

"This!" The yeti whipped out a rose quartz crystal and shoved it in Bellamy's face so he could get a better look at it.

Bellamy's heart sank in his chest at the sight of that beautiful rose quartz stone - instantly realizing that this was all his fault. Everything was always his fault.

The yeti took Bellamy's silence as agreement to his mother's crime and smiled cruelly. "Your mother has earned herself life imprisonment. She will *never* leave here. *We* won't let her. You, however, are free to go." The creature waved her hand at the front door and gave Bellamy an expectant look.

Bellamy fleetingly glanced at the door, gauging the distance he and his mother had to cross before making it out of there. He swallowed and focused his attention on the yeti once more. "We?"

Bellamy hoped that maybe the yeti was bluffing about not being alone. If she were alone then maybe if Bellamy fought against the creature he could buy his mother enough time to escape.

But that's when Bellamy caught sight of movement out of the corner of his eye and glanced around the foyer. He blinked. There were suddenly a bunch of stone statues inside of the foyer that hadn't been there before. The statues had been carved to resemble maids and butlers, and had been made out of a variety of different types of semi-precious stones.

"Statues...?" Bellamy muttered to himself when they started to move and close in around him and his mother. His eyes flared in alarm. The statues...were *alive*? Damn, now they were totally outnumbered. How could he get his mother out of there now? He wracked his brain for a solution. His sickly mother would never last down in that cold, dark dungeon.

A sudden desperate, wild idea came to Bellamy. He turned to look at the yeti and raised his chin. "You're wrong. My mother is *not* a thief. I told her to bring me back a rose quartz for my stone collection. Therefore, the blame lies with *me*. Allow me to take my mother's place down in the dungeons."

A flicker of surprise crossed the yeti's face at Bellamy's suggestion. "You would do that? Aren't you afraid I'll eat you up?" The yeti reached out and caressed Bellamy's cheek with her blue-skinned and clawed hand.

Bellamy gulped as he looked at the sharp, black claws on the yeti's hand. His gaze shot up and he watched as the yeti licked her lips and gave him a predatory look. Or at least, she tried to give him a predatory look...he couldn't help but compare the look to Astonia's. There was something off about how the yeti girl was looking at him. Was she faking her malevolence? "I'm not afraid to die...if it means my mother will be safe."

"Bellamy!" Doris objected, wringing her chilled hands together.

"Very well. You may take your mother's place in the dungeons," the yeti girl said without taking her eyes off Bellamy. "And your mother is free to go."

"No!" Doris grabbed onto Bellamy's arm and shook it. "Bellamy, I can't let you do this! Not for my sake! I'm old, I-"

Bellamy placed his hand overtop Doris's hand on his arm, and gave her a stern look. "Mom, I won't cause you *more* suffering. I'll be alright. Trust me. Go."

The yeti let out a huff, she was beginning to grow impatient with this sappy goodbye and she spoke to her stone servants. "Escort this young man's mother outside and make sure she leaves the estate."

"What? No!" Doris objected as two stone statues shaped like maids grabbed Doris by her arms, picked her up, and unceremoniously carried her towards the front door while her feet dangled above the checked floor.

"Mother!" Bellamy called out in concern, and shot a heated glare the yeti's way. "You don't have to be so rough with her."

"Be gentle with his mother," the yeti called to her servants who obediently set Doris down on the floor and simply walked beside her as she reluctantly made her way to the front door. "Now, you...come with me." The yeti grabbed Bellamy's wrist and began to drag him towards the door that led to the dungeons.

"Bellamy!" Doris cried over her shoulder.

"Mother!" Bellamy couldn't help but call back as he was dragged away. He was taken down into the dungeons and tossed into the cell next to the one that his mother had been in earlier. The yeti shut the cell door and used a large padlock to lock it.

Bellamy flinched at the sound of the padlock clicking into place. It reminded him of a death knell.

The yeti stared thoughtfully at Bellamy for a moment as he stared back at her through the bars. Her gaze left his face and traveled down to his chest. That's when the yeti noticed his open shirt and the small red marks on his pale skin. She frowned, wondering what he was doing in such a state of undress. Surely, he hadn't been outside dressed like that. He must have had a jacket that had somehow gotten lost in the mansion during his rescue attempt. "Why are you dressed like that?" the yeti girl couldn't help but blurt out, her curiosity getting the better of her.

Bellamy closed his shirt with his hand and smirked. "Sorry, but I'm a gentleman. I don't kiss and tell."

The yeti raised a bushy white eyebrow at his words. "Were you having fun with your girlfriend before you came here?"

"She is *not* my girlfriend!" Bellamy panted, suddenly wild-eyed.

The yeti girl took a step back in surprise at the young man's venomous tone. "Oh. Well, that's a strange thing to say. Dressed like that you'll probably catch a cold down here. Sucks to be you, idiot."

Bellamy's brow furrowed in confusion at the yeti girl's odd behavior. "Why would you care? I'm your prisoner, remember?"

"R-Right…who says I care? I *don't* care. You can freeze to death for all I care. Idiot. Hmph!" The yeti flipped her long white hair over her shoulder, turned on her heel, and stalked away in a huff, leaving a bewildered Bellamy behind.

What the hell? Bellamy thought and the corner of his mouth twitched. *I feel like I was just talking to a girl my own age…and not a monster.*

He shrugged lackadaisically since there was nothing he could really do about it, and walked over to take a seat towards the back of the cave. He rested his back against the hard stone, drew his knees up to his chest, and wrapped his arms around his legs for warmth.

Now that the adrenaline had left his system and he'd managed to save his mother, he felt physically and emotionally drained. He was also chilled to the bone. "It's so…cold," Bellamy murmured to himself softly with no one to hear him except for the rocks on the floor as he began to shiver violently.

***

Abigail Snow a.k.a the yeti girl burst into the living room with a frustrated growl. "*Ohhh*, that nerd is so irritating!" She didn't get him at all. He'd surprised her by bravely and selflessly taking his mother's place in the dungeons. Her expression softened. He must really love his mother. Both of Abigail's parents were dead. She couldn't help but envy him a little.

There were other things about Bellamy that had surprised and intrigued Abigail. Like his reaction to finding out that because his mother had stolen a tiny rose quartz stone she'd wound up with a sentence of life imprisonment. She'd expected him to object to the unfairness as his mother had…but he'd seemed to calmly accept it. Why? Abigail remembered Bellamy mentioning he had a stone collection. Did he know the true value of such stones?

Abigail's blue lips dipped into a thoughtful frown. She couldn't seem to predict his actions or words. When Abigail had asked Bellamy about why his shirt had been ripped open like that and obvious love bites covered his chest, why had he been so adamant that whoever did that to him *wasn't* his girlfriend? That just made things weird.

He'd also said something about not wanting to cause his mother *more* suffering. What had Bellamy meant by that? What kind of suffering had Bellamy caused for his mother in the past?

Several strange ideas flitted past her mind due to her overactive imagination. Was Bellamy some kind of male gigolo? Did he seduce rich women for their money and that's what had caused his mom suffering? Or had some old woman attacked him at work? Or maybe even a man? The possibilities were endless.

He was such an enigma when men were usually so easy for her to figure out. Abigail began to nibble on her claws. *He must be cold down in that cell.* She thought. *What if he gets sick and dies? I shouldn't care about a low-class thief's son!* Abigail began to pace across the living room, back and forth.

"Is something troubling you, Milady?" a rich, velvety male voice with a British accent asked.

Abigail turned to face her loyal Head Butler, Jett, who was now a living onyx statue. "No. Why would you think that?"

"Your claws…" Jett pointed out keenly.

Abigail looked down at the claw she'd been nibbling on. She'd nibbled away an inch of nail! Oops. "Oh, ah…it's just…you don't think he'll die of hypothermia down there, do you?" She tried to keep her tone nonchalant.

The corner of Jett's lip twitched. "Ah, you're worried about the young man. Bellamy *was* a tad underdressed to be outside driving a dogsled in this weather."

"I'm not worried," Abigail huffed quickly. "Just *concerned* that my prisoner will die before he's suffered sufficiently for his crime."

"Milady, in case you haven't noticed - your prisoner happens to be a comely young man…" Jett trailed off.

"I am aware of that." Abigail narrowed her eyes at her butler. "What are you getting at, Jett?"

Jett sighed. "He could be the one to break the curse."

Abigail blinked. "Th-That nerd! Did you see those *glasses*? The one to break the curse? Ha! You forget, Jett…I have to fall in love too for the curse to be broken, and he's so…" She waved her hand through the air. "Uncool and low-class. He's *beneath* me."

Jett frowned. "Considering your own appearance at the moment…perhaps, it would be prudent to not be so…picky."

"Picky? Hmph!" Abigail huffed. "You can't control who you fall in love with, Jett. And you know I've only dated handsome guys with nice faces before."

"Yes. Your past boyfriends were all extremely attractive young gentlemen. However…" Jett trailed off.

"However?" the yeti snapped irritably.

"Forgive me for saying so, but…they were all a little vapid, weren't they? They had no notion of *who* they really were. No real sense of individuality. When you asked them *who* they were they would spout a long list of their riches and assets." Jett shook his head disapprovingly.

"Vapid?" A dark cloud fell over Abigail's face. "Then…so am I. I don't really know who I am either, or what I really want in life. The only thing I *do* know is that I *must* break this infernal curse somehow. I must regain my former beautiful appearance so I can get my perfect life back. And get my friends back too."

"Then why not give the boy Bellamy a chance," Jett suggested sagely. "I noticed that he has a muscular physique. He was a little on the plain side with those glasses, but certainly not unattractive, Milady."

"So what you're saying is…I should just try and *use* Bellamy to break the curse, and for that to happen I need him alive." Abigail nodded to herself. "Jett, you're a genius! Come, we must go and fetch him, and take him out of that cold dungeon at once!" The yeti spun on her heel and headed out of the living room with purposeful steps.

A sly, secretive smile curled Jett's lips. "As you wish, Milady." Jett followed Abigail down into the dungeon, and watched as she approached Bellamy's cell.

Abigail stepped in front of Bellamy's cell door, cleared her throat, and placed her hands on her hips. "Hello in there." She tapped the bars to get his attention. "Prepare yourself to be eternally grateful to me, your beautiful and benevolent benefactor." Without waiting for Bellamy's response Abigail continued in a haughty tone. "Out of the goodness of my heart I have decided to allow you the great privilege of having one of the guest rooms in my mansion to stay in. Oh, yes, I know, you're incredibly grateful. But that's to be expected. I knew you must have been freezing in here, so I just...Jett, why isn't he saying anything?" she demanded irritably.

Jett walked over to stand next to Abigail and peered into the cell. He searched the cell for Bellamy and noticed the young man collapsed on the floor towards the back of the cell. He frowned as he took in Bellamy's flushed cheeks. "It appears he fell unconscious due to a fever, Milady."

"What!" Abigail exclaimed and narrowed her eyes, looking into the cell and allowing her eyes to adjust to the darkness therein. That's when she spotted Bellamy collapsed on the floor. She quickly took off the ring of keys that hung from a chain around her neck and unlocked the cell door before rushing inside.

Abigail made her way over to Bellamy's fallen form and sank to her knees beside him. "Hey, wake up." She shook his shoulder. But Bellamy did not stir. His face was flushed and he was panting for breath. Abigail touched his forehead and gasped. "He's burning up! That nerdy idiot! Jett, help me get him to one of the guest rooms!"

"Yes, Milady." Jett walked over and scooped Bellamy's unconscious form up into his arms, displaying a good deal of strength.

With Abigail leading the way, they headed back upstairs, and to one of the guest rooms. Abigail opened the door to the guest room and ushered Jett inside.

Jett strode inside the bedroom that was decorated with a pale blue and gold theme, and deposited Bellamy on the large, four-poster, Queen-sized bed. "I'll go fetch a basin of cold water and a towel. I shall return shortly, Milady." The butler turned to go, but Abigail called out to him.

"Ah, wait, what should I do until you get back?" Abigail questioned as she nibbled on the end of her claw nervously. She was staring down at Bellamy with a concerned expression on her face.

Jett noticed her expression and tried not to smile. "Get him under the covers and keep him warm. We need to get him to break the fever," Jett directed.

"Oh, yes, of course..." Abigail agreed absentmindedly. With some clumsy maneuvering she managed to get Bellamy under the covers. Jett left the room and shut the door behind him. Abigail impatiently waited for Jett to return, and when her butler did finally return she took the bowl of water and towel from him. "I'll do it, Jett. You can go now."

Jett bowed and it served to cover the wide smile that had spread across his face. "As you wish, Milady."

To be continued in…Chapter 3:

Chapter 3:

Meanwhile, Doris had finally reached Yeti Town. Instead of going home she headed straight for the *Polar Bear Pub* - the usual hangout for all the Hunters living in town. "Whoa." Doris pulled back on the reins to bring the dogs to a halt directly in front of the pub.

Doris quickly got off the sled, walked over to the front door, and let herself inside. A blast of warm air hit her as she entered, coming from the blazing fire in the stone fireplace that took up most of the back wall of the establishment. The sound of laughing, glass beer mugs being clinked together and general merriment filled the place.

Doris spotted most of the Hunters seated at a long wooden table together, and approached them. They were always recognizable by their winter camouflage outfits and their shotguns and rifles that were leaning against the backs of their chairs. "Help! You *must* help me!" she exclaimed with a tinge of desperation to her voice.

The Hunters looked up and gave Doris shocked, confused looks. "Doris? What's the matter?" a young male Hunter questioned.

Doris didn't notice, but also seated at the table with the other Hunters was Astonia Sharpe, who was giving Doris a *very* curious look.

"It's Bellamy!" Doris exclaimed, a frantic note to her voice. "The yeti has him!"

A heavy, uneasy silence descended upon the pub at the mention of the legendary yeti. Astonia's curious look turned calculating. "You actually *saw* the yeti? Where?"

Doris turned to face Astonia, wringing her hands together. "At…the yeti's mansion."

Astonia arched an eyebrow at the middle-aged woman. "Mansion?"

"It's amazing…it's made entirely of blue quartz," Doris began to describe the mansion and her experiences there. "At first, I thought it was made out of ice. Inside the mansion the yeti has powerful servants."

"Servants?" Astonia prompted.

"Yes." Doris nodded, her eyes wide as she remembered the unsettling sight. "Stone statues shaped like maids and butlers that can move!"

"Moving statues?" Astonia repeated in a derisive tone.

Doris frowned at Astonia's sudden change in demeanor from kind to mocking, and looked around at the other Hunters with a beseeching look on her face. "I'm telling the truth. Please. You have to help me save him!"

"Poor Doris." Astonia shook her head while trying to appear sympathetic. "It looks like you've finally gone completely crazy due to all the stress Bellamy has put you through."

Doris blinked. "What? No! I'm *not* crazy! I really *saw* her."

Astonia's eyes narrowed. "Her?" Doris's tale was getting more and more interesting.

"The yeti was a female…a girl," Doris explained.

Astonia laughed loudly and several Hunters joined her as if on cue. "And now you've become delusional. The yeti is just an urban legend, Doris. It's not real." Astonia's tone was patronizing.

"But she *is* real. I saw her!" Doris snapped. "Please, you have to believe me! I'm not crazy!" Her voice cracked slightly on the word 'crazy'.

Astonia turned to her father Gaston who was also seated at the table. "Dad, I think we'd better take Doris to Mother. She's become a danger to those around her with her paranoid delusions of Bellamy being kidnapped by a monster. Although, it's not hard to understand why she has such delusions. Bellamy was kidnapped in middle school by his own teacher, right Mrs. DeWinter?"

A frown formed on Doris's face. "Yes, but-"

"You see, imagine how traumatic that experience must have been for Mrs. DeWinter." Astonia addressed the crowd that was hanging on her every word with rapt attention. "Her own son kidnapped...and maybe even sexually abused by his own teacher. It's the stuff of nightmares, really. After that incident you sought psychiatric help, did you not, Mrs. DeWinter?"

Doris's palms were beginning to sweat. "I did, but...how do you even know about that, Astonia?" she demanded suddenly.

"There's a little thing called the Internet." Astonia's reply was flippant.

"But...why?" Doris's brow furrowed in confusion.

"Oh, I make it my business to know *everything* about Bellamy, and you, Mrs. DeWinter," the Huntress declared. "I'm surprised that Bellamy didn't tell you, but he's my boyfriend."

Doris sucked in a startled breath as she suddenly recognized that crazed look in Astonia's eyes. *Oh, no. Astonia must have seen Bellamy without his glasses. And now she's obsessed with him!* There was no telling what she would do. What she was capable of. "You...you fell in love with Bellamy. You *saw* him-!"

Astonia quickly cut Doris off. "And so you see, everyone, that's why poor Bellamy decided to run away from home, as teenagers tend to do. He just didn't feel safe in his own home anymore, or around you and your paranoid delusions, Mrs. DeWinter. But don't worry. You're in luck. My mother runs the medical clinic in Yeti Town. She also happens to be this town's only psychiatrist. She'll be able to help you...get rid of your delusions." A sly smile curled Astonia's red-painted lips.

A horrified look formed on Doris's face and she began to back away from Astonia. Astonia was the crazy one. Doris shook her head. "No. I don't need your help. I...I must rescue my son from that monster. And if I have to do it alone...so be it." She turned and fled for the front door of the pub.

"Tch." Astonia made a disappointed sound. "Grab her! Don't let her escape!"

Astonia's father, Gaston, was the quickest to react. He'd leapt out of his chair and had managed to reach Doris in seconds. He grabbed her arm to stop her from fleeing the pub and sent a hard chop into the back of Doris's neck to knock her out cold. Doris slumped against him, and Gaston caught her in his arms.

Astonia was smiling triumphantly. "Thanks, Daddy. Let's take her to Mother, shall we?"

"Sure thing, bumblebee." Gaston smiled back at his daughter.

Astonia approached Doris's unconscious form and tucked a stray strand of Doris's gray-streaked brown hair behind her ear in what appeared to be a kind gesture. "Don't worry, Mrs. DeWinter. We'll get you the help you need, and then we'll help find Bellamy."

***

Bellamy was delirious due to his high fever. He thought that he could hear someone humming a song softly by his ear. There was also this fluffy softness embracing him like a cloud. The bookworm nuzzled his head against the softness, wrapped his arms around what he believed was a pillow, and sighed in contentment.

When Bellamy awoke he was in the embarrassing position of embracing his pillow rather romantically with his leg thrown over it and hugging it tightly. There was even a little bit of drool on his pillow that made him flush.

"Ah, it's good to see you awake, Sir," a velvety male voice with a British accent began. "How are you feeling this evening?"

"Uh, I'm doing fine," Bellamy was saying as he opened his eyes and scanned the room to see who was speaking to him. Then he spotted a black onyx statue of a butler. The butler was wringing out the towel that had been on his forehead only moments before into a white, porcelain basin. Bellamy sat up, screamed and pointed his finger at the moving statue. "Y-Y-You can talk!"

The butler statue turned to regard Bellamy calmly. "Well, of course, I can talk, Sir. I am this mansion's Head Butler, and my name is Jett." He bowed. "It's a pleasure to make your acquaintance, Sir. It appears your fever has broken. Milady will be most pleased." A small smile formed on the butler's face.

Bellamy put a hand to his forehead. His head was spinning with the words: 'butler', 'Jett', and 'milady'. Then his memories from the previous day came rushing back to him - his mother's disappearance, the mansion made of blue quartz that looked like ice, the medieval dungeons, the yeti, and her army of stone statues! It hadn't been a dream. It was real.

That's right...the yeti. I'm her...prisoner. Bellamy frowned as he looked around the room he was in. This didn't look like the prison cell he'd first been dumped in. In fact, this was the ritziest room he'd ever been in. He swallowed nervously. "Why am I in this room, and not the dungeon?" he asked warily.

Jett offered Bellamy a disarming smile. "Milady was worried about your health. She ordered me to move you here and to take care of you until your fever broke."

"The yeti was...worried about me?" Bellamy scoffed. "Balderdash." He laughed in order to hide his own nervousness.

"Once you've fully recovered you will take your meals with Milady in the dining room," Jett explained matter-of-factly.

Bellamy gave Jett a suspicious look that quickly turned resigned. He sighed. "So she wants to fallen me up first...before she devours me, huh?" His voice had taken on a dark, bitter edge. Before Jett could respond to that Bellamy's stomach rumbled loudly.

"Ah, you must be hungry," Jett noted in a lighthearted tone. "You've been asleep an entire day. Do you feel up to joining Milady for supper tonight?" There was an odd hopeful note to the butler's voice that made Bellamy even more wary.

"No!" Bellamy burst out, but then quickly composed himself. "I mean, no thank you. I still feel a little...lightheaded. I'd rather stay in my room. If that's alright."

"Of course, Sir," Jett agreed in an amiable fashion. "How about I bring you a nice, warm bowl of stew?"

"That sounds great." Bellamy forced himself to smile at the butler though he knew it must have looked strained.

"I'll be back soon, Sir." Jett headed for the door and exited the bedroom, shutting the door behind him.

Bellamy let out a breath of relief as soon as the butler was gone. He'd been watching the butler's every move closely. *A walking, talking statue that looks like a butler and that is made out of onyx. Unreal.* Bellamy shook his head in disbelief. He felt like he was going crazy. Or maybe he was dreaming. He pinched his arm to make sure. "Ow!" Nope. Apparently no matter how weird everything that was happening was - this was still reality.

Taking the opportunity now that he was alone, Bellamy admired the room he was in fully. It was stunning. The walls, ceiling and floor appeared to be made out of blue, shimmery ice.

With his curiosity overriding his fear, Bellamy gathered his strength, climbed out of bed and approached one of the walls. He reached out to touch it, expecting it to feel cold. Instead it felt smooth and slightly cool. But it wasn't ice. Bellamy suddenly felt stupid for thinking that it could be ice.

"Yeah, I've watched *Frozen* too many times with Mom." He let out a self-deprecating chuckle. "Still, this is…rather fascinating. It appears to be made out of blue quartz. To use this much blue quartz…must have cost a fortune." Bellamy took his hand off the wall and glanced around the room, noting that the furniture appeared to be made out of different semi-precious stones.

The dresser was made entirely out of a dark blue lapis lazuli. There was a desk and chair that at first glance appeared to be made out of mahogany, but upon closer inspection was in fact made out of brown tiger's eye. The two nightstands that were sitting on either side of the four-poster bed were also made of tiger's eye. The lamps on the nightstands were solid jade. The bed was made out of lapis lazuli. Regal, dark blue velvet drapes covered the tall windows in the room and were decorated with golden tassels.

Bellamy had never seen furniture this large made entirely out of stone like this before. It was incredible. Overcome by a sudden chill he rubbed at the goosebumps that had formed on his arms. That's when he noticed that he was shirtless. He flushed, wondering if it had been Jett who'd removed his ruined shirt while he'd been sleeping. That thought was unsettling.

"Seriously, creepy man," Bellamy muttered darkly to himself as he quickly made his way back over to the bed. He buried himself beneath the covers in order to get himself warm.

Just as he was getting himself settled in again, the door opened, and Jett entered the bedroom holding a silver tray with a bowl of stew and a crystal goblet of red wine. Bellamy raised an eyebrow at the wine since he was still underage, but he wasn't about to point that out to the butler. With everything that had happened, he could really use a drink.

Jett walked over and placed the tray on Bellamy's lap. "Here you are, Sir. I hope you like rabbit stew."

Bellamy looked down at the succulent smelling stew and vegetables, and his stomach rumbled loudly. "Yeah, I do." Bellamy picked up the spoon and stared at it for a moment. It was made out of agate. Upon closer inspection he realized that the bowl wasn't blue-glazed ceramic, but solid lapis lazuli. "So, the yeti-" Bellamy started in what he hoped was a nonchalant tone.

"Abigail," Jett swiftly corrected.

Bellamy raised an inquisitive eyebrow at the butler. "That mons-" He coughed into his hand, cutting himself off before he put his foot into his mouth. "Er, the yeti has a name?"

"Indeed, Sir," Jett confirmed. "Abigail Snow."

"Oookay. Well, Abigail sure does like semi-precious stones, huh?" Bellamy shoved a spoonful of stew into his mouth and had to hold back an appreciative moan as it hit his taste buds. The stew was delicious.

Jett's lips thinned. "In a manner of speaking, yes."

"It must have cost a fortune." Bellamy waved his spoon through the air.

"Indeed," Jett said evasively. "Well, I'll leave you to dine in peace, Sir."

"Uh, yeah, thanks, Jett," Bellamy called after the butler who'd suspiciously made a hasty retreat all of a sudden. Bellamy shrugged and continued to eat his stew in silence. He almost regretted scaring the butler off since he couldn't ask for seconds.

Bellamy must have been exhausted from his ordeal since he didn't wake up until the following evening. He did feel well rested though, and his fever was completely gone.

When Jett came in to check on him he caught Bellamy wandering around the room and admiring the stone furniture closely with his magnifying glass.

"Ah, Sir, it's good to see you up and about." Jett smiled, walking into the room. "I suppose that means that tonight you will be able to dine with Milady."

"Ah, I guess so." Bellamy looked down at his bare chest pointedly. "I might be a little underdressed for dinner in such a ritzy place though."

"Oh, dear, I forgot to tell you that Milady has provided you with clothes." Jett walked over to the closet and opened it to reveal that it was now filled with clothes. "Allow me to give you some privacy so you can dress. I shall return shortly to escort you to the dining room."

"Sure," Bellamy agreed halfheartedly. He couldn't think of a way to get out of having to dine with the volatile yeti girl. The bookworm walked over to the closet and began to inspect the clothes that had been provided for him. He frowned when he noticed that they were all designer suits by *Gucci*, *Hugo Boss*, *Prada,* and *Armani*. They must have cost a fortune.

Bellamy's stomach twisted into knots out of unease. This wasn't the first time a woman wanted him dressed up to be her personal 'boy toy'. He rubbed his stomach as he remembered what had happened to him in middle school. Some bullies had knocked his glasses off his face and one of his female teachers had seen his face. She's instantly fallen in love with Bellamy.

A few days after that when Bellamy was leaving school she'd somehow managed to catch him off guard and had held a rag doused with chloroform up against his nose, knocking him out cold. He'd woken up to discover that he was now inside of the woman's apartment. She'd kept him drugged the entire time so that he was too weak to try and escape. His teacher had dressed him up in the most expensive suits she could buy and had touched him inappropriately. She'd stolen his first kiss.

Bellamy dug his fingers into his scalp as he tried to push the memory from his mind. He didn't want to remember about that perverted old hag!

An anonymous tip to the police from someone who lived in the same apartment building as Bellamy's teacher had saved him before things had gotten too out of hand. The police had come for him, and rescued him before his teacher could sleep with Bellamy. Bellamy considered himself lucky that he was still a virgin.

So the yeti girl wants me to be her new boy toy, huh? Bellamy thought bitterly. *Why am I not surprised? It always ends up this way.* He let out a heavy, resigned sigh. *I just have to keep in mind that I'm doing this for Mother. I can do this.* He unconsciously rubbed at his stomach again.

Bellamy selected a dark gray suit with a sky-blue, button-down shirt that matched his eyes. The tie he selected was a gray-blue color. He decided to add a Rolex watch to his wrist. He brushed his shoulder-length brown hair before tying it into a ponytail using a blue silk ribbon. *If it's a boy toy she wants - it's a boy toy she'll get.* He was doing this for his mother after all. He had to keep her safe and out of the yeti's clawed hands.

Twenty minutes later, Jett returned to fetch Bellamy, and then led him to the dining room. The dining room was enormous. There was a long, black obsidian table surrounded by eighteen armchairs that were made out of different semi-precious stones: lapis lazuli, turquoise, tiger's eye, jade, red jasper, and rose quartz. The floor was black and white checkered marble. The dishware appeared to be made out of agate stones.

Bellamy was so captivated by the stone furniture that he barely even noticed the yeti seated at the head of the table until she cleared her throat loudly to get his attention. "Ahem!"

Bellamy was snapped out of his reverie by the sound. He'd been stroking his hand over one of the armchairs appreciatively. This one was solid jade. He flushed in embarrassment. "Oh, sorry," Bellamy apologized swiftly. "It's just…incredible craftsmanship." He warily approached the head of the table.

The yeti's silver eyes were pinned to him - following his every move. It was strange seeing a monster seated at the head of a fancy dining table as if it were 'normal'. Even if she was a 'cute' monster. *Cute?* Bellamy mused, as he stopped walking. Where had that strange, unbidden thought come from?

Abigail Snow's features were simian and she had this cute, button nose. The skin on her face was blue. Her fluffy white fur made him think of a rabbit or cat. But that's where her animal-like characteristic ended. Her posture, poise, and mannerisms were those of a high-class lady.

Two place settings had been arranged on the dining table - one for the yeti and one for Bellamy. Bellamy sat down to the yeti's left, and looked down at the plate of food with interest. The rabbit stew had been delicious so he was slightly excited about what would be served to him next.

This time it was a nice filet of salmon with a caper sauce, *au gratin* potatoes, and colorful steamed vegetables drizzled with garlic butter. It made Bellamy salivate, and he gulped. His crystal goblet was filled with red wine. This was high-quality cuisine alright. Food that he wasn't really used to eating. A frown formed on his face at the thought. He'd feel more comfortable eating a hamburger and some fries.

Abigail noticed his displeased expression, and her eyes narrowed with irritation. "Is something wrong with the food?" Her tone seemed to suggest that was highly unlikely.

"Ah, no...it looks great. Thank you," Bellamy quickly assured. The last thing he wanted to do was piss off a volatile yeti girl.

Abigail sniffed in an uppity manner. "Of course it looks great. Do you have any idea who cooked us this meal? The famous chef Kirsten Dixon."

"Oh, yeah...she works here?" Bellamy questioned tentatively. He wondered if Kirsten was a prisoner there too.

"Yes," Abigail said airily. "She's my Head Chef."

"Is she...human?" Bellamy asked quietly.

Abigail blinked. "Of course, she's-"

"I mean, is she made of stone like the others?" Bellamy braced himself in case the yeti decided to attack him or something.

"Oh. Yes. She's a stone statue like the others, for the moment." A shadow fell over Abigail's carefree expression then and she turned thoughtful. "Hurry up and eat before it gets cold," she snapped.

"Sure," the bookworm quickly agreed.

As they dined Bellamy watched Abigail eating out of the corner of his eyes. She was eating very slowly and very carefully. Using the utensils with her clawed hands must have been awkward and difficult, he realized sympathetically. Her back was incredibly straight and she knew which cutlery to use with each course. She was a lady. Or rather she *had been* a lady.

The more Bellamy continued to observe her the more obvious it became that Abigail Snow had the proper upbringing of a high-society lady. Bellamy suddenly became curious about the yeti who was now his captor. She wasn't really a monster, was she? She'd been human once, probably. What had turned her into a monster? Bellamy wondered. He believed in curses after all. "You...you're not really just a yeti, are you? You were...human once, right?" He gave her an expectant look.

Abigail's gray eyes widened like saucers. "Yes...that's right. How did you know that?" Her brow furrowed in confusion.

A cocky smirk formed on Bellamy's face. "I doubt many *real* yetis would bother using a fork and knife." He waved a hand at her and at how she was currently cutting a green bean in half with delicate movements.

Abigail looked down at her clawed hands and at what they were doing. "Ah, I suppose you're right."

Bellamy gazed at Abigail intently. "So…how did you get cursed like this?"

Abigail looked up at Bellamy with a start. "Cursed? You…*believe* in curses?"

The bookworm let out a low, bitter chuckle. "More than you know."

"Well, the *why* doesn't really matter. What's done is done." The yeti waved her hand through the air in a careless gesture. "And I don't wish to talk about it. I'm more concerned with finding a way to undo the curse."

Bellamy licked his lips and leaned towards Abigail, eagerly awaiting her response to his next question. "Do you know how?" If he'd known there was a way to break his own curse…he would have done everything in his power already to break it.

"As a matter of fact…yes," Abigail revealed and a twinkle formed in her eye. "That's where *you* come in, Bellamy."

"Me?" Bellamy sat back in his chair, looking startled.

"Yes. I believe we can make a deal that will be mutually beneficial to the both of us." A sly smile curled the yeti's blue-painted lips. "So, tell me, Bellamy DeWinter, how much does your 'love' cost?"

"Excuse me?" Bellamy blinked in confusion.

"How much would it cost…to make you love me? For instance…" Abigail snapped her blue fingers. "Lazuli, bring it."

A maid statue made out of lapis lazuli entered the dining room carrying a small wooden chest that resembled a pirate's treasure chest, but on a smaller scale. She carried the chest over to Bellamy and set it down on the table next to his place setting. Lazuli opened the chest to reveal that it was filled with hundred dollar bills.

"How about a million dollars?" The yeti offered.

Bellamy gawked at the money. "Uh…"

"No? Still not enough?" Abigail snapped her fingers again. "Ruby."

A maid statue made out of solid ruby entered the dining room with a chest next. She carried the chest over to Bellamy, set it down next to the other one, and opened it to reveal that it was filled with a variety of precious stones: diamonds, rubies, emeralds, and sapphires.

Abigail couldn't stop the wide smile that was spreading across her face. No man could resist so much money. She had this cat in the bag, so to speak. "Will this be enough to make you love me?" Of course it would be…

Bellamy's blood was boiling in anger and his body began to tremble. He clenched his hands into fists on his lap as he tried to contain himself. Abigail Snow wanted to 'buy' his love? In other words…she wanted to buy him. "Love isn't something that can be bought!" he snapped hotly.

A flash of confusion crossed the yeti's face and she frowned. "You don't have to mean it. Maybe even a kiss would suffice-"

Bellamy slammed his hands down on the table with enough force to make the heavy stone tableware rattle. He stood up, his blue eyes blazing. "You…just want my body! You're just like all the others! You really are a *monster*," he sneered at her, his lip curling in disgust.

Abigail gawked at Bellamy in shock. She wasn't used to anyone speaking to her with such blatant disrespect. When she'd been an heiress people had always spoken courteously to her because of her social status. And after she'd become a yeti people had treated her with respect out of fear.

Now this strange, nerdish young man didn't seem to care that she could snap him in two like a twig if he rubbed her the wrong way. He was incredibly brave…or maybe just stupid. She watched in stunned silence as he stalked out of the dining room, leaving her behind in a state of bewilderment.

"Well, that didn't work out at all like I thought it would," Abigail grumbled as she began to unconsciously nibble on one of her claws. "I really don't understand him at all. No human man should have refused that kind of money. Everyone has a price. And what did he mean by 'others'? How…unsettling."

***

Bellamy was royally pissed off. How dare Abigail ask him how much his 'love' would cost! *She's just after me because of my handsome face! Just like all the others!* Bellamy fumed as he began to pace across his bedroom floor.

But then he stopped and frowned as he realized what he'd just been thinking. *Wait a second; Abigail hasn't seen my face yet. So this isn't about my curse. It's about her wanting to use me to break some kind of fairytale curse.*

Bellamy didn't know if he should feel more or *less* insulted. Either way, Abigail was treating him like an object and *not* a human being. How could someone think they could actually *buy* sentiment anyways? Just what kind of messed-up person would they have to be? What kind of life experiences had caused such bizarre notions to form in Abigail's furry head? He wondered sourly.

I'm probably over-thinking things, as usual. Bellamy let out an angry huff. *She's just a monster…on the inside as well as the outside. I don't know why I expected different.*

Bellamy stripped off the expensive suit and tossed it to the floor. The Rolex and Ferragamos joined the pile on the floor next. It felt somewhat satisfying to treat those expensive items so carelessly.

The bookworm decided to turn in early and try to get some sleep. "Why is she like that…?" Bellamy murmured sleepily to himself before his heavy eyelids drooped and he fell asleep.

Perhaps due to his current line of thought, Bellamy DeWinter ended up dreaming about Abigail Snow's past that night…

FLASHBACK

Abigail Snow's family had always been filthy rich. Abigail's father, Aspen Snow, owned a gold mine as well as a gemstone mine where Aurora Borealis quartz, red garnet, jade, and cabochon were mined.

Abigail's mother, Holly Snow, was renown throughout Alaska for her beauty. Holly had long, platinum blonde hair that cascaded down her back to her waist, and intelligent silvery-gray eyes. Holly was always drenched in diamonds that Aspen had gifted her with. She literally seemed to sparkle when she entered a room, and was the envy of all the women who saw her. They would emulate her. They wanted to *be* her.

The glamorous Snows were the picture perfect high-society family. Unfortunately, not all the money in the world can buy good health, and Holly's health was poor, her constitution weak. Like a man possessed Aspen had tried to find a way to improve Holly's health. And when modern medicine failed him, Aspen turned to more... *unconventional* means. Magic. Charms. The occult.

It was around this time that Aspen had purchased the gemstone mine. Gemstones and semi-precious stones were known for their metaphysical healing properties - quartz was known to purify one's aura, rose quartz could help a person find true love, turquoise and lapis lazuli were known for bringing a person luck and happiness, jade instilled wisdom, red jasper brought about justice, and black onyx protected one from negative energies and the Evil Eye.

When Abigail turned twelve, her mother fell gravely ill and became bedridden. Abigail remembered just how desperate her father became with finding Holly some kind of mystical 'cure' for her health.

Abigail recalled sneaking to her mother's room one night, and opening the door just a crack to see that her father was seated at her mother's bedside while holding her hand. "Don't worry, my love. I will find a way to cure you. I will find *it*. You'll see. I will save you. I promise."

It? Abigail wondered curiously.

After that every night Abigail had gone to peek through her mother's bedroom door she'd found her father already there with Holly's hand in his, and he'd keep repeating that he would find 'it' and that he would save her.

One night, when Abigail had snuck to her mother's room she'd been surprised to find that her father wasn't there. She'd searched around the mansion for him and spotted her father acting suspiciously. Aspen made sure no one was watching when he opened a door that led down to the basement level of the mansion that was only used for storage.

Abigail counted to a hundred before following after her father. She descended the steps and entered a long, dreary hallway with doors on either side. One closed door towards the end of the corridor had light shinning underneath it, and Abigail headed in its direction.

Abigail placed her ear against the door to gauge where her father was inside of the room. He sounded pretty far back, and so

Abigail risked opening the door and sneaking inside. Her eyes bulged at the sight before her, and she had to cover her mouth to stifle her startled gasp.

A mad scientist's laboratory. Abigail thought to herself in awe. It was like something right out of a science fiction movie. There were several long worktables arranged throughout the room, and each appeared to have a different purpose. The table that had a chemistry set sitting on it also had an assortment of beakers and test tubes filled with neon-colored liquids. Another table had a strange device sitting on it that was made out of round glass globes filled with different colored liquids. The glass globes were connected by metal. Some of the liquids were frothing or bubbling suspiciously.

Apparently, her father was conducting some kind of scientific experiment. On one of the worktables there was a tiny black cauldron that looked like it fell out of a *Harry Potter* book. Also, on that particular table a lot of old tomes and books had been laid out. Some of the books were open and Abigail could see their aged, yellowed pages. *Magic books?* Abigail wondered uneasily. *Daddy's gone crazy.* There was a sinking feeling inside of her stomach.

Abigail watched her father work from her hiding place. She watched as he mixed different chemicals together and caused different chemical reactions. Sometimes the concoctions would froth or bubble, other times they'd even explode. But none of the reactions seemed to be satisfactory since her father would frown, shake his head, and jot down some notes in his notebook. Most of these experiments seemed to have one strange thing in common though - the use or incorporation of an Aurora Borealis quartz stone.

During one such failed experiment Aspen grew angry, picked up the stone he'd been experimenting with and had thrown it across the room. The stone hit the wall and had shattered upon impact. "Damn, useless fake! But I can't find *it*. I've tried so hard to find *it*. I have to make *it* myself. It's the only way!" There was a crazed gleam in Aspen's eyes that made Abigail tremble in fear as she watched.

When Holly fell into a coma, Abigail recalled the deafening sound of the entire household staff crying in their despair. Holly had been kind to the staff, and was well liked as a result. Their sadness for the lady of the house was sincere.

Abigail had covered her ears to try and block out the sound of everyone crying. They were already acting like her mother was dead. Abigail ran to her mother's room and flung open the door. Her father was seated at Holly's bedside, and Abigail noticed that he was holding a glass vial filled with a rainbow-colored liquid in his hand.

Tears were streaming down Aspen's face. "I cannot bear to lose you, my love. For now *this* is all I can do."

Abigail watched with baited breath as her father forced the contents of the vial down her mother's throat. Abigail watched in horror as her mother became *very* still. Holly's chest stopped rising and falling as her breaths just stopped. A heavy silence permeated the bedroom.

Abigail swayed on her feet as the gravity of what she'd just witnessed began to sink in. Her father...had just poisoned her mother! A chill of fear for her own safety crawled up her spine, and she turned and ran from the room.

Abigail ran until her legs ran out of strength and she collapsed to her knees in the garden. Alone with her pain and grief, Abigail was filled with a sense of betrayal that her beloved, scholarly father had poisoned her beautiful, kind mother.

No one ever did find out what happened to Holly's body after that. A funeral was held for Holly Snow...but the casket that was buried in the family cemetery was empty. Only the household staff was aware of this discrepancy, of course, and they kept their mouths shut out of loyalty to Mr. Snow and Abigail.

Only a day after the funeral, something strange happened. It was early in the morning and Abigail was making her way down the curved staircase into the foyer when she noticed a statue sitting in the center of the checkered floor that hadn't been there before.

Abigail continued her way down the steps more slowly, and approached the statue from behind. It was the statue of a woman with long, flowing hair and a floor-length gown. The statue had been carved entirely out of blue quartz.

As she rounded the statue she continued to admire its craftsmanship until she looked up into its face and gasped. She raised a hand in front of her mouth as she just stared because she was looking into the face of her dead mother. "M-Mother!"

It was a statue of Holly Snow. Her delicate, sophisticated features, high cheekbones, and witty smile tugging at her bow-shaped lips were unmistakable. The dress she was wearing was her silk nightgown - the last thing Abigail had seen her mother dressed in before the poisoning.

Abigail nearly jumped a foot in the air when her father placed a hand on her shoulder. "Abigail, have you welcomed your mother back home yet?"

Abigail turned to gape at her father in confusion. "W-What?" She swallowed thickly when she noticed that the crazed look in her father's eyes had returned.

"It's so good to have your mother back here with us again, isn't it?" Aspen prodded in an insistent manner. "Go on, go and give your mother a hug."

An image of her father poisoning her mother flashed through Abigail's mind and she was suddenly filled with anger. "That hunk of rock is *not* my mother!"

Before Aspen even realized what he was doing he'd backhanded Abigail hard across the face with an audible *smack*.

Abigail raised a trembling hand to her red cheek and stared at her father in disbelief. He'd never struck her before. Why now? Abigail's gray eyes quickly filled with tears. "I hate you! I *hate* you!" Abigail turned and ran, heading for the garden, her sanctuary.

With a stricken look on his face Aspen called out to her. "Abigail, wait!" He sank to his knees in front of the statue and reached out to touch the stone foot. "My love, what have I done? Forgive me. Please, forgive me...but don't worry, I *will* save you. I'll find *it*. I know I will. I'll never give up the search. I can sense *it*. It's close now! We'll find it. Yes, we will, and then we'll be a family once more."

The following day, Aspen Snow could not be found. He'd mysteriously disappeared. Most of the household staff assumed it was suicide and that'd he'd probably just walked off into the forest to never return, unable to cope with Holly's death.

Oddest of all, a stone statue that looked just like Aspen appeared in the foyer standing next to the statue of Abigail's mother. The statue was made entirely of blue quartz. As Abigail stared at the statue she couldn't help but think about how uncanny the likeness was to her father. Both of the statues were so exquisitely carved that they almost appeared *alive*.

Abigail's lips thinned into a stern line. But they *weren't* alive. They were just statues - useless, worthless, hunks of rock that could not speak, feel, or touch.

With the death of Abigail's mother and disappearance of her father, Abigail inherited her family's vast fortune and became a socialite overnight. In a twisted attempt to keep her mother's memory alive Abigail started dressing like her mother in fine designer clothes, mostly *Prada*, and her mother's valuable, glittering gemstone jewelry.

Without her parents' presence the huge mansion became suffocating to Abigail. With only the serious household staff to keep her company, the place became unbearably quiet and lonesome. When left alone with her own thoughts, they'd stray to how Abigail's father had poisoned her mother and she'd squeeze her head with her own hands as she tried futilely to crush the memories out of her head.

In order to rid the mansion of its heavy silence, Abigail started to throw grand, extravagant parties, and invited only la crème de la crème. The deferential way her guests treated her began to go to her head, and her ego swelled. The more beautiful her clothes or jewelry, the more her guests would praise her.

Abigail started to *live* for their praise. She spent thousands on new clothes, and hundreds of thousands on new jewelry she didn't need. It took Abigail hours to get ready for her parties. She'd sit in front of her dressing table for nearly an hour holding up different earrings and necklaces to herself before finally deciding which set to wear for the evening.

Her guests started to grow competitive with each other, and began wearing their best clothes and jewelry when they went to one of Abigail's parties. Abigail noticed how they fought for her attention and reveled in it. She started to grow particular about who could attend her parties until only the richest and most beautiful people were allowed to attend.

On her eighteenth birthday, Abigail decided to throw herself the most extravagant and lavish dance party yet. The best caterer available in Alaska had cooked the food for the buffet. A popular band had been hired for the evening's entertainment, and her guests were suitably impressed.

The ballroom had been decorated with blue, white and silver balloon sculptures. More helium-filled balloons floated along the ballroom's frescoed ceiling. One long table served as an open buffet while another long table was arranged entirely with decadent desserts, and fancy, novelty cakes with colorful, fondant icing. One of the cakes had been commissioned to look like a yeti, or Abominable Snowman. Just for fun.

Standing on the table where the champagne was already served in delicate flute glasses was an ice sculpture of a yeti. It was a hideous, monkey-like creature with fluffy fur and abnormally long arms. Abigail had laughed amusedly at the ice sculpture when she'd first laid eyes upon it, and smiled wickedly. "Oh, it's *so* hideous. I absolutely love it!" She'd praised the man who'd carved the ice sculpture for her, and had tipped him outrageously.

As unobtrusively as possible, Abigail's maids and butlers flitted through the guests while holding silver trays arranged with glasses of champagne for the guests to take. Abigail had made it quite clear to her servants that they were meant to be seen, not heard.

Abigail took a flute of champagne from a butler that passed her by and took a sip as she took that moment to admire her dancing guests. A pleased smile curled her lips. Her party was perfect, and so were her guests. The women were dressed in designer gowns by *Gucci, Chanel, Prada* and *Dolce and Gabbana*. The men were, of course, dressed in designer suits, and had sparkling watches on their wrists by *Cartier* or *Rolex*.

As Abigail made her way through the crowd on the dance floor while looking for a man handsome enough to ask to dance with her, her guests complimented her on her wonderful party, the food, the music, the champagne, and, of course, her appearance. She was wearing a new *Gucci* gown, and the diamond jewelry she was wearing was quite showy. Abigail preened the most when her guests would tell her that she looked like her late mother.

Abigail felt like a goddess in that moment. Her guests practically worshipped and adored her. And that was because she was stunning, wasn't she? Just like her mother Holly.

Her party was going quite smoothly until it started to rain outside. This caused Abigail's lips to dip into a sullen frown. If the weather remained foul that evening she wouldn't be able to have her impressive fireworks display. Thunder boomed so loudly that people cried out, and then laughed at their own fear in a self-deprecating manner.

Unfortunately, the storm didn't abate, and only seemed to get worse. Rain lashed violently against the tall, latticed windows in the ballroom causing the windows to vibrate in an unnerving fashion.

The branches from the trees that were just outside the windows began to scrape along the windowpanes in an unsettling manner that had Abigail hugging her arms around her torso. It was like the trees wanted to get inside out of the harsh rain…

A loud, booming knock on the front door startled Abigail out of her strange thoughts. It seemed to echo throughout the entire mansion. Something made Abigail go answer the door herself when usually she would have had a servant do it for her. Heaven forbid one of her *honored* guests was out there in the pouring rain, getting soaked though.

When Abigail opened the front door it was to reveal an old man who was hunched over, and wearing tattered clothing. Abigail's gray eyes raked over the old man critically and scrunched up her nose in disgust. He was quite ugly, the skin on his face wrinkled, his gray hair wiry and plastered to his face. He smelled and was obviously poor, perhaps even homeless.

"What do you want here?" Abigail demanded with a haughty air. "This is private property and you're trespassing."

"Lady Abigail, may I please come in for just a moment to get out of the rain, and warm myself by your fire? I'll even pay you. I'll give you the very thing your father was searching for all this time." The old man reached into his pocket and pulled out a rainbow-colored Aurora Borealis stone.

Abigail snootily stared down her nose at the rainbow-colored stone. "You would offer me that worthless rock to receive the privilege of sitting by *my* fire!" she sneered, her lip curling. "I think not. Shoo." She waved her hand in a dismissive gesture towards the old man. "Before I call security to remove you from my presence."

A disappointed look fell over the old man's face, and he shook his head. "Pity. You are not yet worthy to wield the Philosopher's Stone. I will have to teach you a lesson in kindness and humility. Then perhaps, one day, you shall be worthy."

Abigail's brow furrowed in confusion. "What nonsense are you babbling about, old man?"

But then the old man straightened until he was towering over Abigail at six-five. He lowered his ragged hood and with the motion the man's appearance changed. The old man became young and handsome. He had short, wavy, golden-blonde hair, sparkling blue eyes filled with a kind of ancient wisdom, and an attractive dimple in his square chin. The ratty, wool material of his hooded cloak turned into lush, dark blue velvet that was embroidered with golden stars.

Abigail gasped in surprise as the odious old man turned into a handsome young man. "W-Who are you?"

"I am known as the Sorcerer Agathon." Agathon executed a mocking bow.

"But, you're so handsome-" Abigail was saying.

"And you are so very ugly," Agathon retorted as he touched the stone to Abigail's chest, directly over her heart, "in here."

Abigail's heart began to beat faster inside of her chest, and she was abruptly filled with excruciating pain. It felt like someone was stabbing her body with tiny daggers, all over. A scream was wrenched from her lips as her body began to transform. Thick, white fur began to sprout all over her body, except for her face and hands. Her skin turned a sky-blue color, and her eyes turned solid silver with no whites. Her short nails lengthened into sharp, black claws. Lastly, two short, black horns emerged from out of the top of her head.

At that point the pain was so excruciating Abigail nearly passed out. She swayed on her feet and struggled to remain standing. When the pain finally began to recede, Abigail was on her knees on the floor, tears in her eyes. She looked up at the sorcerer helplessly. "W-What have you done to me?" she croaked, her voice hoarse from all her screaming.

"Here." Agathon took out an antique silver mirror, and handed it to Abigail. "Why don't you take a look for yourself?"

Abigail peered into the mirror, and screamed at her own abominable appearance. "No! This can't be happening. Why me? Mother!" Abigail looked around frantically, her eyes glazed with terror. "Mother! Help me!"

"Now you are as monstrous on the outside as you are on the inside, Abigail Snow." The sorcerer declared as he stared down at her coldly. "This is your punishment. Your curse. Your test."

With trembling arms Abigail pushed herself up off the floor. She had to get help. Someone had to save her from this evil sorcerer. Once on her own two feet, she made a mad dash for the ballroom and entered. "Help! Someone, please, help me! This man...he...this sorcerer, he-!"

The music stopped playing and everyone turned to stare at Abigail and what she'd become. Their eyes widened and several people screamed in terror. Others were too shocked or surprised to scream, but were equally afraid. "Ah, it's a monster!" "It's the legendary yeti!" "Run for your lives!" "It's...the Abominable Snowman!"

Abigail's brow furrowed in confusion until she realized how she must have appeared to her guests in this new form. *I've been transformed into...a yeti.* Abigail reached her hand out towards one of her friends that ran past her, and headed for the exit. "Wait! Please. Won't anyone help me?" she cried desperately.

Agathon calmly strolled into the ballroom at a languid pace as people ran past him. "You must help yourself, Abigail Snow. There is only one way to break the curse - a young man must fall in love with you despite your monstrous appearance, and *you* must fall in love with *him*. Only the power of true love can break the curse."

"True love?" Abigail scoffed bitterly, remembering her parents and how they'd appeared to be so in love, and how her father had poisoned her mother. They'd been the picture perfect couple, but it had all been a lie. "There is no such thing as true love. That's just a fairytale!"

Agathon shrugged carelessly. "Believe what you will, but true love is the most powerful force in the universe, and the only power that can activate the Philosopher's Stone." The sorcerer handed Abigail the rainbow-colored stone. "Take heed, your time to break the curse is limited. A crack has already formed in the stone. Once the stone shatters, you will no longer have the chance to regain your humanity." The sorcerer spun around, his cloak billowing out behind him and headed for the open double doors.

Abigail panicked as she watched him go. "No! Wait!" Her voice was tinged with desperation. "Where are you going? You can't just leave me here alone like this! I can't do this alone!"

Agathon glanced over his shoulder at the yeti girl. "You will not be alone. Your loyal servants will be here to help you. Their fate is tied with yours now."

"W-What do you mean?" Abigail gave the sorcerer a searching look.

As if in response to Abigail's question, her servants began to appear and reveal themselves. Abigail gasped when she noted that they'd all been turned into stone statues that could move and talk.

Abigail looked down at the Aurora Borealis quartz sitting in the palm of her hand. When the Philosopher's Stone shattered - they too would shatter into dust. She gulped.

"Their lives are now in your hands, Abigail Snow," Agathon called as he left the ballroom. "It is up to you to break the curse. Save them, and save yourself."

To be continued in…Chapter 4:

Chapter 4:

The following morning Bellamy awoke with a gasp and sat up in bed. That dream had felt so real. No. That hadn't been an ordinary dream. It'd been more of a *vision* of the past. The bookworm knew deep in his gut that the young heiress from his dream had to be Abigail Snow a.k.a the yeti girl.

In the vision he'd been unable to see her face - it had been shrouded in a kind of mystical mist. Perhaps, Bellamy was unable to see Abigail's true appearance because of the curse that the sorcerer Agathon had placed her under.

Bellamy had to admit to himself that he understood Abigail a little bit better now, and understood why she felt people's emotions could be *bought* and that *love* wasn't real. He remembered the stricken expression on Abigail's face when she'd been turned into a yeti and had called out to her friends for help. They'd all ignored her, and had run away screaming. In the end, those friendships had all been superficial.

As for Abigail's opinion on love - it would be hard to believe in love if your father decided to poison your mother. A thoughtful frown formed on Bellamy's face. He wasn't entirely sure Aspen had tried to poison Holly though. From his perspective it had appeared to be more of an experiment…gone wrong, perhaps. This would mean the poisoning had been *unintentional*, at least.

It must have been hard on Abigail to first lose her mother, and then so soon after that her father. Everyone assumed it was a suicide, but again Bellamy wasn't entirely convinced. It was strange how that stone statue had turned up more or less *in his place*.

That's right...the statues. Bellamy thought, before leaping out of bed. He was freezing dressed only in pj bottoms, so he threw on a robe that had been provided for him, and put on some slippers before he left the bedroom. He didn't even want to wonder why Jett had decided to give him fluffy, white bunny slippers.

With purposeful steps Bellamy padded down the hall, heading for the grand staircase that led down into the foyer. As he descended the staircase he spotted the two statues he'd never really bothered to pay too much attention to before, and sucked in a breath. *There they are. Mr. and Mrs. Snow.*

Bellamy walked over, stood directly in front of the statues, and studied them intently, taking in their exquisite craftsmanship. There was such detail - even Mrs. Snow's eyelashes had been carved into the blue quartz stone. The statues looked so...*lifelike.*

But maybe the statues *were* alive - just like the living statues that the household staff had been turned into by that pompous sorcerer Agathon.

Bellamy cleared his throat and raised his hand in an awkward greeting. "Uh, hi...I'm Bellamy. It's a pleasure to meet you, Mrs. Snow." The bookworm held out his hand for Mrs. Snow to shake. He closed his eyes, and held his breath. Several seconds ticked by and nothing happened.

"What *are* you doing?" a condescending female voice reached his ears. He may have imagined it but it also sounded slightly amused.

Bellamy glanced up to see Abigail descending the staircase in an oddly graceful manner. She was wearing a sky-blue silk robe that billowed out behind her regally. It made Bellamy smirk. Abigail was ever the heiress, despite her current form.

Feeling bashful by his own silly actions, Bellamy scratched the back of his neck. "Oh, I was just, ah…"

Abigail narrowed her silver eyes at Bellamy keenly. "They won't speak." She walked over to stand beside Bellamy, and gazed upon the statues along with him. "They're not like the rest of the household staff."

"Are you sure?" Bellamy asked tentatively.

Abigail looked at him strangely. "Yes. That statue there is of my dead mother, Holly. My father, Aspen, carved it out of love, no, *guilt.*"

"Who carved the statue of your father?" the bookworm questioned.

Abigail's blue lips dipped into a thoughtful frown. "It just turned up after his... *disappearance*."

"I see." Bellamy stroked his chin with his index finger and thumb. "Interesting."

"Interesting!" Abigail snapped heatedly, and her furry white eyebrow was twitching with her irritation.

"No, I didn't mean it like that," Bellamy quickly amended, raising his hands before him in a surrendering gesture. "I'm sorry for your loss. It's just…I wonder *who* carved the statue of your father."

"Well, *someone* did," Abigail huffed, blowing a long strand of white hair out of her eyes. "It's standing right there, isn't it?"

"Uh…right," Bellamy agreed carefully. He still found it to be incredibly suspicious.

Abigail gave him an exasperated look. "Come on, let's go get some breakfast. It's freezing in here." She sauntered off, expecting Bellamy to follow her.

Bellamy barely heard her as he continued to study the statues for a moment longer. Abigail glanced over her furry shoulder and raised an eyebrow at Bellamy. "Coming?" she asked with an impatient edge to her voice.

"Uh…sure." Bellamy followed Abigail to the dining room obediently. The yeti took her usual seat at the head of the table, and Bellamy sat down to her left.

Throughout breakfast Bellamy was lost in his own thoughts about an evil sorcerer, the Philosopher's Stone, and a cursed damsel in distress. A mystery was beginning to unfold in this enchanted mansion. Bellamy felt like he'd fallen into a fairytale.

Bellamy tried to recall what he knew about the Philosopher's Stone. He'd read about it before in one of his books about stones and their healing properties. The Philosopher's Stone was a legendary alchemical substance capable of turning base metals into gold. It was also known for being an essential ingredient in the elixir of life, which supposedly granted rejuvenation and immortality.

Bellamy's thoughts went to his vision and how Aspen had created what must have been a 'fake' Philosopher's Stone.

Perhaps, Aspen had used one of these fake stones to create the elixir he'd given his wife…but which had ended up poisoning her, instead of curing her.

The sorcerer Agathon had offered Abigail the *real* Philosopher's Stone in return for shelter from the rain, but she'd witlessly refused. Where was the stone now? Bellamy wondered. And was true love really the only way to break Abigail's curse? Was there no other way to activate the power of the Philosopher's Stone?

Were those statues of Abigail's parents - really just statues? Bellamy's attention turned to the stone servants and began to watch them closely. They didn't appear to be all that different from the statues in the foyer.

Abigail was beginning to grind her teeth. Bellamy hadn't noticed that he'd been completely silent throughout breakfast, making Abigail suspect that he was still angry with her for last night, and for having offered to pay outrageous sums of money for Bellamy's love.

Throughout breakfast, she'd tried to start a conversation with Bellamy so that she could apologize for her actions. But he was completely ignoring her! He wouldn't even *look* at her. Well, why would he want to look at her? Abigail thought venomously to herself. She *was* a hideous monster.

The yeti tugged at her hair in frustration, and Bellamy still didn't notice her inner turmoil. *Oh my God, I just don't get him! Argh! Oh, that's it! I don't know what I should do!* Abigail abruptly stood up from her seat, her stone chair scraping across the marble floor loudly, and approached Jett. She grabbed Jett's arm and dragged him over to a corner of the dining room so that they could speak without Bellamy overhearing them.

"Is there something I can help you with, Milady?" Jett arched an eyebrow at her.

"Jett, I'm dying here. What should I do? He's completely ignoring me now. It's like I don't even exist," Abigail complained.

"First, you should apologize for last night," Jett advised sagely.

Abigail threw her hands up into the air out of exasperation. "What does it *look* like I've been trying to do for the past hour!"

Jett tilted his head slightly as he regarded her. "Imitate a fish, Milady?"

Abigail's eyebrow twitched, and she let out a sigh. Jett was right. She needed to speak up already. "Okay, I'll apologize to him. But then…what should I do to make him fall in love with me?" She lowered her voice conspiratorially. "If he can't be bought then I don't know how else to win his *affection*."

"Win?" Jett shook his head at Abigail. "You gain a person's affections by first earning their trust and respect."

Abigail snorted. "And *how* do I gain his trust and respect?"

"Why don't you start with showing him that you're a *good* person." Jett nodded knowingly to himself.

"How?" the yeti asked bluntly.

Jett pondered this for a moment before he spoke. "Why don't you show him your father's laboratory? Show him all the hard work you've been doing as you try to find a 'cure' for us - a way to turn your servants back to their former human selves."

"The laboratory?" The yeti's silver eyes widened and she shook her head. "You can't be serious. He's going to think I'm crazy. Just like how I used to think my father was crazy…until I met that evil sorcerer Agathon, and he cursed us all. Only then did I come to accept the existence of *magic*. What will make *him* accept it?"

Jett's eyebrows rose. "You don't think *seeing* living statues and a yeti are enough to make him a believer in the supernatural?"

"Right…good point," Abigail allowed and nodded in a chagrined fashion. "Okay. I'm going back over there." The yeti smoothed her hair with her clawed, blue hands, and licked her chapped lips nervously. "How do I look?" She flashed her fangs at Jett.

"Absolutely hideous," Jett replied honestly.

A muscle beneath Abigail's eye ticked in irritation. "That *would* have been a good time to lie to me, Jett." The yeti took a deep breath to steel her nerves. "Alright, back in the game, girl!" She slapped her cheeks as she tried to psych herself up.

The yeti gracefully took her seat at the head of the table, and cleared her throat to get Bellamy's attention. "I'm sorry," she said though gritted teeth. Bellamy did not respond. Abigail tried again, a little louder this time. "I'm sorry!" Still no response. "I'M SORRY, OKAY!"

Bellamy was snapped out of his inner thoughts by Abigail's yelling. "What?"

Abigail flushed. "Look, I'm sorry, okay? About last night...when I tried to buy your love." She twirled a strand of white hair around her index finger nervously.

Bellamy just gave Abigail a blank stare.

It made Abigail even jitterier. "I-I didn't mean it in a *sexual* way if that's what you thought." Her cheeks were turning a strange magenta color as she blushed.

The corner of Bellamy's lip twitched and he had to hold back a smile. Yeti girl was acting surprisingly...*cute*. He decided to remain silent a little while longer, just to see what she'd say.

"I mean, why would you think I'd want to sleep with *you* anyways," Abigail blazed on. "You're just a *nerd*!"

Nerd? Bellamy reached up and touched the round glasses on his face. He kept forgetting that Abigail hadn't seen him without his glasses. Thank God. He wanted to keep it that way. He didn't like the idea of a monster girl chasing after him like a tigress in heat. He shuddered at the thought.

Bellamy pushed his glasses up his nose smartly with his index finger. "You're right. I *am* a nerd, and a total bookworm."

Nice segue. "*Ohhh* you like books?" Abigail began in what she hoped was a nonchalant tone. "Well, I happen to have a *lot* of them downstairs in my-"

"Torture chamber? Dungeon?" Bellamy helpfully supplied in a wry tone.

"No!" Abigail snapped, her eyes flashing. "My laboratory, okay?"

Laboratory? She must mean her father's. Bellamy realized with growing interest. "Really?" His look turned hopeful. "I'd like to see...the books."

"Great." Abigail stood up from the table. "Let's go."

"In our pajamas?" Bellamy arched an eyebrow at the yeti girl.

Abigail flushed, her cheeks turning magenta again. "I don't really wear clothes. Now that I have all this horrible fur - nothing will fit," she muttered darkly to herself. "But, um, you should probably go get dressed first or else you'll end up getting another fever and I'll be forced to nurse you back to health again."

A deep scowl formed on Bellamy's face. "You want me to put on one of those penguin suits, don't you?"

Abigail blinked. "You don't like them? They were incredibly expensive."

Bellamy shrugged. "I'm not used to being so...dressed up." He waved his hand through the air.

"Well, what kind of clothes *do* you prefer?" The yeti found herself asking.

Bellamy lifted his shoulders into another shrug. "I dunno. Normal clothes - jeans, T-shirts, sweaters, boots and sneakers."

Abigail snapped her fingers imperiously, and Jett was at her side in an instant. "You heard the man, Jett. Please find Bellamy some clothes he will feel more comfortable in."

Jett bowed. "As you wish, Milady."

After Jett managed to find Bellamy some normal clothes the bookworm met up with Abigail in the foyer. Abigail tried not to scrunch her nose up at the sight of Bellamy dressed in a navy blue sweater, black jeans, and lace-up boots. *So not handsome.* She pouted mentally. *Those are...pauper clothes. Ugh, I can't believe I have to fall in love with him. Boring!*

"Come on, follow me." Abigail led the way to the door, which opened upon a staircase leading down to the laboratory. The duo descended the steep, narrow steps, and when they reached the bottom of the stairs Abigail flipped on a light switch, which flooded the laboratory with light from the overhead fluorescent lights.

Abigail had kept her father's laboratory pretty much the same. There were still worktables piled with chemistry sets, small bubbling cauldrons, and beakers and test tubes filled with glowing, neon-colored substances. The yeti knew that Bellamy would be impressed, and puffed up her chest with pride as she waved her hand to encompass the whole lab. "This is it. My laboratory. Pretty impressive, huh?"

But Bellamy barely spared the lab a second glance. What had immediately captured Bellamy's full attention were the enormous wooden bookcases standing against the back wall of the lab filled with *hundreds* of books. "Are those the books you mentioned?" A starry-eyed expression formed on his face as Bellamy strode over to one of the bookcases and began to peruse the shelves excitedly. "Ooo, these are all First Editions! This one is really rare! These must have cost a *fortune*!"

Abigail sighed, and walked over to stand beside Bellamy. She'd never seen someone get so excited over a bunch of old, dusty *books* before. In fact, she didn't think any of her past boyfriends had even known how to read. *I can't believe I'm letting this peasant touch my First Editions. Argh.* "You really like books, don't you? Then...they're yours." Abigail declared generously while her stomach was tying itself up into knots. "Feel free to come down here and read whenever you'd like."

Bellamy's head snapped in Abigail's direction and he gawked at her in wide-eyed astonishment. "You're really giving these to me?"

"Ah, yeah, sure." Abigail was beginning to feel uncomfortable with the amorous way Bellamy was beginning to look at her. She coughed into her hand. "I've read most of them already anyways. And will you *stop* looking at me like that!"

Bellamy reached out and took one of Abigail's hands into his own two hands. "Thank you." He squeezed her hand softly.

The yeti's cheeks were turning magenta again. She was surprised that he was willing to touch her - especially touch her blue-skinned, clawed hand like that. "It's no big deal, really."

Bellamy just smiled before releasing Abigail's hand and returning his attention to the books. His sharp blue eyes began to scan the different titles, and he started to select a few books to read from the shelves, creating a tall stack in his arms.

"Aren't you at all curious about my lab?" Abigail asked. "Most people would say something like 'This looks like Snape's classroom' or something."

Bellamy paused with his hand on the spine of a book. "Oh. Right. What's it for?" His tone was bland and his expression was carefully neutral.

"I'm trying to find an alternative way to turn my servants human again through transmutation experiments." Abigail raised her chin proudly and gave Bellamy an expectant look. He probably thought she was some kind of genius now.

"That so?" Bellamy said dryly.

A vein in Abigail's temple throbbed in ire. "Aren't you at all surprised? What I'm trying to do isn't easy. I'm combining alchemy and magic."

"I thought only *true love* could break the curse?" Bellamy reminded pointedly.

"Pffft." Abigail snorted and waved her hand through the air. "What if I never find true love? What then? My servants will crumble to dust! I can't let them die." Her shoulders had begun to tremble. "Not when this is all *my* fault!"

A surprised look flitted across Bellamy's face when he noticed the passion swirling in the yeti's silver eyes. "That's…actually very nice of you. *Heh*."

Abigail huffed. "Don't sound so surprised, Nerd! I can be nice, if I try. I mean, I happen to be a *very* nice person!" she quickly amended.

"Uh huh." Bellamy didn't sound all that convinced.

"Don't use that tone with me, Mister. It's true! I would do *anything* to save them. Pay any price. I'd give up all my riches so long as Jett and the others could be human again!" Abigail insisted fervently.

"And what about you?" Bellamy asked, curiously.

"What about me?" The yeti blinked.

"What about…you staying a yeti?" The bookworm prompted.

Abigail frowned. "Right now my priority is trying to find a way to turn everyone back to normal. As for myself…it's better to be realistic. There's not much hope. The chances of someone falling in love with me are slim." *And even slimmer I'll fall in love with someone. I don't believe in love.* The yeti thought sourly to herself.

Bellamy gave Abigail a searching look. "That's…commendable. I could help you. I don't know much about alchemy or magic, but maybe after I read up a bit on it I might be able to give you a different viewpoint that could prove useful."

It was Abigail's turn to look surprised. "You would help me?"

The bookworm's shoulders raised in a lackadaisical shrug. "Sure. Why not? It's not like I have anything better to do while I remain your prisoner here."

"My hero." The yeti's voice was dripping with sarcasm. But maybe it wouldn't be so hard being nice to Bellamy DeWinter after all.

***

Contrary to Abigail's belief, Bellamy had in fact been *very* interested in Aspen's laboratory. But since he'd already seen it in his dream vision he thought that it was wise to pretend to be indifferent, and not look overly interested in it lest Abigail grow suspicious.

Yes, the books were amazing and interesting too, but what was even more interesting was the locked room in the laboratory. Was the Philosopher's Stone in there? Bellamy couldn't help but wonder.

After their first visit to the lab, Bellamy and Abigail started to spend their time together down there, giving each other company. While Abigail would work on her strange alchemy and transmutation experiments, Bellamy would usually be found seated in a comfy armchair reading a book. There was a pile of books on the table next to him with the following titles: *Splendor Solis*, *Astronomia Nova*, *Codex Imperium*, *Key of Solomon*, and the *Book of Cagliostro*.

While Bellamy read he surreptitiously watched Abigail out of the corner of his eyes as she performed her experiments, several of which seemed to include a rainbow-colored stone. His eyes widened dramatically when he watched her turn a live rat into jade. But when Abigail tried to turn the jade rat back to flesh and blood - nothing happened. And the times something did happen…weren't pretty.

Apparently, it was easy to turn a living creature to stone, but not easy to return them to their original state. Trying to keep his tone as nonchalant as possible Bellamy spoke, "Is that rock thing you're using…the Philosopher's Stone?"

Abigail's shoulders stiffened, and she gave Bellamy a suspicious look. "Where did you learn that name?"

"From one of the books," Bellamy replied with an innocent wave to the bookcases.

"Oh. This." Abigail held up the stone she'd been using in her latest experiment. "Is not the *real* Philosopher's Stone. I'm using fakes or replicas for my experiments. It's much too dangerous to risk the real stone until I'm confident it won't be destroyed during one of my experiments."

"Where's the real stone?" Bellamy worked to keep his expression carefully neutral.

"None of your damned business!" Abigail had roared in Bellamy's face, suddenly losing her temper. Heat rose to her cheeks in embarrassment for her outburst though.

Bellamy put his hands up before him in a surrendering gesture. "Whoa. I was just curious. That's all."

Abigail was panting for breath, her chest heaving as she tried to rein in her temper. "That'd better be all. Don't ask about the stone again! *Ever*."

"Alright, I won't." Bellamy glanced askance at the locked door. He didn't need Abigail's permission to see the stone. He just needed the key. Unfortunately he had no idea where the key could be and began to feel frustrated. That's when a silvery glint caught his eyes, and he looked at Abigail.

He'd never noticed the thick silver chain that was dangling from around her neck before, or the key that was hanging from that chain since it was slightly buried in the fluffy white fur that covered most of Abigail's body.

Bellamy ducked his head to hide his stunned, elated expression. *The key! It's been right there all along! I need to get that key somehow. If I can study the Philosopher's Stone myself maybe I can figure out why Abigail's experiments keep failing.* Bellamy was confident in his own genius to solve this puzzle.

In order to steal the key, Bellamy decided to wait until he was sure Abigail had gone to sleep that night then carefully snuck into the yeti's bedroom. As Bellamy stealthily crept inside, his curiosity got the better of him and he looked around the room. It wasn't everyday that one got to see a yeti's bedroom after all.

Bellamy's lips dipped into a frown though since the room was incredibly normal, and surprisingly feminine. The long brocade curtains that covered the almost floor-to-ceiling windows were a beige color with the pattern of red roses on them. The comforter that was draped over Abigail's four-poster bed matched the curtains, and also had a rose pattern. The lamps sitting on the two nightstands that were situated on either side of the bed had pastel pink shades.

Then he caught sight of Abigail's dressing table. His eyebrows rose to his hairline when he saw that the mirror had been broken. It looked like someone had punched the glass and had caused the mirror to shatter. Bellamy approached the dressing table and inspected the items on the counter. There were several silver hairbrushes with lots of white fur stuck in the bristles, and nail files littered the counter as well.

Bellamy picked up one of the hairbrushes and inspected the white fur. He glanced over at Abigail's sleeping form and his frown deepened. It must have been hard for a young woman to be turned into a *monster*. With a pang of sympathy, his chest tightened.

For the zillionth time he felt the sorcerer Agathon had gone too far in cursing Abigail and turning her into a monster. She'd been recently orphaned, parentless, alone. Who would ever be able to see past Abigail's monstrous appearance, and love her, in this day and age? It seemed highly unlikely. His heart went out to Abigail Snow, and her plight.

Bellamy noticed that the pewter and silver picture frames sitting on her dresser were devoid of photos, and suddenly wondered what Abigail had looked like before the curse. If she was cute now then she must have been gorgeous-

Bellamy's thoughts skidded to an abrupt halt.

Did I really just think a yeti was cute? What the hell is wrong with me? Bellamy inwardly berated himself, startled by his own train of thought.

The bookworm shook his head to clear it, and carefully approached Abigail's bedside as quietly as possible, his footfalls silent on the Persian carpet. Abigail was lying on her back and snoring loudly. *Cute.* He shook his head vigorously again.

Bellamy reached out and gingerly began to remove the chain from around Abigail's neck. The yeti let out a breath, blowing his bangs away from his face. Bellamy held his breath as he continued to remove the chain and key as carefully as possible.

"Phew," Bellamy let out a breath of relief as soon as he had the key safely in hand. The bookworm left Abigail's room and shut the door softly behind him. He felt bad breaking Abigail's trust like this, but…he was a gemologist. He was confident he could figure out the mystery behind the Philosopher's Stone.

Once Bellamy was inside of the lab, he swiftly strode over to the locked door and used the key to open it. He opened the door, and flipped on a light switch. There sitting on a marble pedestal was the Sorcerer's Stone. It was similar in appearance to an Aurora Borealis quartz since it was rainbow-colored and slightly translucent. But this stone was glowing softly with an inner light that was most decidedly *magical*.

Enthralled by the stone, Bellamy approached it in a sort of trance. When he was only a foot away that's when he noticed the tiny cracks on the stone's surface. He frowned, that couldn't be good. He wondered what was causing the stone's deterioration, but it had to be Agathon's curse. Bellamy reached his hand out towards the stone concernedly.

"What are you doing in here?" Abigail's harsh demand had him freezing.

Then Bellamy spun to face her. "Abigail!" He couldn't stop the guilty look that formed on his face.

Fear flickered in Abigail's silver eyes as she eyed the stone. "Get the hell away from it!" The yeti rushed Bellamy, and shoved him aside, hard.

Bellamy flew through the air and hit the wall with a smack. He groaned as his back and the back of his head hit the wall painfully. He slid down the wall until his butt was on the cold, concrete floor.

Abigail approached Bellamy with predatory steps, leaned over and growled in his face. "How dare you get close to the stone! Did you touch it? Do you realize what you could have done?" Her silver eyes flashed in anger.

Bellamy pushed himself up off the floor. "Ow." His arm has been dislocated. "I'm sorry…I was just trying to help. I'm a gemologist-"

Abigail's eyes narrowed suspiciously at Bellamy. "You knew all along, didn't you? You knew the Philosopher's Stone was somewhere in this mansion! *That's* why you came here and befriended me. It was all a ruse to get the stone. You just want *immortality* like everyone else who has come here! You…*imposter*!" The yeti shouted in his face.

"What? No, I-" Bellamy protested with his back pressed against the wall.

"Get out!" Abigail shouted at him and when Bellamy just stared at her in disbelief she raised her voice. "GET OUT! Before I kill you, you imposter! You thief!" The yeti roared right in Bellamy's face, showing her pointed fangs.

A tremor of fear slid up Bellamy's spine. *Shit.* In that moment, Abigail was truly frightening. She looked like a monster. Bellamy knew better than to stick around a crazy, pissed off yeti, and so he ran. He ran out of the lab and then out of the mansion.

Jett tried to stop him on his way out, calling out to him concernedly, "Master Bellamy, wait!"

But Bellamy ignored the butler, exited the mansion, retrieved his team of dogs from the stables, hooked them up to his sled, and then he was off with a snap of the reins. "Mush!"

The dogsled flew down the graveled path that winded its way through the beautiful, stone gardens. Bellamy didn't bother to even admire the stone formations as he passed. When Bellamy and the dogs passed through the front black wrought-iron gate, he could breath easier. It didn't appear as though Abigail was going to stop his escape.

The dogsled passed through a bit of forest before Bellamy and the dogs exited onto the frozen lake. "Mush!" Bellamy snapped the reins so that the dogs ran even faster as they began to cross the precarious, iced-over lake. He wanted to put as much distance between himself and that crazy yeti girl as possible.

That's when a feral roar split the air, causing the ice beneath the sled to vibrate - the roar was so loud. Then a white blur was charging towards Bellamy and his team of dogs. Bellamy narrowed his eyes at the approaching white blur. Was it Abigail? He wondered frantically, his heart pounding inside of his chest. But as the creature drew closer Bellamy was able to see it for what it truly was. *Holy shit. A polar bear!* "Mush!" He snapped the reins, urging his dogs to run faster.

The dogs didn't need much encouragement when the seven hundred pound polar bear came charging after the sled with thundering footfalls. The polar bear abruptly sprang through the air from behind the sled.

When Bellamy glanced over his shoulder his eyes flared in alarm as he watched the polar bear soaring through the air and about to barrel into the sled. He had no choice but to jump off the sled. Bellamy hit the ice hard and rolled across it.

Bellamy watched as the polar bear crashed into the back of the sled, and immediately raked its claws over the burlap sack that contained all of Doris's woodcarvings. The animal woodcarvings fell out of the bag, and spilled and skidded across the ice in all directions.

Bellamy quickly scrambled to his feet, and a few wooden figurines skidded to a halt in front of him.

The polar bear let out a frustrated roar that Bellamy had escaped its wrath and set its sights on the team of dogs next.

The dogs! Bellamy inwardly panicked. *Mother loves those dogs.* A determined expression settled over his face. He looked down, spotted the wooden figurine of a yeti, picked it up, and threw it at the polar bear. "Hey! Get away from *my* dogs!"

The wooden figurine hit the polar bear's backside and it glanced over its shoulder at Bellamy. The polar bear languidly hopped off the sled and began to approach Bellamy with menacing steps, growling low in its throat.

Fuck me. Bellamy thought grimly. Even if he ran - he'd never escape the polar bear. He decided that he'd rather face his death head on rather than letting the polar bear attack him from behind and dying in a cowardly fashion.

Bellamy bent over and picked up a dog-shaped figurine next. "That's right. It's just you and me now, buddy. Bring it!" Bellamy threw the figurine at the polar bear's head - it hit him right between the eyes.

The polar bear blinked stupidly for a couple of seconds before it roared angrily at Bellamy. "Yep. I am so dead." The polar bear charged towards Bellamy, and leapt through the air at him.

That's when a white blur slammed into the polar bear's side and knocked it away from Bellamy. Was it another polar bear? Bellamy wondered wildly as he watched the two creatures wrestling and rolling across the ice. But then he caught a glimpse of distinctive blue skin.

Bellamy's eyes flared. It was the yeti girl, Abigail!

Abigail and the polar bear fought viciously. The yeti blocked the polar bear's claws with her own claws. But there was really no way for Abigail to protect herself from a snapping maw full of sharp teeth.

Aghast, Bellamy watched as the polar bear sank its teeth into Abigail's shoulder, and she screamed in pain. In retaliation, Abigail slashed her claws across the polar bear's throat before digging her claws into the wound that was already gushing blood in order to finish the beast off.

The polar bear struggled against Abigail for several minutes, but she kept her claws buried deep in its flesh until finally the polar bear went still and its slack maw fell away from the yeti's shoulder. As soon as she was able to Abigail shoved the polar bear away from her and stood. She turned to face the shocked Bellamy. Bright red blood was staining the yeti's white fur. Abigail smiled lopsidedly. "Are you alright, Bellamy?"

Bellamy was stunned that she was asking if *he* was okay when she'd been heavily injured during her fight against the polar bear. Abigail started to walk towards him, but the ice beneath the yeti's feet suddenly cracked and gave way.

Bellamy watched in horror as Abigail fell into the icy water. Just like that. "Abigail!" He shouted and ran towards the hole in the ice. Bellamy flattened himself on the lake's iced-over surface, and reached into the cold water with both of his hands. His hands wrapped around Abigail's wrist.

Bellamy began to tug upwards, but Abigail weighed a ton with all that wet fur. He was starting to get pulled forward too. At this rate, he'd end up in the lake along with Abigail, he realized. There'd be no escape. But...he couldn't let go of the wrist of the person who'd just saved his life.

If she goes...I go too. Bellamy thought with grim determination as he was pulled forward until his head went under water.

All of a sudden, he was being pulled back. *What the?* Bellamy was yanked out of the water, and Abigail was being pulled up right along with him!

Once Bellamy was fully out of the water, he glanced behind him and saw his team of five Husky dogs. They'd latched onto Bellamy's jeans and were pulling him backwards. A wide grin spread across Bellamy's face. "I love you guys! Keep it up! Good job!"

Bellamy tightened his hold on Abigail and in less than a minute she'd been pulled completely out of the water and now lay on the surface of the iced-over lake. She appeared to be unconscious.

The bookworm shook the yeti's shoulder concernedly as he tried to rouse her. "Abigail? Abigail!" Bellamy turned Abigail over onto her back, and realized she wasn't breathing. *Shit!* Without hesitation Bellamy started to perform CPR on Abigail - alternating between doing rescue breaths and chest compressions.

A few seconds later, Abigail was coughing up a great deal of water. The yeti blinked and looked up. Bellamy's face swam in her vision, and she blinked. "B-Bellamy, what happened?"

"You fell into the lake," Bellamy explained. "I rescued you."

"You...?" Abigail's brow furrowed.

Bellamy scratched the back of his neck awkwardly. "I performed CPR..."

Abigail's silver eyes widened as Bellamy's words began to sink in. "You...CPR...." A shocked expression settled over the yeti's face and she touched her lips unconsciously with her fingers. "You *kissed* me." Abigail's voice was tinged with confusion, shock and anger.

"Well, that depends on how you view kissing. I mean, you could call it a kiss...but it was just our lips pressing together without any emotion behind it which makes it meaningless," Bellamy rambled carelessly as he remembered all the kisses that had been forced on him by crazy, lovesick girls.

Abigail's eyes flashed with anger and she slapped Bellamy, sending him skidding across the ice from the force of that killer yeti slap.

"Ow." Bellamy sat up and rubbed his jaw, a chagrined expression on his face. "So much for a 'thank you for saving my life'." He pushed himself up off the ice, and shot the yeti an exasperated look.

Abigail became flustered by her own overreaction. "Sorry. That was rather ungrateful of me. It's just..." She shouldn't have been so affected by a simple kiss. "No, never mind. It's nothing."

Bellamy made his way over to the sled and stroked the dogs' heads to calm them down. He owed them a lot. He hopped on and held his hand out to Abigail. "Come on, let's go home, monkey face." A fond smile curled his lips.

Abigail hesitated for a moment before standing up. She swayed on her feet due to blood loss. She realized she had no choice but to accept Bellamy's help to get back to the mansion.

Abigail approached the sled warily, hopped up behind Bellamy and hesitated a moment before wrapping her arms around Bellamy's waist. Even if Bellamy didn't consider them as having kissed, it was still impressive that Bellamy had managed to give a monster like her CPR. She was oddly touched by his heroic actions.

The yeti wondered if she would have been able to do the same if she'd been put into a similar situation. Would she have been selfless enough to give a monster CPR? Why had Bellamy decided to save her? He could have just let her drown. But he hadn't. Did he perhaps…care for her? As a friend, at least?

Bellamy snapped the reins to get the dogs to go a little faster. He wasn't outwardly showing it but he was worried about Abigail. She was heavily wounded, and had been wounded for his sake. It was making him feel funny. And the feeling of her arms wrapped around his waist was making him feel…odd. He owed Abigail his life.

As soon as he'd pulled the sled up in front of the stone staircase that led to the front door of the mansion, Bellamy hopped off the sled and turned to Abigail.

Abigail thought Bellamy was going to give her a hand up and so reached out her hand. But Bellamy surprised her by swooping her up into his arms bridal-style.

"Eek! W-What are you doing? P-Put me down this instant! I'm…too heavy!" Abigail objected, as she stared up at Bellamy in disbelief, her silver eyes as wide as saucers.

Bellamy stared down at her and grinned wolfishly. "You're not that heavy. Actually, I expected you to be a whole lot heavier. All that fluffy fur makes you appear bigger than you are. Besides, I can't let an injured *girl* walk on her own!" Honestly, Abigail was heavy, but Bellamy didn't mind the strain she put on his muscles.

Girl? Abigail thought dizzily to herself. *He sees me as a 'girl' now…and not a monster?*

"Especially, when that girl saved my life," Bellamy added softly.

Abigail looked up to meet Bellamy's stare, but had to look away. There were so many emotions shinning in his blue eyes that were mostly obscured by his round, nerdy glasses. She nibbled on her lower lip, wondering just what Bellamy was thinking about.

Bellamy carried Abigail up the front steps and by the time he'd reached the front door his arms were trembling so he was incredibly grateful when Jett opened the door for him.

"Master Bellamy! Mistress Abigail!" Jett greeted, his voice laced with concern as he ushered them inside with wide eyes. "What happened?"

"A polar bear attacked me…" Bellamy started and noted that Lazuli the maid and the little girl Kristal were also present in the foyer. "Abigail saved my life."

A proud expression formed on Jett's face as he turned to look at Abigail. But then he noticed the blood on her white fur and frowned. "Come, let's get milady up to her room immediately." He turned to address Lazuli and Kristal. "Lazuli, go fetch as many towels as you can find. Kristal, I want you to bring the first-aid kit."

"Yes, Sir, right away," Lazuli said with a curtsey.

"You can leave it to me, Daddy!" Kristal chimed with a salute.

With Jett leading the way, Bellamy carried Abigail up the grand staircase, down the hall, and to Abigail's room. Jett opened the door for Bellamy and they made their way inside. The bookworm walked over and deposited Abigail on her bed, right on top of the floral print comforter.

"Ack! Don't put me on the bed, you imbecile!" Abigail snapped hotly. "Do you have any idea how much these sheets cost? They're from France! And I'm soaking wet and covered in blood. *Ohhh!*" The yeti tried to get off the bed, but Bellamy reached out and pushed her down onto the covers. She glared up at him, but he glared back with a stern look on his face.

"Fuck the French linen!" Bellamy snarled and Abigail was rendered silent by his venomous tone. "You're *hurt*. And that's all that matters right now."

Abigail gave Bellamy a look of disbelief, and finally huffed. "Alright, fine." She crossed her arms over her chest. "I suppose I'll just have to get new ones."

"That's more like it," Bellamy said.

When Abigail tried to get into a sitting position she winced at the pain that flared up in her shoulder. A few minutes later, Lazuli entered the bedroom with a tall stack of fluffy, white towels balanced precariously in her arms. "I've brought the towels, Jett," Lazuli informed him.

Jett turned towards the door and gave Lazuli a grateful look. "Good work. Bring them over to the bed. Lazuli, Bellamy, I want you both to help dry Abigail off."

A horrified expression formed on Abigail's face. "Jett, you can't be serious. You're not thinking of towel drying me, are you? What about blow-drying?"

Jett shook his head at Abigail with a stern expression on his black onyx face. "This is no time for vanity, Milady. You're freezing. You could get deathly ill."

Abigail crossed her arms over her chest and scowled. At this moment, Kristal entered the room with the first-aid kit. She walked over and set it down on the bedside table and watched what was going on with a curious tilt of her head.

Bellamy watched Abigail having her tantrum while his lip twitched in amusement. Lazuli handed him one of the towels, which he gratefully took and began to dry himself off. "Thank you, Lazuli." He grabbed another towel and approached Abigail with it, a mischievous look on his face. "Now, it's your turn."

"Don't you dare," Abigail started to object.

Kristal giggled, grabbed a towel and followed Bellamy's lead, approaching Abigail with an impish smile.

Abigail fussed the entire time Bellamy, Kristal and Lazuli towel dried the yeti off and Bellamy couldn't figure out what the big deal was - that is until all of a sudden Abigail's white fur puffed out and she suddenly resembled a gigantic sheep. Bellamy snorted as he tried to hold back his laughter at the amusing sight.

Abigail's cheeks were turning magenta out of embarrassment. This is *exactly* what she'd been afraid of. "Don't you dare laugh!" she warned.

But it was impossible for Bellamy to contain his mirth. He broke out into boisterous laughter, and was soon joined in by Jett, Lazuli and Kristal.

"*Ohhh!* Do shut up! It's not that funny!" Abigail complained as she glared at them all. "That's enough. All of you. Stop laughing at once!" the yeti demanded imperiously as she sat up in the bed and winced at the pain in her shoulder. A pained groan slipped past her lips.

Bellamy's mirthful expression fell and instantly turned concerned. "Abigail."

Jett grabbed the first-aid kit off the bedside table and approached the bed with it. "I believe it's high time I tended to your wounds, Milady." Abigail huffed but didn't object to Jett's treatment of her wounds. He skillfully cleaned and disinfected the bite wound before stitching it closed. Abigail fretted about scars. Lastly, Jett applied some sort of salve and bandaged the wound with white, cloth bandages.

"Is she going to be okay?" Bellamy asked as he hovered behind Jett.

"Not to worry, Master Bellamy, Abigail has impressive healing capabilities as a yeti," Jett informed him.

"Phew," Bellamy let out a sigh of relief. "Glad to hear she's like Wolverine."

Abigail scrunched up her nose at being compared to the X-man. "I do hope you learned your lesson for running away, Bellamy."

Bellamy gawked at Abigail for a moment. "I only ran away because you scared the bejesus out of me!"

"And I only grew angry because you could have broken the Sorcerer's Stone!" Abigail argued back.

"I was only trying to help," Bellamy groused. "I'm a gemologist. You should have just *trusted* me!"

"I trust no one!" Abigail snapped.

Bellamy rolled his eyes at the yeti girl. "You're going to have to trust someone sometime! You can't go through life *alone*!"

"I'm...not alone," Abigail argued. "I have my servants!"

"Yeah, right *now* you have them," Bellamy grudgingly agreed. "But what happens if you don't find a way to break the curse? They'll turn to dust...and you'll be left all alone."

Abigail flinched at Bellamy's harsh words. "You think I don't know that! I won't let that happen to them. No matter what."

Bellamy's expression softened upon noticing the distressed look on her face. "Then…trust me." He gave the yeti a beseeching look. "Let me help you to find an alternative way to break the curse."

"Why do you want to help me?" Abigail asked, feeling a little suspicious. It was still hard for her to trust people. "This has nothing to do with you."

"I know what it's like to be cursed," Bellamy revealed.

The yeti's fluffy white eyebrows rose. "You do?"

Bellamy nodded solemnly. "My curse is that if a woman sees my face without my glasses on they instantly fall madly in love with me."

A heavy silence descended upon the bedroom and a minute ticked by before Abigail burst out laughing. "You're joking, right?" She gave Bellamy an incredulous look.

Bellamy stiffened and his expression turned grim. "I wish I were. But no, I'm telling the truth. In the past, the girls who saw my face became obsessed with me. When I couldn't return their affections they became crazy and dangerous. Being a lady's man is definitely not all it's cracked up to be." Bellamy tried to smile through his painful memories.

"Alright then. Show me," Abigail challenged, a strange glint in her silver eyes. "Come on, take your glasses off, and let me see this handsome face of yours." She reached out to swipe the glasses off Bellamy's face.

Bellamy instantly panicked. "No!" He shouted in fear and quickly backed up, away from Abigail. He stumbled backwards and ending up falling onto the floor.

Abigail looked at the fearful expression on Bellamy's face and her eyes widened. His breathing was beginning to become irregular, coming in and out in short pants. He looked like he was about to have a panic attack. She frowned since this meant he wasn't lying. Her disbelief turned to concern. "Bellamy! Snap out of it! I won't remove your glasses. I…promise."

Bellamy stared at Abigail and concentrated on slowing down his breathing to a normal pace. He hung his head, feeling pathetic.

Abigail was slightly mystified by what had just happened. "You...you're telling the truth, aren't you? You really are cursed too? Who cursed you?"

Bellamy swallowed the lump that had formed in his throat and licked his lips. "I don't know. The curse was passed down from my mother to me when I was born, and she never told me who cursed her."

Abigail's expression turned sympathetic. "I'm...sorry. It won't happen again."

Bellamy let out a sigh of relief. "Thanks." He pushed himself up off the floor and dusted his damp clothes off. "I'm...going to go get some rest. It's been a long day."

"Alright," Abigail readily agreed. "Goodnight, Bellamy." She watched Bellamy leave her bedroom with his shoulders slumped and his head hanging dejectedly, and felt something twist in her gut.

To be continued in...Chapter 5:

Chapter 5:

Bellamy returned to his bedroom and shut the door softly behind him. He leaned his back against the door, and let out a heavy sigh. Talking about his curse had never been a comfortable subject for him. In fact, he realized that he'd never talked to anyone about the curse except for his mother. But he'd told Abigail. Why?

Bellamy's body was shivering slightly due to his damp clothes and he decided to take a quick, hot shower before going to bed. After he finished his shower, he dressed in the silk pj's that Abigail had provided for him. Those flashy pj's made him feel like a gigolo, or pimp or something. The corner of his mouth twitched and he shook his head ruefully. He really needed to ask Abigail for some normal sleepwear.

Bellamy padded over to the bed, buried himself under the covers, and fell into a restless, troubled sleep. He began to have another dream vision…

FLASHBACK

Nineteen years ago, Doris had been living in Alaska in the town that would someday be known as Yeti Town. Her parents were Hunters, but she really had no interest in pursuing the family trade. Instead, she concentrated on getting a college degree online so that she'd eventually be able to leave and get a job elsewhere.

Doris *hated* living in Alaska. In the small, isolated town there weren't a lot of things one could do for fun or entertainment. The town always seemed to be buried under at least a foot of snow. Doris was *sick* of snow. She longed to move to New York City where she'd be able to go to the mall or movie theaters, and act like a normal teenaged girl.

The only joy Doris found was when she took her team of five dogs and went for a drive on her dogsled. She loved her dogs. They were her only true friends. Her life continued to be uneventful, until one day as Doris was crossing a frozen lake on her dogsled she heard a male voice inside of her head:

Doris, please, help me…

Pulling back on the reins Doris stopped the sled and looked around wildly, wondering where the voice had come from. "Hello?" she called out with a slight tremor in her voice.

Doris, only you can help me. Free me from my prison. I'll die if I remain here much longer. There was a note of urgency in the voice now.

Doris frowned, and her brow furrowed. "Who said that? Hello? Where are you?"

I'm here. Hurry, Doris. You must save me. The rich, velvety male voice continued.

Doris hopped off the sled and began to wander across the ice.

Below you. The voice informed her suddenly.

Doris glanced down at the ice beneath her feet, and gasped. Directly below her and trapped inside of the ice was a man. "Oh my God," she breathed in shock.

Hurry, Doris, get me out of here. Free me. The voice insisted.

Doris shook her head helplessly as she looked down at the trapped figure. "But…how?"

Fetch the icepick you have on your sled and return. The voice instructed.

"Oookay." Doris wasn't sure how this trapped man knew she even had an icepick with her, but followed the man's instructions, fetched the icepick, and returned to the same spot on the frozen lake.

Now, break the ice. The voice directed.

Doris gulped. "I don't think I'm strong enough to do something like that." A skeptical expression had formed on her face.

You can do it, Doris. You are my only hope. The voice urged passionately.

"Well, alright, if you insist." Doris raised the pick and brought it down upon the ice again and again until the ice miraculously began to crack. Doris blinked down in surprise and smiled before she kept on bringing the icepick down upon the ice. She worked until the calluses on her hands started to bleed. When a single drop of her blood fell onto the ice it suddenly shattered away completely.

Doris cried out as she was blasted back by some unseen force. "Eee!" She landed on her behind and groaned. "Ow." Then she looked up to see that a very handsome man was standing directly in front of her.

Doris had never seen such a handsome man before. His short, wavy, hair was the color of spun gold. His sparkling blue eyes were the color of the sky on a clear summer day. Although his face was youthful in appearance, especially with that dimple in his chin, his eyes seemed to hold untold wisdom. He was wearing a hooded, dark blue velvet cloak. The pattern of stars had been embroidered into the material with gold thread.

Doris gawked at the mysterious, otherworldly man. "You…who…*what* are you?"

"I am a sorcerer and a Wish Granter," the man said with a slight nod. "My name is Agathon."

Doris blinked slowly. "You can't be serious."

"Doris, you have saved my life. I now owe you a single wish," Agathon informed her in a commanding tone. "What is thy desire?"

Doris was startled, confused, and half-incredulous with this sudden turn of events. "My desire…? I thought genies granted three wishes?" She added in a lighthearted tone, which simply caused the sorcerer to arch an eyebrow at her. Doris had only one desire that came to her mind. And that was the love of a young man who lived in town. His name was Raul DeWinter.

Raul was extremely handsome. He had hair the color of midnight, blue eyes the color of periwinkles, and alabaster skin. Raul had a lean, muscular physique due to his training as a Hunter. He was known for being quite skilled with his rifle and could take down most prey with a single shot. Raul was also known for being a notorious playboy due to his good looks.

Doris had tried to flirt with and get Raul's attention upon several occasions, but to no avail. She was simply too *plain*. She wished she were beautiful enough to get Raul's attention. If she had Raul's love she knew she would be happy, even living in this isolated Alaskan town, and she wouldn't feel so lonely anymore.

A determined expression formed on Doris's face and she met Agathon's inquisitive stare. Even if this were just a dream, she decided to be honest about her one true desire. "I wish for Raul DeWinter to fall madly in love with me."

The sorcerer blinked, and then let out a heavy, disappointed sigh. "You want me to cast a love spell? Why is it always a love spell?" He muttered the last darkly to himself in a low voice so that Doris wouldn't hear.

Doris nodded eagerly. "Yes."

"Very well. But before I grant you your wish, Doris, I feel I must tell you *why* I ended up trapped in my icy prison. It's because I granted someone a wish and they didn't like how the wish was granted. But, you see, wishes are dangerous. All magic has a price. The balance of the universe must be maintained.

"For example, you could wish to save someone's life, but unwittingly cause the death of someone else instead. A life for a life. The principle of equal exchange. You cannot make something out of nothing. This ungrateful cur grew angry with me and decided to imprison me here." Agathon's blue eyes glittered dangerously as he remembered this unjust betrayal.

"So if Raul falls in love with me," Doris began to muse aloud, "what will happen as a result?"

The sorcerer shrugged. "I cannot foresee how the universe will choose to grant you your wish. I can only warn you that there *will* be a price for your wish being granted, in order to maintain the balance of the universe. That being said, do you still want me to grant your wish?" Agathon's eyebrows rose in question.

Doris nibbled on her lower lip as she considered what Agathon had told her for a moment. That's when she glanced around the cold, icy, desolate landscape. Doris rubbed at her arms where goosebumps had formed due to the cold. The silence was heavy without her or Agathon speaking. The loneliness was starting to seep into her bones again. She was so tired of being alone.

I don't want to be alone anymore! Doris thought desperately to herself. *I'm willing to try something crazy.* She looked up, met the sorcerer's eyes, swallowed a lump of nervousness in her throat, and nodded. "Yes. Please, grant me my wish. Make Raul fall in love with me."

Disappointment swirled in Agathon's blue eyes, but he nodded just the same. "Your wish...has been granted."

As Doris headed home on her dogsled, she didn't *feel* any different. But she was thrumming with nervous, expectant energy. She couldn't wait to go and see Raul at his usual hangout - the *Polar Bear Pub* - in order to see if his feelings for her had miraculously changed in some way.

Once at home, Doris took a quick shower, blow-dried and styled her hair as best she could and brushed her teeth. She didn't want to have bad breath in case things worked out and Raul wanted to kiss her. She picked out a cute outfit - well, as cute as it could get in this cold weather. She'd decided on a tight, long-sleeved, low-cut black shirt, a knee-length black and white skirt, stockings and knee boots. She only owned one expensive coat - a floor-length, black mink one and this was the coat she chose to wear.

Doris didn't want her parents to know she was going out again at such a late hour and had to stealthily sneak out of the log cabin. Trembling with excitement, Doris hopped onto her dogsled, grabbed the reins, and drove to the *Polar Bear Pub*.

She parked the sled right outside the pub, hopped off, made her way to the front door, and entered. A pleasant gust of warm air hit Doris as soon as she entered, turning her pale, frozen cheeks pink.

Doris took off her mink coat and hat, and hung both items by the door. As Doris began to make her way deeper into the pub she could feel eyes on her. She looked around and was surprised to see that the men inside of the pub all had their attention on her. Doris stilled and took in their admiring glances with disbelief.

Something *was* different about her. She smiled to herself. Usually she was invisible to the men in this town, but now...

Doris quickly searched the pub for Raul and spotted him seated at the bar on a tall barstool with two women seated on either side of him on their own stools. The women were both clinging to one of his arms and rubbing their cleavage against him.

Oh, Raul, always the playboy. Doris thought. *Perhaps you will never change.* She swallowed and nervously began to make her way towards him. This was it - the moment of truth.

Raul felt someone's intense stare on him and spun on his barstool curiously to see who would dare to stare at him so blatantly. He was wearing his usual cocky expression, but when he met Doris's plain brown eyes his expression changed. First, he looked surprised, then intrigued, and finally amorously shy.

Raul slid off the stool with his usual confident movements, and approached Doris. Doris walked towards Raul with stiff, awkward steps. The rest of the pub seemed to disappear for Doris until it was just her and Raul.

Raul's brow furrowed as he looked over Doris's face. "Doris, is that really you?" His voice had grown low, husky.

Doris nodded and offered Raul a timid smile. "Hi Raul. I, um…"

Before Doris could finish her sentence, Raul reached out, cupped Doris's cheek, and smoothly leaned in for a kiss.

Doris's eyes flared in surprise, and she inwardly squealed. *Eeee!* Raul was kissing her! She shut her eyes and eagerly kissed him back even though she didn't really know what she was doing. But Raul didn't seem to mind her unskilled kissing. It felt so good to be kissing him and to be in his arms like this. It felt like a dream. Doris was on Cloud 9. However-

Abruptly Raul was yanked away from Doris. "Hey! Why the hell are *you* kissing Doris? Doris is *my* gal!" one young man announced right before he punched Raul hard across the face.

Doris blinked at this guy she barely knew claiming that she was *his*. What the hell…? She raised her chin, and clenched her hands into fists at her sides. "You're *not* my boyfriend. I don't even *know* you, buddy."

Raul rubbed his cheek where a red mark was beginning to form. A feral grin curled Raul's lips before he punched the young man right back. "Doris is *mine!*" he growled possessively.

Raul's declaration made Doris's heart flutter inside of her chest. Until-

"No, Doris is mine!" another man stood up from one of the nearby tables.

"No, mine!" another man objected.

Doris stared around the pub wide-eyed, wondering what the hell was going on. What was wrong with these men? Then Doris remembered the sorcerer's warning. Was this the 'price' he'd mentioned she'd have to pay for gaining Raul's love?

Doris realized in that moment she had to do something before things escalated inside of the pub into a crazy bar fight. She grabbed Raul's hand, raised her chin, and spoke loudly, "Listen up, everyone, the one I *love* is Raul!"

Raul gave Doris a surprised, pleased look. "*Doris,*" he said dreamily.

Several men moaned in despair while a few other men grew angrier than before. *Shit!* A tremor of fear crawled up her spine. She didn't like that crazed look in their eyes. "Time to go, darling." Doris pulled Raul along with her and they made a hasty exit from the pub.

Doris mounted her dogsled, and Raul hopped up behind her. Raul wrapped his arms around Doris's waist, and off they went. "Mush!" Doris snapped the reins with a flick of her wrists.

Doris was so frazzled by what had just happened that she didn't even know where she was really going. All she knew is that she had to put as much distance between them and the pub as possible.

Raul leaned in and whispered in Doris's ear, his hot, minty breath wafting over her ear causing her to shudder. "Doris, turn left up ahead. Let's go back to my place. My parents are out of town for the weekend."

Doris blushed at the implication behind his husky words. She nibbled nervously on her lower lip, but this is what she'd wanted all along, right? She wanted Raul, his body, his love, his companionship, his everything. More than anything she wanted him to fill this empty void of loneliness inside of her.

"Alright," Doris agreed, pulling on the reins in such a way that the dogs were steered into taking a left. They headed towards a huge log cabin that Raul's parents owned.

That very night, Doris gave her virginity to Raul. It was better than anything she had imagined. She felt so...*connected* to Raul now. In the afterglow of sex, Doris had wrapped her arms around Raul's muscular, sweaty chest and thought about how they'd be inseparable now. She was feeling hopeful too. Surely, the other men in the village would have to back off once they saw how serious Doris and Raul were about each other.

The following day, Doris and Raul walked around town together hand in hand. Doris expected to see resigned expressions on the men's faces, but was disappointed to see venomous glares being directed Raul's way. Her grip on Raul's hand unconsciously tightened in response.

Perhaps, the men in town weren't taking their relationship seriously since they were just 'dating' and Raul did have the reputation of being a playboy. Feeling desperate and fearful, Doris decided that she and Raul needed to get married as soon as possible in order to have their relationship accepted by everyone in town. Then…those men would have to leave her alone. Wouldn't they?

After Doris and Raul were married, she sadly noted that the strange attitudes of the men in the village towards her didn't change. It was like they'd all become *obsessed* with her for some reason. They'd all turned into crazy, lovesick fools. But Raul was different. She thought, stubbornly to herself. Raul *really* loved her.

But then Doris noticed the murderous glare Raul was shooting at the other men to keep them away from her. Of course, when he turned his attention to her his expression would soften, and become tender and loving. Still, she couldn't forget the crazed glint in his eyes when he was glaring at the other men. It unsettled her and caused her to shudder with unease.

As time passed, Doris began to accept the cold, hard truth. Raul really was just like the other men in town. He'd simply been *enchanted* by her. His feelings for her weren't sincere, or of his own free will.

What have I done? Doris wondered to herself morosely as she realized she'd made a grave mistake by *forcing* Raul to love her. She'd taken away his free will, and now they were both paying the price. Sometimes, Raul even scared her with the intensity of his feelings for her, and his possessive attitude.

Doris eventually came to the painful decision that she should leave Raul and the little Alaskan town far behind. With her absence, she'd free Raul from the curse.

However, on the very day she'd decided to leave as she'd started to pack, a sudden wave of nausea hit her. Doris ran into the bathroom, sank to her knees in front of the toilet, and puked her guts out. *Shit.* What could be wrong with her? She wondered dizzily. Was she sick? Was she...? *No, no, no...*

She couldn't be pregnant? Could she?

Doris reluctantly took a pregnancy test, and discovered that she was indeed pregnant. The little plastic stick had fallen out of her limp hand to clatter onto the cold, tiled bathroom floor. With a sinking feeling inside of her stomach she realized that there was no way she could leave the father of her child behind.

When Doris informed Raul that she was pregnant, he appeared to be incredibly happy and excited by the news, but Doris was unable to share in his happiness since she doubted whether his reaction was sincere, or if it had been forced by the curse.

Eight months passed by without event, and the baby continued to grow inside of her. Until, on a day, just like every other day, something happened that would change Doris's life forever.

Raul had left to go hunting early that morning as he oftentimes did. Doris was just making a second pot of coffee when she heard a knock on the front door. She warily approached the door with a frown on her face, and peeked through the keyhole to see who it was. If it were a man there was no way she was opening the door, especially without Raul around to protect her.

But it turned out to be Doris's friend Samantha. Doris let out a sigh of relief and opened the door. "Hey, Sam, what-?"

Samantha pushed her way inside of the house, and quickly closed and locked the door behind her. She turned to face Doris with a stricken look on her face and started to wring her hands together. "Doris, I have to tell you something. I overheard my boyfriend Robby and his friends talking to each other on game night. They said they were going to get rid of a 'pest' in the forest today. When I asked Robby about it, he said they were going to hunt down a lynx that had been terrorizing Mr. Stone's cattle at his ranch. But when I asked Mr. Stone about it this morning, he told me that as far as he knew all of his cattle were safe and sound."

Doris gave Samantha a confused look. "What are you trying to say, Sam?"

Samantha placed her hands on Doris's shoulders and squeezed. "I'm saying...that if Robby and the others aren't going to hunt a lynx then *what* are they going to hunt exactly? I know this is really none of my business, but ever since you and Raul got married all of the men in town started to act strange. Even my Robby. Not that I'm jealous or anything. I understand since you're gorgeous."

Doris gave Samantha an apologetic look, and felt a wave of guilt crash through her. Especially since the only reason why Sam would think that she was 'gorgeous' was because of the curse. Sam was the gorgeous one with her long blonde hair and curvaceous figure. "Sam, I'm sorry…"

But Sam shook just her head. "No. It's okay. But this morning my Robby was acting extra suspicious. He usually makes a pot of coffee for me before he leaves to go hunt so that the smell will wake me up. But today he didn't make me that pot of coffee which can only mean he didn't want me to wake up yet. I have this bad feeling that maybe Robby and the others are going to do something stupid…like hurt Raul."

The blood slowly began to drain out of Doris's face as Robby and the other men's intentions became horrifically clear. There was no lynx out in the woods that needed killing. They planned to hunt down and kill her Raul! Doris swayed on her feet as a wave of dizziness swept over her, and she had to reach out and put her hand on the wall in order to remain standing. "Oh, no, Raul…"

"I didn't know what I should do," Samantha said, nibbling on her pouty lower lip. "I thought about telling the Sheriff, but…he looks at you funny too."

Doris nodded her agreement. "It's good you didn't go to the Sheriff, Sam. He's also a little…taken with me. Shit. I have to find Raul and stop those guys from doing something stupid! Thanks, Sam!" She rushed out of the house and hopped onto her sled that was always parked out front.

Sam's eyes were wide as she chased after her friend and exited the cabin. "Wait, you can't go out there in your condition! What about the *baby*?"

Doris placed a hand over her rounded stomach and smiled thinly. "He'll be alright. He's a kicker. He's tough. Take care, Sam. Mush!" With a snap of the reins the sled dogs took off, heading for the forest.

Doris drove the sled towards the forest area where Raul usually hunted deer and the occasional bear. She leaned over to tell the dogs, "Find Raul, boys. Go! Mush!"

The Huskies easily picked up Raul's scent and were on the trail. *Oh, Raul.* Despite their tumultuous love affair, Doris really did love Raul. She knew she didn't deserve him. He'd turned out to be such an adorning husband. *I have to protect the father of my child. This is all my fault. I put him in this danger.*

The sled zigzagged through the pine trees until Doris spotted a familiar silhouette ahead. "Raul!" she called out. With a sinking feeling in her stomach, Doris noted that he wasn't alone. Five other young men were surrounding Raul in a circle, and had their shotguns and rifles raised and pointed at him. "No!"

Raul had his own shotgun raised in retaliation, aimed and ready to take one of the men with him. The sound of the sled approaching them got the men's attention, and they glanced Doris's way. "Everyone…just stop!"

Doris maneuvered the sled so that it came to a stop directly in front of Raul. She strategically placed herself between Raul and the other men. Deep down she knew the other men would never actually hurt her. They fancied themselves in love with her, after all.

"Doris, what are you doing here?" Raul asked, worry swirling in his clear blue eyes. "You shouldn't be out here in your condition."

"Raul, I want you to run," Doris said softly so that the other men wouldn't hear her. "It's not safe for you here."

Raul looked startled by her suggestion, and shook his head in disbelief. "No way. I won't leave you."

Doris shot Raul an urgent, frustrated look. "You must. *Please.*"

"Hello, Doris, it's good to finally see you again," Robby began conversationally. "Raul has been keeping you all locked up for himself."

Doris shook her head while giving the man a pitying look. "That's not true, Robby. I've been at home because…I'm pregnant."

"Pregnant," Robby echoed darkly. "With whose child?"

"With Raul's, of course," Doris said indignantly. "He's my *husband!*"

Robby raised his shotgun and pointed it at Raul again. "That son of a bitch, knocked you up? He has some nerve when you belong to *me*!"

"No, she belongs to me!" One of the other men pointed his gun at Robby threateningly.

"She's mine, guys," another man argued, pointing his gun at the man who'd just spoken.

"No, mine!" A forth man pointed his gun at the third man who'd spoken.

"I thought we all decided she doesn't belong to anyone. *Especially* not Raul." A fifth man pointed his shotgun at Raul along with Robby.

"That *was* the plan," Robby nodded his agreement. "But you know what, boys? Doris is mine. All of you should just back the fuck off."

"No fucking way!" one of the men objected hotly.

"Why don't *you* back off!" another added.

Doris started to tremble in fear as the situation began to spiral out of control with the men pointing their guns at each other. "No, please, stop this. All of you," Doris begged while giving the men a beseeching look. "The only one I love is Raul."

"So I just need to kill Raul first," Robby said nastily, a menacing gleam in his dark brown eyes. "Then you'll be mine, Doris."

"Doris will *never* be yours, Robby!" The man who already had his shotgun pointed at Robby pulled down on the trigger and fired. A shot rang through the air and a bullet imbedded itself right between Robby's eyes.

Robby's body crumpled to the snowy ground where it lay still. Robby was dead.

"No, Robby!" Doris screamed, immediately thinking of her best friend. *Poor Samantha! This is all my fault!* Her scream made the other men nervous and they began opening fire on each other. Doris forced herself to stay perfectly still as bullets whizzed past her dangerously.

It was a gut feeling, but she knew these men would never hurt her. Not on purpose anyways. Doris would have flung herself in front of Raul in order to act as a shield, but…she was pregnant, and this made her hesitate. Her life wasn't her own now. It belonged to her unborn child.

Doris did cry out in horror though when she watched Raul get shot, and fall back to the snow. "Raul!"

Only one man was left standing at this point and he was panting for breath. He approached Doris, who was still seated on her dogsled. The man had a hungry gleam in his eyes and he leered at her, reaching out to grab her arm. "Come along, Doris. You belong to me now."

"No!" Doris yelled in protest as she tried to yank her arm out of his iron hold. "Let go of me!"

A shot rang through the air and hit the man in his temple. He fell over sideways.

Wide-eyed, Doris turned to see Raul standing, shotgun in hand, and expression grim. "Get your hands off my *wife*!"

"Raul!" Doris cried happily. But then Raul crumpled to the snowy ground as his strength left him. "Raul!" Doris climbed off the sled and rushed to her husband's side. She cradled his limp body in her arms. "Raul, come on, get up. I'll take you to the town doctor."

Raul weakly opened his eyes and looked up at Doris. "Doris?"

"Yes, Raul?" Doris asked.

"I...love you," Raul managed to croak out.

Guilty tears began to well up in Doris's eyes. "Raul, please-"

"It's too late for me now, Doris." Raul shook his head slightly at her. "I can feel it. I got shot right in the heart. I'm dying."

"Oh, Raul. I'm so sorry. This is all my fault. *I* put you in this dangerous situation. It's because of *me* that these men were acting this way," Doris began to explain with haunting shadows in her dull brown eyes. "You see, I'm cursed. I had someone cast a spell to make you love me. You don't *really* love me. I took away your free will, and we've both paid the price. I did it because I loved you, but that's no excuse."

"I...*know*," Raul replied, startling her. "All this time there was a voice inside of my head, compelling me to love you. And I couldn't resist it. But, later, I fell in love with you for real, and then the voice grew silent. I fell in love with the mother of my child."

Doris's heart began to pound inside of her chest loudly. Raul...loved her. Truly? "Oh, Raul."

With the last of his remaining strength Raul reached up to brush a tear from Doris's cheek away with his thumb. "Take care of our son for me. I'm sure he will be as beautiful as his mother. Call him…Bellamy. Promise me."

Doris placed her hand over Raul's that was on her cheek. "I promise, darling."

Raul offered her a weak smile before his eyes closed, and his breath stilled.

"No…Raul! No!" Doris sobbed into his chest. It was all just too much. She felt the baby kick inside of her, and her eyes flared in alarm. *No, not now. Please, not now!*

But Doris couldn't stop it. She'd gone into labor. Doris lay down on the blood-soaked snow with her back supported by Raul's dead body and gave birth to her son, surrounded by the dead bodies of the men who thought they loved her.

As soon as she was able, Doris scooped the baby up into her arms to protect it from the biting cold. The baby was crying his little lungs out. When the baby opened his eyes he revealed that they were blue - just like his father's. A broken smile formed on Doris's face at the sight. "You truly are beautiful, my son, my Bellamy."

A few days later, Doris left the small Alaskan town, and traveled to New York City to get a job, and start a new life with her newborn child. She managed to find a job as a seamstress since Doris had always been good with her hands, and she rented a small apartment for Bellamy and herself to live in.

At first, Doris had been worried about the curse, but had been surprised when the men around her seemed to ignore her, just like in the old days before she'd encountered the sorcerer Agathon. Because of her job, she needed to hire a babysitter to watch over Bellamy. And that's when Doris discovered the truth of what had become of the curse.

Bellamy's female babysitter tried to kidnap Bellamy, but didn't get very far when someone spotted the young woman acting suspiciously while leaving Doris's apartment with Bellamy, and had reported it to the police. It was in that moment that Doris realized that the curse had been passed on to Bellamy.

After that incident, Doris tried to come up with a way to protect her son from the curse. Acting on a hunch she decided to cover Bellamy's face and see how women would react. When Bellamy's face was hidden by a mask, a scarf, or a pair of sunglasses the effects of the curse appeared to be blocked somehow.

'The eyes are the windows to the soul' Doris had thought to herself, thinking she was on to something. When she put a pair of nonprescription glasses on Bellamy's face to see if they worked to block the effects of the curse and discovered that they did, she knew she'd figured out a way to not break but at least stop the curse from activating. And the rest was history…

END OF DREAM

Bellamy awoke with a start the following morning. "Mother! Father! No!" He shouted into the heavy silence of his room. Sweat beaded his brow. What the hell was that? A dream? No. A *vision* about his own past origins.

The dream vision was still painfully fresh in Bellamy's mind - his mother's rescue of the sorcerer Agathon, Raul falling in love with his mother along with all of the men who lived in town, his parents' marriage, and Doris's pregnancy. But most of all Bellamy remembered *that day*.

The day the Hunters had tried to hunt down and murder his father Raul like an animal. All because of the curse.

Bellamy's mother had never mentioned his father. Bellamy had assumed he'd been a good-for-nothing, but Raul had protected his mother and *him* with his last breath. Raul had *named* him. His father had *loved* him.

And his poor mother had given birth to Bellamy in the middle of that bloodbath.

Bellamy couldn't get the horrifying images out of his mind. He gripped the sides of his head and dug his fingernails into his scalp painfully. How could he get the images out? He needed to get them out! A sudden idea came to him.

Bellamy got out of bed and took a quick, hot shower. Afterwards, he dressed in a white sweater, some faded blue jeans, and a pair of sneakers. He chose a gray coat with a white fur lining to finish his winter outfit that was sure to protect him from the cold.

As Bellamy was heading for the front door of the mansion, Jett called out to him. "Master Bellamy, are you leaving us so soon?" His voice was laced with concern.

"No." Bellamy glanced over his shoulder at the butler. "I just...I need to go outside and clear my head. Do you mind if I borrow some tools from the tool shed?"

Jett arched a quizzical eyebrow at Bellamy, but nodded. "Not at all, Master Bellamy. Please, help yourself."

Bellamy exited the mansion, entered the expansive front gardens of the estate, and headed for the tool shed. Inside the shed he found exactly what he'd been looking for - a pick, chisel, and hammer.

Bellamy took the tools with him and headed to an area of the garden where large chunks of ice lay scattered across the frozen lawn. The bookworm picked an especially large chunk of ice to start with, set the chisel against the ice, and set to work.

***

When Abigail made her way to the dining room for breakfast, she'd been expected Bellamy to already be seated at the table waiting for her. She pouted upon noting his absence.

When the minutes ticked by and Bellamy still didn't arrive, Abigail took an irritated sip of her coffee and addressed Jett, "And where is Bellamy? Probably still asleep. That lazy bum."

"Actually, Master Bellamy is outside in the front gardens," Jett began to inform her. "He hasn't had breakfast yet."

Abigail shot her butler a questioning look. "The garden? Whatever for? It's *freezing* out there!"

"He's appears to be...working on something," Jett said evasively.

"Working on *what*?" Abigail demanded, but Jett just remained silent. "Oh my God, I'm going out there to see for myself." She began to get up from the table.

But Jett tutted at her. "Ah, ah, ah, you're not going out there until you have finished your breakfast, Milady. You're still recovering from an injury and need to build up your strength."

Abigail huffed. "Alright, fine. I'll finish breakfast first. Then I'm going to see what that bookworm is up to." As soon as the yeti finished her last bite of omelet she quickly sat up from her chair and rushed outside to the gardens. Her curiosity about what Bellamy could be up to was killing her at this point.

It was in that moment that Abigail realized she didn't really know anything about Bellamy DeWinter. Just that he was a nerd, a bookworm...and maybe a hero. She remembered how he'd given her CPR to save her life. Even though Bellamy had told her not to fret about their *almost* kissing and had said something about how a kiss without any emotion behind it being meaningless, Abigail couldn't help but feel that they'd still shared a kiss. Even if it hadn't meant anything to Bellamy, it had meant something to her.

Abigail shook her head of such confusing thoughts and made her way into the garden. Where the hell was he? She sniffed the air and caught a whiff of Bellamy's unique scent. The bookworm smelled like pinesap and maple syrup. It was a manly, woodsy scent that reminded her of the forest.

Abigail tracked Bellamy's yummy scent to the section of the garden where huge chunks of ice had been scattered across the lawn. She gasped since the shapeless chunks of ice were no longer shapeless. Now covering the lawn were several highly detailed ice sculptures that appeared to be telling a story.

The first set of sculptures were of a homely looking woman kneeling before a man who looked like some kind of wizard with his hooded cloak that was billowing out behind him dramatically. The wizard was holding a wooden staff with a familiar looking stone decorating the top of it. Abigail's eyes bulged when she recognized the sorcerer Agathon.

"Agathon? What the hell is going on here?" Abigail muttered to herself as she kept walking in order to inspect the next set of statues. The next two statues were of a handsome man and a woman kissing each other while locked in a passionate embrace.

Abigail's blue cheeks turned magenta at the romantic atmosphere surrounding these two statues. The yeti realized that the woman who was kissing the good-looking man was the same plain looking one from the earlier scene with the sorcerer Agathon.

Abigail continued walking and entered a very different frozen scene from the one before. This scene looked more like a grisly crime scene. The plain woman was in this scene again, only this time she was seated on a sled that was pulled by a team of five

Huskies. A man had grabbed onto the woman's arm and had an evil leer on his face.

The woman's expression was one of sheer terror. But the handsome man from the earlier scene was standing with his shotgun in hand and had it pointed at the man with the leer. There was this fierce, protective look in the handsome man's eyes. Scattered around the scene were four dead bodies. It was easy to see that the handsome man was trying to rescue the plain woman from the guy who'd grabbed onto her arm.

Bellamy was hard at work, using a chisel to carefully craft the look of pain and horror on one of the fallen men's faces.

"Bellamy," Abigail called out hesitantly.

Bellamy looked up and met Abigail's inquisitive stare with haunted eyes. "Hi, Abigail."

"What's all this?" The yeti waved her hand at the sculptures.

"This was the only way to get it all out of my head," Bellamy began to explain. "Last night, I dreamed about my own past. It was like a vision. I'm pretty sure it was real. That everything I saw in my dreams last night - really happened." Bellamy stood up and approached the ice sculpture of the woman on the sled. "This plain looking woman...that's my mother Doris when she was younger. And that man there with the shotgun protecting her...is my father Raul DeWinter."

Abigail started and looked at the ice sculpture of the plain woman again. "That's...Doris?" But that meant that Doris had met the sorcerer Agathon when she was younger. Her brow furrowed. Pieces of the puzzle were slowly falling into place. "But then, that means, your curse, the sorcerer-"

"Agathon," Bellamy finished her sentence and nodded grimly. "Yep. Apparently, the same evil sorcerer who cursed you...cursed my mom a while back. What are the chances that charlatan would curse us both, huh?"

"The stone on his staff, it's-" Abigail started.

"The Philosopher's Stone," Bellamy finished. "Yep." The bookworm began to explain his past origins to Abigail from the beginning, recounting how his mother Doris had saved Agathon from his icy prison and had earned a wish from the sorcerer. He told Abigail about how Doris had wished for Raul's love, how Raul had indeed fallen in love with Doris along with all of the men in town. Bellamy went on to tell Abigail about how his mother Doris had intended to leave Raul in order to free him from the curse, but had then discovered she was pregnant.

A dark cloud fell over Bellamy's face as he got to this point in the story. He then told Abigail about that fateful day. The day the Hunters in town tried to hunt down and murder his father. But how his mother had bravely gone to try and stop this from happening. Things had spiraled out of control and the men had ended up shooting each other. Raul had died protecting his mother.

Bellamy walked over to stand by the ice sculpture of his father Raul. "I never got to know my father. I'd always assumed he was some deadbeat since Mom never talked about him. But he saved my mother's life and mine that day." He placed his hand over the bullet wound on the front of Raul's chest. "With his dying breath he named me. My father was a good man. A *hero*. And he didn't deserve to die that way!" Bellamy clenched his hands into fists at his sides. He was so angry at the injustice of it all.

"Then what happened?" Abigail questioned softly.

"My mother went into labor. She had me right here," Bellamy swept his hand at the macabre scene, his expression dour. "Surrounded by the dead bodies of her enemies and of the man she loved. Surrounded by blood and death…she gave birth to me."

Abigail sucked in a startled breath. "That must have been a truly horrifying experience for Doris." Her heart went out to Doris. *Poor Doris.*

Bellamy dragged his hand back through his brown hair; a few strands had escaped from his ponytail and had moved in front of his face. "My mother has suffered so much, and partly because of me. I wish there was something I could do for her. I'm worried about her. I hope she's alright. I…want to apologize to her too. Sometimes I wondered what *awful* thing my mother had done to get herself cursed. But she was just another victim of that charlatan Agathon."

Abigail nibbled on one of her claws. Her heart went out to Bellamy too, and his obvious inner turmoil. "You miss your mother that much?"

"Yeah." Bellamy nodded. "If only I knew she was okay, I could relax."

"Then…I'll let you see her," Abigail announced.

Bellamy's sour look turned hopeful. "How?"

"Come with me." Abigail took Bellamy to her bedroom and showed him the enchanted mirror the sorcerer Agathon had given her. "Here. Use this. Just ask it what you want to see."

Bellamy nodded and took the mirror from Abigail. He stared into its silvery reflection. "Show me my mother - Doris DeWinter."

The reflection in the mirror shifted, glowed, and stilled to reveal the inside of a hospital room. His mother Doris was strapped to a padded chair, and electrodes had been attached to her temples. Some kind of gag was inside of her mouth, probably to prevent her from biting her tongue.

"Maybe this will jog your memory about where my beloved Bellamy is!" Astonia declared before flicking the switch on the ECT machine.

Doris cried out as electricity was sent coursing through her head uncomfortably.

Bellamy's eyes flared in alarm and he clutched at the mirror tightly. "Mother! No! Get away from her, you crazy bitch! Shit!"

"Oh my God, what's wrong?" Abigail asked with obvious concern.

"It's my mother…this girl who saw me without my glasses has captured my mother and appears to be torturing her in order to discover my whereabouts," Bellamy snarled out through gritted teeth.

"Torturing?" Abigail shuddered and rubbed her arms. "Then, you must go and rescue your mother."

Bellamy shot the yeti a surprised look. "Abigail…?"

"But I want you to bring her back here," Abigail explained in a haughty tone. "Deal?"

Bellamy quickly nodded his agreement. "Deal."

"Then, you're free to go," Abigail said airily. "For now. It's a son's duty to protect his mother."

Bellamy rushed over to Abigail, grabbed her hands in his, squeezed them and gave the yeti a grateful look. "Thank you, Abigail."

Abigail snatched her hands out of Bellamy's grasp and made a shooing motion with her right hand. "Go on, shoo. You shouldn't keep your mother waiting."

Bellamy tried to hand the mirror back to Abigail, but she shook her head and pushed it back into his hands. "No. You're going to need it. The mirror will help you find your mother, and…" A magenta tinge rose to Abigail's blue cheeks. "It will help you find your way back to *me*."

The bookworm nodded. "Understood. Thanks again." He spun on his heel and exited the bedroom.

Abigail went over to her bedroom window so that she could watch as Bellamy exited the mansion, hurried his way down the steps and mounted the dogsled. She watched as he grabbed the reins, snapped them, and the dogs began to take off, heading for the front gate.

Jett entered her bedroom at this moment. "Master Bellamy has left the estate."

"I am aware," Abigail said. "I let him go on a little rescue mission to save his mother. He's supposed to bring her back here. Or else."

The corner of Jett's mouth twitched in amusement. "That was a very kind thing for you to do, Milady. I'm proud of you."

"Oh, do shut up," Abigail grumbled and had to duck her head to hide her magenta colored cheeks.

To be continued in…Chapter 6:

Chapter 6:

Bellamy used the enchanted mirror to find the location of the clinic that was run by Astonia's mother, Dr. Glacia Sharpe. He drove his dogsled as fast as he could, and executed another impatient snap of the reins to get the dogs to go a little faster. "Mush!"

Less than an hour later, Bellamy was pulling the sled right in front of the clinic. As soon as the sled came to a halt he hopped off and stalked towards the front door. When Bellamy burst into the reception room a flurry of snow followed him inside due to it being windy outside.

The nurse, who was sitting behind the front desk, gave Bellamy a wide-eyed stare as she watched his abrupt entry and how he slammed the door shut behind him. "Um, can I help you, Sir?" the nurse questioned tentatively, noticing the determined expression on Bellamy's face.

Bellamy chose to ignore the nurse completely, and looked down at the surface of the enchanted mirror instead in order to find out what room his mother was currently being held captive in. He began to stalk down the hall in the appropriate direction.

"Sir! You need to fill out this form first before you...*ohhh!*" the nurse let out a frustrated sound, and dropped the clipboard with its attached forms onto the surface of her desk.

Bellamy made his way down the hall with swift, purposeful steps, took a left and continued his way down the hall all the way to the end where he came to a stop in front of a door. This was it. His mother was inside of there.

Without hesitation Bellamy brought up his booted foot and kicked the door in, using all of his strength. He entered the room to see that his mother was still strapped to a chair with electrodes attached to her temples that were connected to some kind of machine.

Doris's eyes widened at the unexpected appearance of her son and she tried to call out to him through the gag in her mouth. Tears were streaming down her fearful, pain-filled face. "Mmph!"

Standing next to Doris was Astonia who looked shocked and worried to see Bellamy there all of a sudden. She was wearing a red tube dress with black fur trim and a black mink shoulder wrap along with a pair of thigh-high leather boots.

Bellamy didn't fail to note that Astonia was standing directly next to the ECT machine with her hand outstretched towards the machine as if she were considering turning it on again. *That bitch.* Bellamy thought venomously to himself.

Astonia's surprised expression turned pleased, and she inconspicuously lowered her hand away from the machine. "Bellamy! You came back to me!" A wide smile spread across her face. "Oh, how I've missed you!" The Huntress sauntered over to Bellamy and tried to hug him.

But Bellamy reached up, put a hand over Astonia's face, and unceremoniously shoved her backwards, hard.

Astonia let out an indignant squawk as she stumbled backwards and fell onto her behind. She stared up at Bellamy, hurt and bewilderment swimming in her brown eyes. "*Bellamy?*" Her tone was petulant.

Bellamy narrowed his icy blue eyes at her behind his glasses. "Astonia, what is the meaning of *this*?" Anger laced his words. "Why were you *torturing* my mother?"

Astonia blinked slowly, and gave Bellamy an innocent look. "Torturing? I was merely trying to *help* her. She's gone completely crazy..." She waved her hand through the air. "Talking about a yeti and living statues."

Bellamy's blood was boiling. He angrily clenched his hands into fists at his sides, and he could feel his nails digging into the palms of his hands. "My mother is *not* crazy!" he boomed.

Astonia flinched at Bellamy's harsh, raised voice. "Well, do you have any proof?" There was a calculating gleam in the Huntress's intelligent dark brown eyes.

A muscle beneath Bellamy's eye ticked in irritation. "Here's your proof - right here!" Bellamy shoved the mirror in Astonia's face. "Show me the yeti!" he commanded the mirror.

The silvery surface of the antique mirror glowed and shifted until the image settled and revealed the yeti girl, Abigail. Abigail was standing outside on her bedroom's balcony, gazing off in the direction of Yeti Town with a sad, wistful expression on her face. Her long white hair was whipping around her blue face in the fierce, chill wind that was blowing around her.

A look of astonishment settled over Astonia's face at the sight of the creature. "The yeti…she's real. What is that mirror-?"

Bellamy yanked the mirror back and stuck it behind him in the waistband of his jeans to keep it out of Astonia's reach. "You see, *not* crazy. I'm checking my mother out of this creepy Clinic California. She doesn't belong here," Bellamy announced before swiftly walking over to the chair his mother was still secured to and crouching in front of her.

The bookworm offered his mother a reassuring look. "Don't worry, Mom. I'm getting you out of here." Bellamy removed the gag from his mother's mouth and furiously tossed it aside where it clattered on the floor. He wiped the tears from his mother's cheeks with his thumbs. "You okay?" He gave his mother a searching look.

Doris sniffled and nodded. "Bellamy, you came for me." Her voice was laced with surprise for some reason.

Bellamy offered her a reassuring smile. "Of course I did. We have a *lot* to talk about. But don't worry, Mom. I'm getting you the hell out of here." Bellamy removed the electrodes from his mother's temples, and started to undo the leather straps that were keeping Doris's wrists pinned to the arms of the chair.

Astonia was carefully watching what Bellamy was doing and waited until he seemed completely focused on his task before she made her move. She stood up and dusted herself off before sneaking up behind Bellamy and grabbing the mirror from the waistband of his pants.

Astonia quickly put some distance between herself and Bellamy. A devious smile curled her red lips. "I'm afraid I can't let you do that, Bellamy. You belong to me. And I'm not letting you leave me again! Douglas, Colden, get your butts in here! I need you!" Astonia called out loudly.

At that moment, two burly male nurses burst into the room. One of the male nurses held a white straightjacket in his hands. The other male nurse held a syringe filled with some kind of liquid that was most likely a sedative.

Astonia waved her hand imperiously in Bellamy's direction. "Bellamy DeWinter has gone crazy too, I'm afraid." She tried to look worried and disappointed. "Restrain him!" she ordered.

Douglas and Colden shared a conspiratorially sinister look before leering smiles spread across their faces. They were *always* ready to obey Astonia's whims. Especially, if that meant taking out the competition.

Douglas and Colden turned their attention to Bellamy and began to approach him with menacing steps. Bellamy looked at the straightjacket and syringe in disbelief. "You have got to be kidding me! Just how crazy is your mom's clinic, Astonia? Whatever happened to human rights?"

Astonia cackled merrily. "What mother doesn't know…won't hurt her! Get him, boys!"

"Yes, Astonia," Douglas and Colden chimed at the same time as they continued stalking towards Bellamy.

Douglas cautiously approached Bellamy first with the straightjacket raised before him. He lunged forward abruptly and tried to wrap Bellamy in the jacket like a taco, but Bellamy quickly dodged out of the way with a quick sidestep.

Bellamy decided to take advantage of Douglas's obvious surprise and stepped up to the male nurse, grabbed the jacket, and flipped it over the man's head in order to blind him. "Argh! I can't see!" Douglas complained as he tried to get the jacket off his face.

Bellamy brought his fist back and then sent it flying right into Douglas's face in a straight right punch. Douglas let out a grunt before he toppled over to the floor like a felled tree with a loud thud against the cold, hard linoleum floor.

Bellamy shook his throbbing hand. Punching Douglas in the face had felt like punching a wall, and he wasn't really used to violence. He was a bookworm and gemologist, after all.

Astonia was grinding her back molars in frustration. "Colden, hurry up and sedate him already," she snapped.

"Yes, Astonia." Colden stalked towards Bellamy and started to lunge the syringe at him with his right hand. Bellamy dodged the attacks and when he saw the opportunity he grabbed Colden's right wrist. They began to struggle for possession over the syringe.

Somehow Bellamy managed to bend Colden's wrist back until the male nurse cried out in pain and dropped the syringe. "Dammit! Fucking nerd is tougher than he looks!" Colden complained before sending a left hook flying into the side of Bellamy's face.

The punch caught Bellamy by surprise, and he staggered sideways before falling to the floor and landing on his backside. For a moment, Bellamy thought he could see tiny dogsleds orbiting his head in a circle. He gripped his head, groaned, and tried to push away his dizziness. Colden hit hard.

Unnoticed by Bellamy, Colden was sneaking up on him and once he was close enough lunged at Bellamy. Colden practically fell right on top of Bellamy, and they began to wrestle across the floor. The male nurse was physically stronger than Bellamy, however, and the bookworm wouldn't be able to hold out much longer.

"Bellamy!" Doris called out in an urgent tone.

Bellamy glanced at his mother and as soon as their eyes met she kicked the syringe across the floor and in his direction.

Colden raised his fist and prepared to send it flying into Bellamy's face. This time the blow probably would have broken Bellamy's nose. Abruptly, Colden's fist dropped and his eyes rolled into the back of his head. The male nurse heavily collapsed unconscious on top of Bellamy with a syringe sticking out of the back of his neck where Bellamy had injected him.

"No!" Astonia shrieked in denial, stomped her foot, and started to chew on her lower lip.

Bellamy rushed over to his mother, quickly undid the rest of her restraints, and helped her to stand up from the chair. "Come on, Mom, now that Tweedledum and Tweedledee have been taken care of we're getting out of here." He looped his arm around his mother's waist to help support her as she walked unsteadily towards the door.

"You're not getting out of here that easily!" Astonia screeched and slammed her hand down on the emergency call button.

Shit. Bellamy inwardly swore.

All of a sudden, a group of five female nurses stepped into the room with concerned looks on their faces. "What's going on, Miss Astonia?" one of the nurses questioned.

Astonia pointed her trembling finger at Bellamy and his mother in an accusing manner. "They're trying to escape!"

"Escape?" The nurse raised a quizzical eyebrow at Astonia. "We can't hold people here against their will, Astonia," the nurse chided.

"Who do you think pays for your salary!" Astonia barked. "Or do you want me to get my mother to fire you for negligence?"

"No, I..." the nurse stammered nervously.

"Then just do as I say and restrain them, at once!" Astonia ordered snootily with her nose in the air. "They're both dangerous and unstable mental patients."

The nurses let out resigned sighs as if they were used to dealing with Astonia's over-the-top requests before approaching Bellamy and his mother with apologetic looks on their faces. "We're sorry about this Bellamy, but orders are orders," one of the nurses said while all five nurses whipped out syringes filled with a sedative.

Shit. There were just too many nurses to fight off on his own. And really...Bellamy didn't want to have to hit a woman. That was pretty low and cowardly. There was really only one thing that Bellamy could do at this point.

The bookworm whipped off his glasses, folded them neatly, and slid them into his pants pocket. He ran a hand back through his messy brown hair to move his bangs out of his blue eyes. Then he lifted his chin and met their curious gazes.

The nurses looked at Bellamy's handsome face and their eyes turned into pink hearts.

Bellamy smirked at their now amorous expressions. "Oh ladies, how would you like...a kiss?" he asked them in a singsong voice.

Astonia was starting to frown.

"Oh, I'd love one!" "I want one!" "Oh, yes, please!" the nurses cried out excitedly.

"Then restrain Astonia," Bellamy instructed them. "And I'll give you girls your reward." He tossed a roguish wink their way.

"Eeee!" the five nurses squealed before setting their now predatory sights on Astonia.

Astonia instinctively took a step back at the suddenly crazed look her nurses were giving her. "W-What? What do you think you're doing? Stay back!" She raised her hand before her and took another step back. "If you girls don't stay back...you can just forget about your Christmas bonuses!"

But Astonia's threats were falling on deaf ears. The nurses were acting like lovesick zombies. "*Bellamyyy, kiss, Bellamyyy, kiss,*" the nurses moaned as they approached Astonia.

"Time to go," Bellamy said softly to his mother as he quickly guided her out the door.

Astonia's terrified scream followed them on their way out.

Luckily, they weren't met with any more resistance and Bellamy was able to get his mother safely outside of the clinic. He helped her up onto the sled before joining her. Just as Bellamy was getting the reins in a firm grip in his hands he realized something. *Shit!* He no longer had the enchanted mirror. How the hell was he supposed to find Abigail's mansion now? A funny idea came to him and he decided it was worth a shot. He leaned over and spoke to his Huskies. "Go back to Abigail! Mush!" He snapped the reins.

"Woof!" The Huskies barked loudly and took off, heading towards the forest.

"Who is Abigail?" Doris questioned curiously.

"The yeti girl," Bellamy revealed.

Doris suddenly felt faint and raised a hand to her forehead. "We're going back to that haunted mansion?" There was an incredulous note to her voice.

"Abigail only let me leave the mansion so that I could save you from Astonia," Bellamy explained and his grip tightened on the reins. "That was the deal. Now we have to go back there, or else. But don't worry, Mom, Abigail is a lot nicer than she looks." The corner of Bellamy's mouth quirked up into a lopsided smile.

Doris eyed the back of Bellamy's head with a skeptical look on her face. "If you say so, Son."

The four dogs impressively and unerringly took Bellamy and his mother to Abigail's mansion. As they approached the towering wrought-iron gate it opened of its own accord to let them pass through the estate's outer wall.

Bellamy abruptly pulled back on the reins, stopping the dogs from heading directly to the mansion. "Before we go to the mansion there's something I need to show you first, Mom."

"Alright," Doris agreed.

Bellamy drove the sled to the section of the garden where he'd carved and chiseled the ice sculptures that depicted the dream vision he'd had of his mother's past and his origins.

Doris gasped when she recognized her younger self carved out of ice and confronting the comely sorcerer Agathon. Doris's plain brown eyes flared in shock. "But that's...*me*," she exclaimed in a small, cracking voice.

When Bellamy drove past the sculptures he'd carved of Raul and Doris sharing their first kiss, tears filled Doris's eyes. "*Raul.*"

Bellamy pulled back on the reins to stop the sled directly in front of the ice sculptures that depicted the moment when Raul had saved not only his mother's life, but his own.

Raul had been so brave and heroic in that moment, Bellamy thought with a pang in his chest.

Crystalline tears began to slide down Doris's face as she looked at that moment literally frozen in time - the moment Raul had saved her and the life of her unborn child.

"What *is* all this?" Doris asked, shaking her head in confusion. "How...?"

With a myriad of emotions swirling in his blue eyes Bellamy began to explain, "Ever since I came here I've been having these...dreams. Dreams that I think are actually visions of the past. First, I dreamed about the yeti girl Abigail, and discovered how she was cursed. Then I dreamed about you, Mom. I dreamed about how you saved the sorcerer Agathon, how he offered to grant you a wish, and how you wished for Raul DeWinter to love you. I saw it all - how Raul fell in love with you, but how all the men in Yeti Town that met your eyes did too.

"I saw how even after you married Raul, their obsession with you did not stop - it only grew worse, more poisoned, venomous. You were going to leave Raul and free him from yourself, but when you became pregnant you decided not to. I saw...my *father*. I saw how Raul saved your life, and mine. I saw how Raul *named* me with his dying breath." Bellamy turned to give his mother a searching look. "Why? *Why* didn't you ever tell me about him?"

A flash of guilt crossed Doris's face. "I...thought it would be easier this way. And it was painful for me to remember Raul, and how in the end he did truly love me...*us*."

Bellamy could feel the anger pulsing through his veins. "I thought my father was some deadbeat loser or maybe he'd been unfaithful to you...and that's why you never talked about him. I always assumed he abandoned us. That he was a bad person. I *cursed* him. And now...I find out my father was a hero. He protected us. Saved us!" He slashed his hand angrily through the air in a gesture of frustration.

"Bellamy, I'm sorry," Doris apologized with an ashamed look on her face. "I'm sorry about *everything*."

Some of Bellamy's anger began to deflate at the sad, lost look on his mother's face. "I know. I blamed you too, you know? I used to wonder what horrible thing you did to get yourself *cursed* by someone. Some days...I wanted to hate you because of everything I was going through."

"What I did *was* horrible, I-" Doris started.

"No!" Bellamy burst out and took his mother's hands in his. He noticed that Doris's hands were like ice and began to rub them. "Just, no. None of this is *your* fault. I know that now. It's all because of him...the sorcerer Agathon. That evil charlatan! Everything is *his* fault. He cursed you in the guise of granting you an innocent girlish wish. What teenage girl doesn't wish her crush will magically fall in love with her? Your *wish* was not evil, Mother. You just didn't want to be alone in this frozen, barren wasteland. Who could really blame you for that? The sorcerer Agathon...*he's* the evil one!"

Doris remembered how the sorcerer Agathon had warned her that magic has a price. The balance of the universe must be maintained. She shook her head. "Bellamy, I appreciate you saying that, but I am partly to blame for all this. I made a choice - I made a wish. And Agathon warned me about the possible consequences. I should have heeded his warning. It's my fault. I don't know if the sorcerer Agathon is truly evil or not."

"Oh, he's evil alright," Bellamy snarled, his lip curling with disgust as he thought about how the sorcerer had turned Abigail into a monster just for being a little superficial. "And if I ever encounter him, I'll..." He trailed off.

Worry and fear clawed at Doris's insides at her gentle son's vengeful words.

Bellamy's grip on Doris's hands tightened unconsciously until it began to hurt. "Bellamy, you're hurting me."

The bookworm instantly let go of his mother's hands, and his expression turned sheepish. "Sorry, Mom, I was lost in thought for a moment there. Anyways, let's go back home."

"Home?" Doris asked hopefully thinking of their small log cabin back in Yeti Town.

"To the yeti's mansion," said Bellamy.

"Oh, right." Doris's shoulders sagged disappointedly. "Of course."

Bellamy drove the sled the rest of the way to the mansion and stopped the sled in front of the stone staircase that led to the front door. He helped his mom up the slippery quartz steps to the front door and knocked using the yeti-shaped lapis lazuli doorknocker. The door opened and Bellamy guided his mother inside.

"Welcome back, Master Bellamy," Jett greeted amiably.

Bellamy flashed Jett a grin. "Thanks, Jett. It's good to be back."

Doris stared at the talking black onyx statue that looked like a butler in shock. "It…the statue just *talked*."

"Jett, I'd like you to meet my mother Doris," Bellamy introduced with a nod of his head in his mother's direction.

"It's a pleasure to meet you, Madam," Jett greeted politely.

Doris was a little caught off guard by Jett's prim, velvety British accent. "Likewise."

Bellamy noticed that his mother was trembling slightly and frowned. "You look cold, Mom."

"Oh dear, let's get you warmed up by the fire, Madam," Jett offered as he took Doris's hand and started to lead her in the direction of the living room. Doris nodded numbly for a moment and murmured an assent.

However, that's when Jett and Bellamy heard a thud and turned to see that Doris had fainted to the floor. "Goodness, I must have startled her," Jett said reprovingly.

"Don't worry about it, Jett," Bellamy assured the butler. "She's just had a long day." He swooped his mom up into his arms and carried her into the living room, followed close behind by a concerned Jett.

Bellamy set his mother down on the jade armchair that was sitting in front of the fireplace. There were now two soft, emerald green velvet cushions on the chair that hadn't been there before, which made the hard chair much more comfortable. Bellamy was touched by the gesture. A fire was crackling pleasantly in the marble and stone fireplace.

"Jett, do you have any smelling salts?" Bellamy asked skeptically.

"Why, of course, Sir," the butler said. "I'll fetch them right away." Jett walked off to fetch the smelling salts and returned a few minutes later with Lazuli the maid in tow. Lazuli was holding a silver tray arranged with a crystal pitcher filled with water and a matching goblet.

Jett handed Bellamy the jar of smelling salts. "Here you are, Sir."

"Thanks, Jett." Bellamy held the jar beneath his mother's nose and waited for a reaction. In seconds, Doris regained consciousness with a gasp, and blinked, glancing around her with obvious confusion.

"Hey, Mom, how are you feeling?" Bellamy's voice was laced with concern.

Doris looked around the living room and spotted the statue made out of lapis lazuli that was shaped like a French maid, and her eyes flared in alarm. "Uh…"

Lazuli poured Doris a glass of water and held it out to her. "Would you like a glass of water, Madam?"

"Now *it* talked too." Doris was surprised by the maid's sultry French accent. She felt dizzy as she swayed in her seat a little. "I think I'm going to faint again."

"Mom, don't freak out," Bellamy soothed. "They're *not* ghosts."

"They're not?" Doris questioned.

Bellamy shook his head. "Nope. They're human. Just like you and me. The sorcerer Agathon cursed them into being stone statues." A hard edge had come to his voice.

"Agathon did?" A flash of surprise crossed Doris's face and her eyes narrowed. "Why?"

"Now, that's a long story," Bellamy sighed as he raked a hand back through his hair. "But I think you ought to know it before you meet Abigail again."

Doris gave her son a reluctant nod. "Alright."

Bellamy told his mom all about the dreams he'd had about Abigail, and how Holly Snow had been sick, how Aspen Snow had been trying to find his wife a cure through magic and alchemy, and how eventually both of Abigail's parents died making her a rich heiress.

Bellamy went onto tell his mother about how Abigail had these over-the-top, extravagant parties where only the best-looking socialites were invited. Then he related how Agathon had shown up in the guise of a homeless man during Abigail's eighteenth birthday party and had offered her an Aurora Borealis quartz stone in exchange for shelter from the rain. Bellamy had explained that Abigail had refused due to her disgust of the homeless man and had been subsequently cursed. "So you see, even though Abigail *looks* like a ferocious yeti she's actually an eighteen-year-old girl suffering from a horrible and totally unfair curse," Bellamy finished with an adamant look in his blue eyes.

Sympathetic tears were leaking out of Doris's brown eyes. "That really is horrible."

Jett offered Doris a silk handkerchief. "Here you are, Madam."

Doris took the handkerchief and dabbed at her eyes with it before blowing her nose loudly. "Thank you, Jett." She shot the butler a grateful look before turning her attention back to her son. "What do you intend to do now, Bellamy?"

Bellamy blinked. "I plan to help Abigail find a way to break the curse. Duh."

A proud expression fell over Doris's face. She reached out to cup Bellamy's cheek fondly, and gave him a watery smile. "I'm so proud of you, my son."

Bellamy beamed at his mother and leaned into her comforting touch. "Mom."

At that moment, Kristal entered the living room with shy steps, and curtsied nervously. "Milady would like you all to join her for dinner," she announced in her tiny, girlish voice.

Doris glanced towards the doorway and caught sight of the little girl made out of blue quartz crystal that resembled Shirley Temple. She couldn't stop the smile that curled her lips. "She's adorable." Doris stood up from her chair, approached Kristal, and crouched before her. "And what might your name be, young lady?"

"Kristal," she answered timidly while shifting from one foot to the other.

"My name is Doris. It's a pleasure to meet you, Kristal." Doris held her hand out to the girl. "Can you show me where the dining room is?"

Kristal beamed and took Doris's hand. "Of course, Doris!"

Bellamy sauntered over and took Kristal's other hand. "I guess it's time for you to meet Abigail Snow." He addressed his mother. "Properly this time."

Kristal giggled at that as she led the guests to the dining room.

***

Abigail could hardly believe it when she saw Bellamy's dogsled reenter her estate. "He came back." There was a wistful note to her voice. The yeti squinted at the sled and could see that Bellamy's mother Doris was with him. She let out a sigh of relief at the sight. So he'd been able to rescue her after all.

Abigail was just about to run out of her room and go and greet Bellamy and his mother when she looked down at herself and her furry body. Her blue lips dipped into a troubled frown. The yeti realized that she was about to meet Bellamy's mother for the second time, and this time she wanted to make a *good* impression.

I don't want to scare Bellamy's mother by looking like a monster. I can't let her see me like this. Abigail decided to fix herself up as best she could, considering her current form. It took her a little more than an hour, but somehow she managed to squeeze herself into one of her designer evening gowns.

Abigail gazed longingly at her shoe collection for a moment, and wished that her furry, clawed feet would fit into her *Christian Louboutins*, but there was just no way. She pouted and made her way over to her dressing table instead. Abigail got out her curling iron and began to style her hair. Once her hair was finished, she carefully and tenderly took out her mother's jewelry box. She ended up selecting a pair of cascading diamond earrings and a matching necklace.

Once she was finally finished getting ready, Abigail looked at her appearance in the cracked dressing mirror, and touched mirror's surface with her clawed hand. "Do I look even a little bit like you, Mother?" She took a deep breath to steel her nerves. She had guests to attend to! It had been so long.

Brimming with excitement, Abigail headed to the dining room, prepared to meet Bellamy's mother Doris. When the yeti arrived, Bellamy and his mother were already seated at the table and awaiting her presence.

Abigail swallowed the nervous lump in her throat, took another deep breath, raised her chin, and strolled into the dining room as elegantly and gracefully as possible.

Bellamy raised an eyebrow when he caught sight of Abigail all dressed up. He wondered how she'd managed to get herself stuffed into that golden-yellow silk evening gown. Her hair was a series of large, curled ringlets that looked…hilarious, and reminded him of a French wig. Bellamy snorted as he tried really hard not to laugh. He didn't want the yeti to change the main dish of tonight's menu to roasted Belle.

Doris's dull brown eyes merely widened at the unexpected sight.

Abigail walked over and took a seat at the head of the table. As she sat down, however, the back of her dress ripped open slightly and audibly. A faint, magenta-colored blush rose to Abigail's blue cheeks, and she pretended that nothing was amiss. "Good evening, I am Abigail Snow. The owner of this estate."

"Doris DeWinter," Doris introduced herself politely.

"It is a pleasure to make your acquaintance, Doris," Abigail said with a gracious smile. "It would please me greatly if you'd join me for dinner."

"Of course, I would be…" Doris searched for the right word. "Delighted."

Abigail's smile widened. "Excellent. Let's dig in, shall we?"

Before Doris and Bellamy started to eat they shared an amused, conspiratorial look at Abigail's efforts to be a gracious, ladylike hostess. That evening the chef had prepared veal *scallopini* with button mushrooms, wild rice, and grilled zucchini.

Abigail raised her fork and knife, and daintily began to cut into her veal *scallopini*. However, with a popping sound one of the buttons from the front of Abigail's dress suddenly flew off and landed on Bellamy's plate with a *plop* as it landed in the mushroom sauce.

Bellamy had to bite down on his lower lip to hold back a laugh, and used his fork to discreetly push the button to the side of his plate.

Abigail studiously ignored what had just happened, and resumed cutting her veal. This time three buttons flew off the front of Abigail's dress simultaneously - one landed in Doris's glass of wine, another on Doris's plate, and the last button hit Bellamy on the side of his face.

At this point, Bellamy couldn't hold back his laughter, and finally burst out laughing. Doris snorted, but she was unable to hold back her laughter either.

When Abigail decided to put her fork and knife down on the table the entire front of her bodice ripped open revealing a lot of white fur. Tears of humiliation stung Abigail's silver eyes. In a fit of anger the yeti slammed her hands down on the dining table causing the candelabra to rattle and tilt precariously.

Abigail glared heatedly at her guests and growled, "You think this is funny, do you? A monster trying to be a civilized lady. Well, you're right. It *is* funny. I really am just a monster!" She finished her tirade before standing up from her seat and then rushing out of the dining room.

"Abigail!" Bellamy called after her. "Shit."

Doris was looking ashamed with herself. "I shouldn't have laughed like that...the poor girl. It's just like you said, Bellamy. She may *look* like a monster on the outside, but she's just an eighteen-year-old girl."

"I wish there was something I could do for her." Bellamy frowned thoughtfully. "A way to cheer her up. But it's not like a know a lot about girls and the inner workings of their hearts."

Doris grew pensive for a moment. "I think *I* may have an idea." A sly glint came to her brown eyes.
***

In order to put her plan into action, Doris had Kristal take her up to Abigail's room. "Thanks, Kristal," Doris said once they'd arrived at the door to Abigail's bedroom.

"No problem," Kristal said as she skipped away.

Doris took a deep breath before she knocked on the door. "Go away!" Abigail's voice cracked slightly through the door.

"Abigail, it's me, Doris, may I please come in?" Doris asked tentatively.

There was a long pause. Finally, the door opened to reveal Abigail with puffy, red-rimmed eyes, and a magenta nose from crying. Abigail sniffled, looking petulant. "What do you want, Mrs. DeWinter?"

"Please, call me Doris. And I'm here to apologize for my earlier appalling behavior." A sheepish expression formed on Doris's face and she tried to look extra apologetic.

Abigail snorted and looked amused. "There's nothing to apologize for, Doris. You were both right to laugh at me. I'm a circus freak." She let out a heavy sigh before opening her door wider and ushering Doris inside.

"My son doesn't think of you that way," Doris protested as she followed Abigail into the room. "In fact, he told me that the two of you had become good friends."

A flash of bewilderment crossed Abigail's silver eyes. "He *said* that?"

Doris nodded. "Yes. You know, Bellamy told me that you used to have these extravagant dance parties here."

Abigail blinked. "He did? I don't remember telling him about that. Maybe Jett told him."

Doris swiftly continued, realizing that Bellamy probably hadn't told Abigail about his dream visions. "Bellamy wants to make it up to you for his earlier behavior by inviting you to dance with him tonight. He said that he figured you missed dancing."

"Dance?" Abigail arched a fluffy white eyebrow at Doris. "You can't be serious. I can't dance. Not anymore. Not…like this." She waved a hand at herself in despair.

"Balderdash," Doris objected with a wave of her hand. "You have two perfectly good legs. It's not like you got cursed into being The Little Mermaid! Now dancing with a fin? *That* would be hard!"

Abigail couldn't help but laugh at the mental image that produced in her mind. "I suppose it would be." She sighed. "Even if I *wanted* to dance with your son…I have *nothing* to wear.

Nothing that fits me anymore, anyways." A pout formed on her face.

Doris rolled up her sleeves. "You just leave the dress alterations to me, dear. I used to work as a seamstress to make ends meet when I was living in New York with Bellamy."

"Really? You'd do that?" Abigail gave Doris a searching look. "Even after everything I've put you and your family though?"

"You let Bellamy leave this place so that he could rescue me," Doris pointed out. "In a way I owe you one. That crazy Frankenstein girl wanted to electrocute me with her so-called therapy. So, where are your dresses?"

Abigail showed Doris her collection of designer gowns, and Doris immediately set to work.

***

Meanwhile, Bellamy was helping the household staff get the ballroom ready for an impromptu dance party. The marble floor was covered in a thin layer of dust and cobwebs hung in the corners of the spacious room. The maids and butlers immediately set to work sweeping and dusting until the white and gold marble floor gleamed.

Jett informed Bellamy that he planned to play the piano, and so he helped the butler to uncover the piano and dust it until it shone a glossy black. After that Jett shooed Bellamy off and told him to get ready for his dance with Abigail.

Bellamy made his way to his room where he perused the selection of designer suits that Abigail had provided him with. After a moment's consideration he decided on wearing a slick, gray-blue *Armani* suit with a pair of shinny *Ferragamos*. He reluctantly added a gold Rolex to his wrist. He still wasn't used to wearing such fancy, expensive things, but thought that Abigail would probably appreciate the effort to look nice.

After Bellamy was finished getting ready, he exited his bedroom, and began to make his way down the corridor, heading for the grand staircase. Just as he reached the top of the stairs, Abigail emerged from her room. When she spotted Bellamy this cute, shy look formed on her face.

"Whoa," Bellamy breathed softly as he took in Abigail's startling appearance. His mother was a miracle worker. Abigail looked almost...*human*. She was wearing a blue and silver gown that had one point had probably been two separate dresses. It fit her perfectly and since it was long-sleeved and high-necked the dress covered up all of the yeti's white fur.

The skin of Abigail's face was still blue, and she still had a 'monkey face' with her little button nose, but Bellamy couldn't help thinking she looked extremely *cute*. Her silvery eyes had been lined in black and looked really wide, giving Abigail a bit of a puppy dog look. Her long white hair had been tamed and meticulously styled by his mother into an elaborate updo with half of her hair up and the other half cascading down around her shoulders.

Feeling a little tongue-tied and not sure what he should say, Bellamy approached Abigail offered her his hand, and smiled timidly. A magenta hue rose to Abigail's cheeks as she silently took Bellamy's hand, and smiled back at him.

In a gentlemanly fashion, Bellamy guided Abigail down the stairs and into the foyer. They then headed for the ballroom. Two jade butlers opened the gilded double doors that led to the ballroom as they approached.

Upon entering the ballroom, Abigail sucked in a breath at the sight of the previously dusty ballroom once again clean and sparkling in all its former glory. Abigail's silver gaze was drawn upwards to the massive, golden chandelier hanging overhead. The gold velvet curtains that covered the tall, latticed windows had been drawn back to reveal a nice glimpse of the starry night sky outside. The marble floor was so clean that Abigail could see her and Bellamy's reflection on it as they crossed the floor.

Seated at the now uncovered piano was Jett who was currently playing a traditional waltz. This unexpected sight caused Abigail's silver eyes to widen. "It's been so long since this room looked like this." She turned to Bellamy. "Before…I used to throw these lavish, extravagant parties. I spared no expense in order to have the best food, drinks and live entertainment. Only the most beautiful people were allowed to attend. It's ironic since now I am most likely one of the most ugly people on Earth."

Letting his instincts guide him, Bellamy reached out and cupped her face tenderly. "You're not ugly. I think you look really cute tonight, monkey face."

Abigail frowned. "You're just saying that because you're my friend."

"You're right. I am your friend," Bellamy agreed smoothly. "But you remind me of a cute, fluffy bunny." His serious tone had taken on a teasing note.

Abigail let out an incredulous laugh. "A bunny? You can't be serious."

There was a merry twinkle in Bellamy's blue eyes that was slightly obscured by the round glasses on his face. "Abigail, I wanted to thank you for letting me rescue my mother."

A flash of surprise crossed Abigail's face. "I should be thanking *you* for coming back."

"Hey, a promise is a promise." A grin spread over Bellamy's face. "And we still haven't found an alternative way to break the curse. But we *will*."

"Do you know how to waltz?" Abigail nodded her head in the direction of the piano and Jett.

Bellamy nodded. "Yep. But only because my mother taught me." The bookworm whisked Abigail out onto the dance floor and they began to waltz. Abigail's movements were surprisingly graceful for a yeti.

"You and your mother...are very close," Abigail observed.

"Well, when two people go through a lot together they inevitably become close." Bellamy lifted his shoulders in a shrug. "I feel bad that I used to secretly blame her for my curse though. Sometimes I even *hated* her for it. But now, I know my mother is a victim in all of this. Just like you, Abigail." There was suddenly a sharp gleam in Bellamy's eyes. "You're both Agathon's victims. He's the evil one here. The villain in this twisted tale."

A conflicted look fell over Abigail's face as she thought of the sorcerer Agathon. "Perhaps...but I accept that I was at fault too. I was vain and superficial and uncaring, and I paid the price."

Bellamy snorted. "What teenager isn't a little selfish? You didn't deserve *this*, Abigail." His eyes blazed with righteous anger.

It was strange seeing someone grow angry for her sake. It made butterflies flutter in Abigail's stomach. "Thank you for...feeling that way."

Bellamy arched an eyebrow at her. "So were all your parties 'classy' like this? Everyone did ballroom dances?"

Abigail giggled. "No! It's 2018! What do you think?" She turned to Jett. "Jett, hit it!"

Jett stood up from the piano stool, made his way over to the entertainment center, popped in a CD and pressed play. A pop dance song started playing. Jett pushed some other buttons on a console and a glittering disco ball lowered from the ceiling and colored lights began to zigzag across the marble dance floor.

Bellamy's jaw gaped open in surprise as the classy ballroom was suddenly transformed into a modern discotheque. "Whoo," he let out an appreciative whistle. "Nice."

Abigail grinned wolfishly. "Now, let's *really* dance!"

"Sure," Bellamy easily agreed.

The yeti and the bookworm began to dance to the pumping, upbeat song, swaying their bodies from side to side, and occasionally throwing their hands up into the air.

As Abigail blushed and giggled and smiled at Bellamy shyly, the bookworm's heart skipped a beat. *Too cute.*

Oh man...what did I just think? Bellamy thought to himself uneasily. *I can't be falling for yeti girl, can I? Talk about Stockholm Syndrome. But what about Abigail? How does she feel about me?*

If we end up falling for each other...we might be able to break the curse that way, but..

I doubt she'll fall in love with a nerd like me. I'm...boring. Dull.

And if she sees me without my glasses...then she'll just end up like my father Raul.

Besides we've become friends and have decided to try and find an alternate way to break the curse. Together.

Bellamy returned his attention to Abigail, grinned, and spun her like a top. For now, he just wanted to enjoy this moment, and decided he'd worry about the curse later.

To be continued in...Chapter 7:

Chapter 7:

Meanwhile, just outside the ballroom Astonia Sharpe was watching Bellamy and Abigail dance together with a look of sheer disbelief playing on her face. "My darling Bellamy is dancing with that hideous monster? What the *hell* is going on! The yeti girl must have bewitched Bellamy. Yes, he must be under some kind of spell. I *must* save my darling Bellamy from her evil clutches!"

The Huntress loaded her shotgun with two cartridges, aimed at the yeti and waited until she had a clear shot before firing. The bullet flew through the air, pierced the window, and zoomed towards Abigail before hitting her in the center of her chest, right in her heart.

Abigail's silver eyes flared in shock and pain, and then she fell back to the floor where she remained unmoving.

"Abigail!" Bellamy let loose a shout of alarm.

Astonia grinned triumphantly as she watched her prey fall. She was an expert markswoman. She never missed a shot, and she always took down her chosen prey with just one shot, giving them a quick, merciful death.

The Huntress kicked the latticed glass and wood door open, and waltzed inside of the ballroom, her long black mink coat billowing out behind her in a dramatic fashion.

"Bellamy, darling," Astonia called out as she laid her shotgun across the back of her shoulders in a casual, confident pose. "Rejoice, for I am here to save you from that hideous monster!"

Bellamy gawked at the sudden and unexpected appearance of Astonia. How the hell had she even gotten there? The bookworm wondered frantically and with growing unease.

Bellamy was more worried about Abigail, however, than his own safety. His blood was boiling out of anger. "Astonia, what have you done?" He tried to make his way over to Abigail, but Astonia took her shotgun down and pointed it at Bellamy in a threatening manner.

"Ah, ah, ah," Astonia chided. "Don't move. Now, tell me, why would you *care* about what happens to that monster?"

A muscle beneath Bellamy's eye ticked in irritation. "Abigail...is *not* a monster. She's my *friend*."

The corners of Astonia's red lips dipped into a dark scowl. "It's just as I thought. You must be *bewitched*."

"You have no idea how ironic that sounds coming from you." Bellamy shook his head, thinking about how Astonia was currently enthralled into loving him because of his curse. "I'm *not* bewitched, and I don't need to be rescued. I am here of my own freewill. I'm here to help my friend, Abigail!"

"Your *friend*?" Astonia sneered, her lip curling. "You must be joking. Anyways, we need to get going...there's a storm coming."

Bellamy took a step back and shook his head at the Huntress. "I'm not going anywhere with you, you crazy bitch."

"Oh, really?" Astonia suddenly pointed her shotgun at Doris. "I suppose you don't care if your mother kicks the bucket?"

"Astonia, you..." Bellamy clenched his trembling hands into fists at his sides as a wave of rage crashed through him. "You're the *real* monster here!"

Astonia's eyes narrowed into thin slits at the insult. "You belong to me, Belle. Now, what's it going to be? I'm beginning to grow impatient and my finger is getting tired."

Bellamy let out a resigned sigh. "Alright, fine, I'll go with you." His expression turned haggard. "Just don't hurt my mother. Or Abigail. If she's still alive..."

Astonia lowered her shotgun and smiled winningly. "Excellent. And don't worry, as long as you stay with me no harm will befall your mother or the yeti girl." The smile on the Huntress's face widened at her own thinly veiled threat. "That is, if she's still alive." A wicked cackle slipped past Astonia's lips.

With his shoulders slumped dejectedly, Bellamy began to walk towards Astonia. But Doris objected as she watched her son start to walk away from her. "Bellamy, no! I can't let you go with her!"

"Mom, it's okay," Bellamy soothed. "Please, take care of Abigail for me." The bookworm shot a worried look Abigail's way. She was still lying on the floor unmoving, but there didn't appear to be any blood on the front of her ball gown, so that had to be a good sign, right?

A subdued expression fell over Doris's face and she gave a stiff nod. "I will."

The first thing Bellamy caught sight of when he'd exited the ballroom along with Astonia was the 2-up snowmobile that was parked right outside, its motor running loudly. Bellamy frowned thoughtfully, thinking that they probably hadn't heard the snowmobile because of the pounding dance music. The snowmobile reminded Bellamy of a quad that had its wheels replaced with metal tracks like those on a sled.

Astonia motioned to the snowmobile with her gun. "You'll ride in front so I can keep an eye on you, Belle."

"Fine." Bellamy hopped up onto the snowmobile, and straddled it. Astonia got up behind him, slung her shotgun strap over her shoulder, reached out to grab the handlebars, and off they went.

The wind was beginning to pick up speed, and snow had started to fall. Bellamy mused that it would cover their tracks. Not that he expected a rescue party or anything. Astonia was right though - a snowstorm was approaching.

Astonia's ample breasts were pushing up against his back causing him to frown. "How did you even find this place, Astonia?"

"The magic mirror, *duh*," Astonia explained offhandedly.

"Oh, right, the mirror," Bellamy muttered darkly to himself. He should have realized that nothing would stop Astonia from coming after him - not when she was suffering from the affects of his curse.

"So where are we going exactly?" Bellamy decided to ask.

"Back to my place, of course. My parents recently bought me my very own log cabin just on the outskirts of town. You're going to love it, darling. It will be our little love nest," she cooed happily.

"Whoopee." Bellamy's voice was dripping with sarcasm.

Astonia and Bellamy managed to beat the approaching storm and made it safely to Yeti Town. Just as Astonia had said, her log cabin was located just on the outskirts of town. Even if he were to yell for help - no one lived close enough to hear. And who would really care if he were in trouble anyways? Bellamy thought morosely. Oscar and Crispin both hated him because he'd stolen Astonia's attention. And the bewitched nurses…Bellamy shuddered at the thought of them finding out his whereabouts. He'd be so fucked.

Astonia pulled the snowmobile right in front of her log cabin and turned the engine off. Bellamy dismounted from the snowmobile first with Astonia right behind him. The Huntress told Bellamy to open the door and enter first. Upon entering the cabin he was greeted with a really normal looking foyer. A tall, brass coat rack that was holding several long fur coats and fur wraps stood right next to the door.

Bellamy felt a trickle of sweat slid down the side of his face at the sight of all those fur coats. *Astonia sure likes her furs.* A few wooden pegs attached to the nearby wall provided even more space for hanging fur coats. An antique table with a silver tray on it sat close to the entrance and Astonia tossed her keys into the tray in a practiced way that made Bellamy think she did that every time she got home.

Astonia took off her floor-length, black mink coat, giving Bellamy a good look at what she was wearing underneath - a tight, red leather catsuit. The boots she was wearing were also red leather and had pointed toes and high four-inch heels. *Hello, Emma Peel.* He thought to himself with a tinge of amusement. Bellamy had to admit to himself that she looked smoking hot. Too bad he just wasn't into fur-crazy huntresses with psychotic possessive tendencies. The bookworm put his own suit coat on the rack.

"Welcome to your new home, Bellamy!" Astonia declared as she waved her hand at the entirety of the cabin.

"Yeah," Bellamy mumbled.

Astonia eyed the pale blue vest with gold buttons, white button-down shirt, and gray-blue silk pants he was wearing with a critical eye. "You must be freezing. Silk doesn't really provide a lot of warmth. Come and warm yourself by the fire in the living room." She crooked her finger at him before turning on her heel and sauntering off towards the living room, expecting Bellamy to follow her.

Not really having much of a choice, Bellamy sighed again, and shoulders slouching followed Astonia into the living room. A muscle beneath his eye ticked as he took in the living room's décor. A large chandelier made of antlers was hanging from the ceiling, but the antler motif didn't stop there. There were also lamps made out of antlers sitting on tables and antlers displayed on the walls along with the animal head hunting trophies. Astonia had killed a lot of different kinds of animals: deer, bears, wolves, lynxes, and there was even a poor stuffed bunny rabbit sitting on a nearby table.

"Wow. You've killed a lot of furry woodland creatures," Bellamy noted dryly in order to hide his unease. "I feel sorry for Bambi, Thumper, and Smokey the Bear over there." A dark frown had formed on his face.

Astonia arched an eyebrow at Bellamy, noticing his recriminating stare. "You do realize us Hunters are providing a public service for the people who live in Alaska. Ever since so many predators started appearing around this area…they started hunting farmers' sheep and cattle. They became a *menace* that had to be stopped. And if we get to make a little extra money by selling the meat, furs and pelts…" She shrugged nonchalantly. "I think we deserve it. Hunting is dangerous work. Sometimes prey becomes predator. If the Hunters of Yeti Town didn't keep this bizarre incursion of wild predators in check…northern Alaska would soon be overrun with them."

Bellamy blinked. Astonia *did* have a rather good point there. "I just…don't like the idea of *killing* a living creature." He rubbed the back of his neck in an uncomfortable gesture.

"I don't *enjoy* killing," Astonia said in a voice so soft that Bellamy failed to hear her.

Bellamy had to pull his gaze away from that stuffed bunny rabbit. "Anyways, I wonder what caused the sudden influx of predators to start appearing." Bellamy's angry expression turned pensive.

Astonia stared. "It's *unnatural,* whatever it is. Perhaps, your precious yeti girl is behind it."

"What?" Bellamy started, taken aback by the suggestion. "Abigail has *nothing* to do with it!"

"Oh, really?" Astonia gave him a disbelieving look. "How can you be so sure? A yeti girl, statues that can move and talk - that's not *natural* either, is it? I think all the weird things that are happening close to Yeti Town are all connected. I think it's...*magic*."

"Magic?" Bellamy instantly thought of the sorcerer Agathon who was hiding in the Alaskan wilderness somewhere. Could he have caused the unnatural incursion of dangerous animals close to Yeti Town? *Sorcerer Agathon...where are you, you bastard?* Bellamy wondered to himself venomously.

"Anyways." Astonia waved a hand through the air in a dismissive gesture. "You just make yourself comfortable while I cook us something to eat."

"*You* know how to cook?" Bellamy asked skeptically. He pictured Astonia as being one of those spoiled, rich girls who had her own chef.

"Of course I can cook." Astonia flipped her long black hair over her shoulder with a huff. "I'm multi-talented."

"I already ate. I'm not hungry," Bellamy said.

"Then I'll bring you some hot coco and some dessert." Astonia tossed a flirtatious wink Bellamy's way.

Oookay. Bellamy thought to himself. This was *so* weird. Astonia was being *nice* to him. She had to be up to something. And Bellamy had the sinking feeling that whatever Astonia was up to was most likely X-rated.

Ten minutes later, Astonia returned to the living room carrying a silver tray arranged with two mugs of hot coco, a bowl of fresh strawberries and a bowl of whipped cream.

By this time, Bellamy was seated in a cozy armchair by the fire and wasn't really paying attention to Astonia as he watched the flickering orange and yellow flames in the hearth. He couldn't help but compare the comfortable chair to the hard, stone chairs that existed in Abigail's mansion. His gaze flicked over to note that a tray was being set down on the coffee table next to him.

When he glanced up he saw that Astonia was wearing *way* less clothing than she had been before she'd left the living room. *What the hell is she wearing?* Bellamy inwardly wondered.

Astonia was dressed in a black bra that had orange fur trim along with matching silk panties. There was a headband on the top of Astonia's head with two fuzzy, orange fox ears.

Astonia picked up one of the steaming mugs and handed it to Bellamy - her cleavage suddenly in his face. "Here you go, darling."

Bellamy backed away in horror, pressing himself into the back of his chair as far as he could so that Astonia's boobs wouldn't be in his face. "Whoa. What the hell, Astonia? What's with that fox girl getup? Are you *trying* to seduce me?" He took the mug of coco though - just so she'd back off and give him a little personal space.

There was a mischievous glint in Astonia's brown eyes, and she placed a hand on her jutted hip. "Trying?" She raised an eyebrow at him. "I just figured you had a thing for furries."

Bellamy's brow furrowed in confusion at the unfamiliar term. "Furries?"

Astonia waved her hand through the air in an exasperated gesture. "You *know*, furries. People that like to dress up in cute, furry animal costumes, and go to Comic Con or other conventions dressed like that."

"Oh, yeah. Well, no." Bellamy shook his head. "I'm not into furries."

"But you're *into* Abigail…aren't you?" The Huntress gave Bellamy a keen look.

Bellamy took a slow sip of his coco in order to give himself more time to formulate an appropriate and evasive response. "What makes you say that?"

Astonia took a seat in the plush armchair across from Bellamy and adopted a relaxed pose. "The way you called out her name after I shot her. It sounded like…you might even be in love with her. But *that's* gotta be impossible. Are you sure you're not under her spell?" She gave Bellamy a searching look.

"I'm *not* under her spell. But you're sure under mine." Bellamy let out a heavy sigh.

"What?" Astonia's ears perked up.

"Oh, nothing," Bellamy muttered.

Astonia shrugged, and reached out to pick up a strawberry. She dipped it into the whipped cream before bringing it up to her lips. Without breaking eye contact with Bellamy, she began to suck on the strawberry and swirl her tongue around its tip.

Bellamy swallowed thickly. His throat felt dry and his pants were feeling a little too tight. What? He was a healthy young man, and Astonia was half-naked and sucking on strawberries in a *very* suggestive manner. *Shit. If I get hard...I am so fucked.*

At that moment the doorbell rang. *Saved by the bell.* Bellamy thought to himself as a wave of relief swept over him.

"Who could that be?" Astonia frowned, irritation playing on her beautiful face. "Whatever. I'll just ignore them. They'll have to go away eventually. Now, where were we?" Her expression turned predatory as she once again set her sights on Bellamy.

The sound of the front door being unlocked was heard, and then the sound of approaching footsteps before a short, chubby girl stepped into the living room. Her blue eyes widened like saucers when she saw what was going on in the living room, her jaw dropped, and her pudgy face turned as red as a tomato. "A-Astonia? What are you doing? Why are you dressed up like a naughty fox?"

Astonia rolled her eyes at her best friend Louise. "Hey, Louise. What does it look like I'm doing? I'm obviously in the middle of seducing my *boyfriend*."

"Um, nope. I'm not her boyfriend. More of her captive really. Or prisoner. She kidnapped me after all. Not like you care..." Bellamy was muttering to himself in a bitter tone, not really expecting Louise to listen to his laments.

But Louise heard Bellamy loud and clear. Confusion swam in her gaze until her expression settled on being appalled. "Kidnapped? Prisoner? Astonia, what have you done *now*?" She placed her hands on her wide hips while giving Astonia a recriminating stare.

Bellamy was surprised this Louise chick actually believed him. It made him wonder if Astonia had done something crazy like this before.

"Bellamy, darling, how could you say that to her?" Astonia questioned Bellamy in a scandalized tone. "We're in *love*."

"*Anddd* you're delusional," Bellamy drawled in a droll tone.

Louise began to look angry. "Astonia, you can't just kidnap people! That's a *crime*."

Astonia pouted and stomped her foot in a petulant manner. "But, I want him. I…I love him."

Louise rolled her eyes at her self-centered friend. "Just because you love him doesn't make this okay." She shook her head, causing her short blond ringlets to sway. "You can't force true love. You need to take him back home. Immediately."

Astonia rushed over to Bellamy and clung to his arm desperately, her boobs pressing against his arm. "No way! I'm not giving him back to that yeti girl! Bellamy is mine!"

Louise raised an eyebrow. "Yeti girl?" She shook her head, and offered Bellamy an apologetic look. "I'm really sorry about this. Astonia…can be very impetuous."

"No big," Bellamy assured. After all, this *was* partly his fault. If only Astonia hadn't seen him without his glasses. If only he'd been more careful…Astonia wouldn't be acting this way. Guilt was beginning to well up inside of him. He was beginning to realize how his mother must have felt about what she'd done to Raul.

"Well, we're kind of in the middle of a snowstorm anyways…so it's not like he can go home right now. I suppose he'll have to stay the night. Where were you planning on having him sleep, Astonia?" Louise questioned.

Astonia's dejected expression turned hopeful. "My room?"

Louise's expression turned stern. "Nope. I'm not about to allow you to commit a crime, Astonia. How's the guest room?"

Astonia pouted and looked put out. "It's fine…I guess."

Louise nodded, and turned to Bellamy. "Maybe you should go up and get some rest. I'm going to try reasoning with Astonia."

Bellamy quickly stood up. "Thanks…and good luck with that." Astonia gave Bellamy directions to the guestroom. The bookworm went upstairs, padded down the hall, and stopped in front of the door of the guestroom that'd been designated for him.

Bellamy opened the door, flipped on a light switch, and entered. He blinked because it was a pretty ordinary looking guest room with a woodsy, green, brown and yellow color theme. The walls were pale green, the comforter on the four-poster bed was green and yellow, and the two lamps sitting on the two nightstands were also green and decorated with antlers, of course. The room also contained a small pine desk, chair and a dresser.

Bellamy looked down at his princely threads. He instantly decided that he really didn't want to sleep in this expensive Armani suit. He glanced over at the dresser and figured there might be some old, spare clothes in there that he could use to sleep in.

Bellamy walked over to the dresser and began to open up drawers. His eyebrows rose to his hairline as he reached in and pulled out a geeky *Iron Man* T-shirt that was most definitely his. *Oookay. How the hell did Astonia get her hands on this? Did she really raid my house?*

That was weird and incredibly creepy. And at the same time kind of thoughtful. *No, no, no…no more Stockholm Syndrome!* Bellamy quickly reprimanded himself as he realized the train of his internal thoughts. He was getting way too used to being kidnapped and held prisoner by crazy girls.

Bellamy swiftly dressed in the T-shirt and decided to sleep in his boxers. When he got on the bed and began to make himself comfortable he couldn't help but compare the mattress to the bed he had at Abigail's mansion. Both of the beds were extremely comfortable compared to what he was used to. Both of his captors had given him nice rooms and nice, comfortable beds. Captors. What was he? Some kind of kidnapped damsel in distress? *Shit!* Bellamy inwardly swore as he hit the back of his head against the pillow in frustration.

The bookworm shut his eyes and willed himself to fall asleep. It was hard though when there was a lovesick girl downstairs that wanted to have her way with him. He tossed and turned on the bed while his thoughts strayed to Abigail. Worry swirled in the pit of his stomach making him feel nauseous. He hoped that she was okay.

A little after midnight Bellamy finally fell into a restless sleep, and close to sunrise he began to dream…

Bellamy ran through the forest that was filled with tall pine trees and other evergreens.

The snow was a half a foot deep and kept his progress annoyingly slow. For some reason he felt as though he were in a hurry as he searched frantically for someone while calling out their name. It was so cold out that his breath was coming out in little white clouds.

When Bellamy exited the edge of the forest, he entered a large clearing. In the center stood an enormous white oak tree that was more than a hundred feet high and around five feet wide. He'd never seen anything like it before. It must have been a couple hundred years old.

Standing in front of the tree was a woman. She had her back turned to Bellamy so he was unable to see her face. Her long platinum blonde hair cascaded down past her waist. Her womanly curves were visible through the sheer fabric of the slinky, white dress she was wearing. Even though Bellamy was unable to see the woman's face, he could tell that she was beautiful. At the same time, she also felt strangely familiar. He found himself calling out to her. "Abigail?" He was surprised by the name that slipped past his lips, but even though the woman before him may not have looked like Abigail she *felt* like her.

Abigail turned to face him, revealing that she was wearing a white and gold owl mask with feathers that shielded most of her face from view. "Bellamy?" she questioned as she approached him.

A fierce, chill wind began to blow and stirred up the fallen leaves that had been sitting on the forest floor. A swirl of red, orange and yellow leaves surrounded them in a temporary maelstrom.

Abigail tucked a strand of long white hair behind her ear as she stopped about a foot away from him. "What are you doing in *my* dream, Belle?"

Bellamy chuckled. "It's actually *my* dream."

Confusion swirled in Abigail's silvery gray eyes. "Is that so?"

"Where is this place?" Bellamy questioned as he looked around the spacious clearing. The oak tree in itself was quite odd because at this time of the year it should be without leaves, but instead looked like the tree would usually look during fall.

"I'm not sure," Abigail said, a tiny, thoughtful frown playing on her lips. "But it feels *familiar* for some reason."

Bellamy reached out to cup her cheek. Her skin felt pleasantly warm against his palm. "I must be really worried about you…to dream about you like this."

"Worried?" Abigail's brow furrowed in confusion.

"Astonia shot you." A dark cloud fell over the bookworm's face. Then he narrowed his eyes. "Don't you remember?"

Abigail looked pensive for a moment but then shook her head. "Sorry. I don't remember…"

"Of course you don't." Bellamy flashed her a reassuring smile. "You're *my* dream, remember? I just really hope the real you is okay because I think I might just…" He trailed off and looked past Abigail at the forest beyond.

Abigail was leaning unconsciously closer as she waited for Bellamy to continue. "Might what?"

Bellamy's attention snapped back to Abigail. Letting a primal force guide him, he closed the distance between them, tilted his head, and captured her lips with his own. The kiss started out tentative and tender, but grew hot and passionate. The feathers of the owl mask ticked Bellamy's nose causing the corner of his mouth to twitch.

In that moment, Bellamy didn't care if this was just a dream. Right now he had Abigail safe and alive and in his arms, and that made him so freakin happy.

Abigail eagerly kissed Bellamy back, and of course she did. She was his 'dream girl'.

Bellamy wondered what her *true* face looked like. He was sure it was beautiful. He just had this gut feeling that Abigail would be as pretty on the outside as he found her to be on the inside after having gotten to know her better.

Their kissing grew more heated, and after a few minutes they had to pull away from each other for air. Bellamy cupped Abigail's face in his hands, and wanting to press his forehead against hers did so, but instead of skin he felt the feather's of the mask she was wearing. He felt a twinge of disappointment at this. Bellamy longed for more skin on skin contact with Abigail. He slid his hands down over her neck and her skin felt icy to his touch.

I want to warm her up. Bellamy thought firmly, before remembering that this was his dream. *My dream. So why the hell not?*

Bellamy took a step back from Abigail, removed his long winter coat with a flourish, and laid it down on top of the snowy ground. He then took Abigail's hand and guided her over to the coat. He noticed that her hand was trembling slightly, but that was most likely due to the cold.

Bellamy lay Abigail down on top of the winter coat, and crawled over her body until he was staring directly into those gray eyes that were slightly obscured by her feathery mask. The tip of Abigail's nose had turned bright pink. Bellamy kissed it tenderly.

"Bellamy, I don't think this is just a-" Abigail was saying in a hesitant tone.

But Bellamy placed a finger to Abigail's lips to shush her. "My dream, remember? And…I want you, Abigail. I want my first time to be with you."

Abigail swallowed nervously, and nodded. "O-Okay."

A wide grin spread across Bellamy's lips. He kissed her lips before peppering kisses down her neck to her exposed collarbone. He continued his way, kissing his way down to her cleavage. The pale flesh at the top of her breasts was soft and warm.

Feeling strangely confident since this was his dream, Bellamy slid her dress down past her shoulders and over her breasts. She wasn't wearing a bra, and her beautiful, bare breasts were exposed to him with their rosy nipples. The sight made Bellamy salivate slightly. *Yum.* She looked utterly delectable. *Her skin is the color of freshly fallen snow.*

Abigail appeared to be holding her breath, waiting for Bellamy to say or do something.

"Beautiful," Bellamy breathed before lowering his head and capturing one of her nipples in his mouth. He knew he probably sounded horribly cliché, but he didn't give a damn in that moment. It was the truth.

Abigail gasped at the feeling of Bellamy's hot mouth on her cold, peaked nipple. The bookworm licked and sucked on her nipple until it pearled even more. Then he lavished equal attention on her other nipple until it was hard and straining.

Abigail was rubbing her thighs together unconsciously as heat began to pool between her trembling legs.

Bellamy's cock was hardening in his pants. He could hardly contain his own arousal, but he wanted to savor and enjoy this awesome dream for as long as possible.

The bookworm slid Abigail's dress the rest of the way down her body, exposing her core and long, long legs. A thatch of silvery, white hair that looked incredibly soft covered her sex. "Mmm," a masculine groan of appreciation slipped past his lips at the sight.

Bellamy tossed the dress aside and lowered his head to place a kiss on Abigail's cute, little, outtie bellybutton. *So cute.*

Abigail shuddered, arched her back like a cat, and purred beneath him. The bookworm's eyes widened at this unexpected reaction and felt his cock harden even more at the sexy sight.

Bellamy swallowed, gathered his courage, and began to kiss his way down to her sex. He placed a kiss directly over her core and Abigail bucked her hips against his lips. He grabbed Abigail's legs and spread her legs wide so he could get a better look at her sex. She was glistening with lust and hopefully desire for him. *Yum.*

Letting his instincts guide him since he really didn't know what the hell he was doing, he leaned forward and began to lick and lap up her desire. He felt her clit with his tongue and instinctively began to tease it.

Abigail started to writhe beneath him. "Bellamy, oh my god...*ohhh*...that feels so..." When Bellamy nibbled on her clit she was pushed over the edge. "Bellamy!" she cried out as her orgasm crashed into her and she trembled beneath him as fireworks exploded behind her closed eyelids.

Bellamy pulled back to watch Abigail coming undone, licked his lips, and a cocky smirk formed on his face. *Who's the man? I'm the man.* Even though he had no idea what he was doing and was just letting his instincts guide him he was apparently doing a good job bringing Abigail carnal pleasure.

At this point, Bellamy's cock was aching and throbbing inside of his too-tight pants with pent-up lust. He could feel precum leaking out of the tip of his impatient penis.

Bellamy reached down, undid his pants and pulled out his erection. It was already fully erect so he guided it to Abigail's entrance with his hand. He moved his hips forward and the tip of his penis entered Abigail.

Abigail gasped at the sensation of being stretched open, her gray eyes wide. She reached up to wrap her arms around Bellamy's neck. Her hands rested on the back of his neck and she began to comb her hands through Bellamy's soft brown hair. She decided to undo the blue silk bow that had his hair tied back into a ponytail and Bellamy's hair fell sexily around his face.

Bellamy looked down at Abigail and their eyes met through the mask's eyeholes - gray eyes clashed with sky-blue. Without breaking eye contact with Abigail, Bellamy entered her fully with one powerful thrust.

Abigail cried out, as she was suddenly completely full. Her hands slid down Bellamy's back and she dug her nails into his flesh through his T-shirt as she tried to get herself under control from being so stretched and full so suddenly.

Bellamy groaned with pleasure. She was so hot, wet and tight around him. He wanted to start thrusting in and out of her right away, but he could still feel her sex spasming around him, and gentlemanly waited for her to relax.

Abigail blinked up at Bellamy with a surprised look on her face. "Bellamy...?"

"I'm all the way in, baby." Bellamy smirked at her. "Can you feel me inside you? Can you believe we're actually having sex, Abigail? It's like a dream. Well, it *is* a dream. But you know what I mean."

Abigail smiled impishly. "I agree. This definitely must be a dream since it would probably hurt more if it weren't. So you can hurry up and move, Belle."

Bellamy chuckled at the wanton look on her face. "As you wish. Since this is my dream I bet I'm awesome in bed. I'll make you scream my name, monkey face." He pulled his cock halfway out of her before thrusting back in causing them both to see stars.

Bellamy adopted a steady, forceful rhythm as he surged over her, his hard cock sliding deliciously in and out of her heat. His own body was beginning to tremble slightly and not from the cold. He'd never felt anything like this before. It was crazy good. *Fuck, yeah.*

Abigail started to let out little gasping pants and cries as she continued to claw at Bellamy's back. The slight pain in his back only seemed to heighten Bellamy's pleasure though which was coiling in his gut. He was getting close. Then with one final thrust he came deep inside of Abigail while grunting out her name in a husky voice gone deep with lust. "Abigail!"

The feeling of his hot seed filling her caused Abigail to climax. "B-Bellamy!" She panted, clinging to him tightly. Overwhelmed by the mind-numbing pleasure crashing through her and this odd desire to mark him she sank her teeth into the side of Bellamy's neck in a possessive manner. *Mine!*

Bellamy continued to move in and out of Abigail as her body continued to shake in order to increase the pleasure of her orgasm. When her body finally stilled he collapsed on top of Abigail. Her breasts felt nice squished up against his hard chest, and he delighted in giving her chilled body more of his warmth. It made him feel…needed. Wanted.

For a few minutes, they just lay there panting in each other's arms. Then Bellamy pulled back to look at her with an adoring expression on his face. "You were amazing, monkey face."

Abigail's gray eyes sparkled. "You weren't so bad yourself, Iron Man." She winked and giggled.

Bellamy's brows rose to his hairline. "Huh?" Abigail glanced at his chest pointedly, and he followed her line of sight to note that he was wearing his Iron Man T-shirt even in the dream. "Was my rod of iron pleasurable, Milady?" he teased and waggled his eyebrows at her playfully.

Abigail burst out laughing. "Rod…of…iron!"

However, Bellamy began to hear a female voice calling out to him that wasn't Abigail's. "Oh, Bellamy, someone sure is happy to see me," the voice purred. "I knew you'd warm up to me eventually. *Mmm.*"

Bellamy's eyebrows furrowed in confusion since Abigail's lips weren't moving. "Huh? Did you say something, Abigail?"

"No." Abigail shook her head slightly. "Maybe you should wake up."

Bellamy frowned at the idea of leaving Abigail behind, even if this was just a dream. "But I don't *want* to wake up," Bellamy groaned petulantly and buried his face in Abigail's cleavage, nuzzling her breasts. "I want to stay here with you. Forever."

Abigail's cheeks turned bright pink at Belle's lewd actions. But she began to push at Bellamy's shoulders in an insistent manner. "I really think you should wake up now. Something might be happening back in the real world. Wake up, Bellamy! Wake up!"

Bellamy awoke with a start, and his eyelids snapped open to see that Astonia Sharpe was currently on top of him, straddling him. He was erect and she was grinding herself wantonly against his arousal, but thank God he still had his boxers on.

Astonia leaned over to nibble on his ear for a moment before pulling back to give Bellamy a wolfish look as she licked her lips. "Good morning, darling."

Bellamy screamed right in her face causing Astonia to frown, pull back and plug her ears with her index fingers. "How rude! Is that any way to greet the love of your life?"

At that moment, the door to the bedroom burst open, and Louise rushed inside with an alarmed expression on her face. Bellamy saw that Louise was dressed in pink flannel pj's, and a pair of fuzzy bunny slippers. When her gaze snapped to the bed and she caught sight of Astonia straddling Bellamy anger flashed across her face. "Astonia! Bad, Astonia! Bad!" Louise rushed over to the bed and grabbed Astonia's ponytail. "Come on, we're getting you out of this bedroom before he decides to sue you for sexual harassment!"

"But Louise," Astonia whined. "It was just getting *good*."

Louise ignored her and pulled Astonia off the bed. She offered Bellamy an apologetic look. "Sorry about that. Please don't sue her." Her gaze went to the obvious tent in Bellamy's boxers. "You should probably go take care of *that* in the bathroom. Toodles. See you at breakfast. Come along, Astonia." Louise began to unceremoniously drag Astonia towards the door.

"I don't want to leave," Astonia complained as she tried to dig her heels into the carpeted floor. "Bellamy, save me!"

Bellamy watched wide-eyed as Louise dragged Astonia out of his bedroom. Wow. Louise was something else! It caused a wry smile to form on his face.

His smile fell though when he glanced down at the tent in his boxers and let out a heavy sigh. He'd probably gotten a boner because of that steamy dream he'd had about the yeti girl Abigail in her lost *human form*.

Bellamy shook his head to clear it of his dirty thoughts. What the hell was wrong with him? Having erotic dreams about Abigail? It wasn't like he was in love with her, right?

I can't be in love with a yeti…I just can't be.

Feeling a little blindsided by his own traitorous thoughts, Bellamy stumbled out of bed and went to take a *very* cold shower. After taking care of his 'problem', he finished his shower and exited the chill bathroom. He got dressed in another of his Iron Man T-shirts, a pair of faded jeans, and sneakers before making his way downstairs.

The tantalizing aroma of scrambled eggs and sizzling sausage reached his nose, causing him to salivate. *Yum.* Following the delectable scent Bellamy found the kitchen easily. He expected to see Astonia cooking at the stove, but was surprised to see Louise behind the stove instead wearing a frilly, white apron. There was a pan on the stove containing scrambled eggs and another pan with grilling sausages.

Bellamy suddenly felt awkward as hell remembering how Louise had seen him aroused and practically being humped at by Astonia. "Uh, hi…good morning. Louise, right?"

Louise just smiled airily. "Good morning, Bellamy."

"Um, thanks for earlier." Bellamy rubbed the back of his neck in a sheepish gesture. He wasn't really used to people helping him. Especially, girls. To be perfectly honest, he was used to running and screaming from lovesick girls, so a girl helping him out was a nice change of pace.

Louise's lips dipped into a worried frown. "I really hope you won't decide to sue Astonia."

Bellamy chuckled. "Don't worry. I won't." *It's partly my fault she's acting crazy after all.* He thought the last to himself with a twinge of guilt.

Louise beamed at him. "That's very kind of you, Belle."

"Where *is* Astonia anyways?" Bellamy asked, glancing around the kitchen. He wasn't surprised to note that the counters were black marble, the cabinets mahogany, and the appliances were all chrome. Only the best for Astonia.

"Oh, she's *still* getting ready," Louise replied offhandedly. "She likes to think she's the Queen of England or something."

"Or better yet Cruella de Vil," Bellamy quipped playfully before he could think better of it. Louise was Astonia's best friend and may be insulted by Belle's insult, but Louise just laughed and Bellamy joined her.

After they'd both settled down, Louise's mirthful expression turned serious. "You know, Astonia is not really 'evil'. She used to be very sweet until..." Louise nibbled on her bottom lip, wondering if it was really her place to tell Bellamy these things.

"Until?" Bellamy prompted curiously.

"Well, Astonia's father, Gaston Sharpe, always wanted to have a son, and kind of raised Astonia as if she were a boy regardless. Gaston had it all planned out from the very beginning. He wanted Astonia to follow in his footsteps and become a Hunter. And so he came up with a plan.

"First, he got Astonia a pet rabbit and let her raise it for an entire year. Astonia loved that rabbit. Then, one day, Gaston told Astonia to kill the rabbit and stuff it. He explained it was part of her training to become a future Hunter. Astonia cried and refused. After all, she really loved that rabbit. But Gaston told Astonia that he didn't need a weak daughter...and threatened to disown her if she did not complete the task."

A look of horror had settled over Bellamy's face. "What an asshole. How old was she when this happened?" he asked quietly.

"She was eight-years-old. Astonia loved her 'daddy', and so she killed and stuffed her pet rabbit." Louise shook her head sadly. "After that, Gaston took Astonia along with him on his hunting trips and taught her how to hunt. She learned how to shoot, how to track her prey, and how to never miss her mark. He'd successfully managed to harden her heart. She became different...cold. That's why Astonia is the way she is and acts the way she does. She puts up this tough front, but I know deep, *deeeeep* down she's not so bad. Although, I think everything she's been through has given her a warped view on how to treat the things she loves. Like *you*, for instance."

"And what about her obsession with furs?" Bellamy prodded.

"That started with her pet bunny. After Astonia killed and stuffed him...all that was really left behind was his pretty fur." Louise's gaze drifted over to the stuffed bunny that was sitting on one of the tables inside of the living room that could be seen from the kitchen through the open door. "It was a constant reminder of her bunny. But instead of being sad about it, Astonia decided to be happy instead. The memory of her bunny had been perfectly preserved. Astonia became obsessed with preserving the *memory* of other animals. In a twisted way she thinks she's honoring the animals' memories by wearing their furs."

"Huh," Bellamy said as a knot tied itself up in his stomach. He felt confused. Maybe Astonia wasn't so bad after all. But, right now, she was still his enemy and his captor.

As if his thoughts had summoned her, Astonia swept into the kitchen, back perfectly straight, and chin raised like royalty. "Good morning, everyone."

Bellamy glanced in her direction, and arched an eyebrow at her. Astonia was wearing a black tube dress with golden fur trim at the top, and a pair of thigh-high black leather boots with pointed toes and stilettos heels. To complete her look she was wearing a floor-length gold and black fur coat that billowed out behind her as she sauntered forward while swaying her hips.

"Good morning, Cruella." Louise shot Astonia a harassing smile.

Astonia's expression fell at her best friend's words, and she pouted. "I look *so* much better in furs than that old hag ever did."

Astonia sashayed over to the round breakfast table and took a seat. "What's for breakfast, Louise?" She rubbed her hands together expectantly.

"Scrambled eggs and sausage," Louise informed her.

Astonia let out an irritated huff. "Are you trying to get me fat?"

Louise flinched guiltily. "I could make something else…"

Astonia rolled her eyes and gave her friend an exasperated look. "Did I *say* I didn't want it?"

Louise let out a breath of relief and quickly set plates with scrambled eggs and sausage down in front of Astonia and then Bellamy. She prepared a plate of food for herself, carried it over to the table, set it down, and took a seat.

"Uh…is Louise your maid?" Bellamy questioned Astonia.

Astonia actually laughed at the absurd notion. "No, you fool. She's my best friend. Louise just loves to cook. I do too."

"Oh," Bellamy said, feeling a little dim. Hanging out at Abigail's mansion had gotten him used to servants flittering around to attend to one's every whim.

As the trio ate breakfast together Louise watched Astonia and Bellamy's interaction intently. Astonia was shamelessly flirting with Bellamy the entire time and eating her sausage in a very suggestive manner while Bellamy pointedly ignored her, but he didn't look angry. In fact, he looked amused by her antics. It made Louise smile. Maybe Astonia had made a friend. She could use another of those since at the moment she was Astonia's only one.

***

Abigail awoke with a gasp. She blinked up at her ceiling for a few minutes, the images of the dream she had still fresh in her mind and causing heat to rise to her cheeks. When she sat up, leaning her back against the headboard, and glanced sideways she spotted Doris.

The woman was seated in a chair she'd pulled up to Abigail's bedside and appeared to be asleep. She was in a rather uncomfortable position with her neck at an odd angle and there was a little drool on her chin. "Doris?" Abigail called out softly, not wanting to startle the woman so badly that she'd topple out of her chair.

Doris stirred in her sleep, groaned, and then her eyes snapped open. She turned to look at Abigail, wide-eyed. "Abigail! You're finally awake. We tried everything to wake you, but it was like you'd fallen into a coma…"

Abigail raised an eyebrow at that. "A coma? How odd. What happened?" Her head began to pound as she tried to remember.

"Don't you remember?" Doris frowned worriedly. "Astonia shot you - right in the heart."

Abigail's brow furrowed as she thought back, and then she remembered the impromptu dance party with Bellamy, and the appearance of a stunning woman dressed in a red leather catsuit and a black mink coat. The woman had been wielding a double-barrel shotgun, looking like she'd just stepped out of *Jumanji*.

"Oh my God, that crazy Huntress shot me!" Abigail looked down at her chest, and blinked. There was no blood. She quickly unlaced the front bodice of her gown to reveal her necklace. She'd been wearing the Philosopher's Stone on a chain around her neck during the dance party. Just in case Bellamy decided to confess his undying love for her or something. Hey, a girl could dream.

The rainbow-colored Aurora Borealis quartz stone was pulsing with magical energy and on the very front surface of the stone was a melted piece of metal. Abigail pulled the piece of metal off and inspected it, deciding it must be the bullet. "The Philosopher's Stone...saved me. It must have shielded me from the bullet and placed me into a magically-induced sleep in case I was truly injured."

Doris was now looking at the Philosopher's Stone curiously. It looked oddly familiar to her, but she couldn't remember where she'd seen it before. It was on the tip of her brain...and then recognition lit up Doris's dull brown eyes. "That stone...it used to be a part of the sorcerer Agathon's staff!"

"That's right," Abigail agreed. "We have a common enemy, it seems."

"Enemy?" Doris echoed and a thoughtful frown formed on her face.

Snippets of Abigail's erotic dream about Bellamy began to flitter across her mind, causing her to blush. That dream...it had felt so real. In the dream, Bellamy had desired her. Even though she was a monster. He'd taken her. And she'd let him.

I can't believe I gave myself to that nerd. Abigail snorted. *But why did I? Do I love him or something? Or am I falling for him?* All she knew for sure was that she needed to see him, needed to speak with him, as soon as possible. "Where's Bellamy?" she asked Doris, her voice laced with impatience.

A shadow fell over Doris's face. "Astonia...kidnapped him."

Abigail felt like a truck hit her when she suddenly remembered Bellamy walking away towards the Huntress. Her eyes flared in alarm. Bellamy...had actually been kidnapped by some crazy Huntress who thought it was normal to point guns at people - not just animals or monsters. She was dangerous. "I have to go get him back." Abigail leapt out of bed, a determined expression on her face.

"You can't," Doris said grimly. "There's a snowstorm outside."

Abigail rushed over to the window, pulled aside the velvet drape and peered outside. She could barely see anything it was snowing so hard. She nibbled on her lower lip and hesitated, but just for a moment before she remembered something rather important. She turned and grinned so widely at Doris she showed off her fangs. "I am a yeti."

To be continued in...Chapter 8:

Chapter 8:

Breakfast was peaceful for the most part until someone began to pound loudly on the front door. At the same time the phone began to ring and Astonia's fax machine began to print various pages.

A chill of unease crawled up Bellamy's spine and he broke into a cold sweat at this familiar occurrence. *Déjà vu.* He thought to himself. Bellamy came to the sickening realization that the nurses must have discovered his whereabouts somehow. They were here. *Shit.*

"Who could that be?" Louise speculated aloud. "I'll go answer the door."

"No, don't!" Bellamy shouted at her in alarm.

Astonia shot Bellamy a sharp look. "Are you expecting company, darling?"

Bellamy grit his teeth and remained stubbornly silent.

Her curiosity getting the better of her, Louise went over to the kitchen window and peeked outside through the red and white checkered drapes. "Aren't those the nurses that work at your mom's clinic, Astonia?"

When Astonia joined Louise at the window and peered outside a dark scowl formed on her face as she recognized the five women outside. "Indeed."

"What's going on here? What are you guys not telling me?" Louise asked, glancing back and forth between Astonia and Bellamy in a speculative manner. To Louise's chagrin, they continued to remain silent.

Needing answers, Louise walked over to the scanner and picked up a few of the printed sheets that had fallen onto the floor.

She quickly looked over their contents. Her eyebrows rose in surprise at what she read. The pages appeared to be 'love letters' addressed to Bellamy. Super creepy love letters. She shuddered at the contents. "What the hell is *this*?" Louise demanded, waving the papers at Bellamy.

Bellamy let out a defeated sigh and his shoulders slumped. "You wouldn't believe me even if I told you."

Louise folded her arms in front of her chest and raised her chin. "Try me."

"I'm...kind of *cursed*," Bellamy admitted, and raked a shaky hand back through his brown hair. "If a woman sees me without my glasses on she'll fall madly in love with me. Emphasis on the *madly*."

Amusement played on Louise's face at Bellamy's joke until she noted that his own expression remained serious. He wasn't joking then. Her expression fell. "You're not joking are you? Oh my God...that explains Astonia's over-the-top, lovey-dovey behavior."

"You believe me?" Bellamy blinked at her.

"Yeah," Louise said firmly.

While Bellamy and Louise were distracted speaking to each other about what was going on, Astonia took advantage of the opportunity to grab her shotgun. Astonia opened the kitchen window and called out to the nurses. "Hey! Get off my lawn, bitches! Or else!"

The nurses' attention immediately went to Astonia's face in the window. "Astonia! Let us see Bellamy!" The nurses began to make various demands and exclamations. "We *know* he's in there!" "You can't hog him all to yourself!" "Let us see Bellamy!"

A muscle beneath Astonia's eye ticked in irritation. "No, you cannot see Bellamy! Leave!" Astonia took aim and fired at a snowman that was sitting on her front lawn. The snowman exploded, sending pieces of packed snow flying through the air in several directions.

"Eeee!" The nurses all cried out in fear and surprise, and dove out of the way.

Bellamy shot Astonia a horrified look. "Astonia! What the hell are you doing?" He rushed over to Astonia, grabbed the shotgun, and tried to wrest it from her grasp.

"Get off, Bellamy!" Astonia protested as she tightened her grip on the shotgun and tugged backwards. "I'm just trying to protect you!"

"I don't want you to *kill* anyone for make sake, you crazy woman!" Bellamy countered, his voice laced with anger.

"I won't!" Astonia let out a frustrated huff. "Just what kind of monster do you think I am? I was just warning them. I never miss my mark, you know."

Bellamy reluctantly let go of Astonia's shotgun despite her reassurances. *Shit, shit, shit.* Things would only escalate more if he remained here. This could easily turn into an actual bloodbath. History could repeat itself like with what had happened to his father Raul. The blood began to drain out of Bellamy's face at the thought until he was as pale as a sheet.

Astonia pointed her shotgun at the nurses again. "Get back!" she warned them.

Louise suddenly grabbed Bellamy's arm. He turned to give her a questioning look. Louise put an index finger to her lips. "Shhh." Then she nodded her head towards the back of the house. "Come on, I'm getting you out of here. There's a backdoor."

Without argument, Bellamy allowed Louise to guide him through the log cabin and to the backdoor. He watched as Louise whipped out a key to unlock the door, opened it, and then waved her hand towards the now open doorway. "Go. I'll handle this."

Bellamy gave Louise a warm, grateful look. He really wasn't used to girls helping him in these sorts of situations and he really appreciated it. "Thanks, Louise. You're a real pal." He patted her shoulder in an amiable way.

Louise beamed at him, enjoying the sudden attention. Boys usually ignored her because she was chubby, and any girl that was standing next to Astonia usually tended to get ignored. "You're welcome. Now, hurry! As soon as Astonia realizes I've let you go she'll probably go after you."

"Right!" Bellamy gave her a quick nod before exiting the cabin and into the snowstorm beyond. Louise closed the door and locked it behind him.

As soon as Bellamy was outside he started to run, heading for the nearby forest. It was snowing pretty hard, but blessedly it wasn't *that* cold out. It wasn't like his lungs would explode and he'd drown in his own blood or anything from overexerting himself.

Although, unluckily he'd once again found himself outside without a proper winter coat on, and was dressed in only a T-shirt, jeans and sneakers. He rubbed his arms with his hands as goosebumps broke out along his chilled flesh. Bellamy breathed into his hands and his breath was coming out in white puffs.

Bellamy's sharp blue eyes scanned the wintry expanse searchingly. If he could find a cave, he could hide there and wait for Astonia to give up her inevitable search. After that he could try and find a way to get back to the yeti's mansion.

As Bellamy pressed on through the snowstorm he could barely see anything in front of him and as a result he didn't see the rock in his path either. His foot hit the rock and he fell forward flat on his face with an undignified splat in the snow. "Ugh." Bellamy pushed himself up off the snow and dusted himself off. His face and his bare arms were freezing now. *Great, just great.*

Why was it that he always seemed to be running around outside in Alaska without a proper winter jacket on? When Bellamy tried to take a step forward he winced in pain. "Ow! Shit." He realized that he'd sprained his ankle in the fall. "When it rains, it pours." There he was in the middle of a snowstorm, wearing a T-shirt, and now with a sprained ankle. "Wonderful." He wondered if he'd be able to get through this alive. It would be a miracle.

Bell...amy! A female voice was carried by the icy wind to his ears.

"Huh?" Bellamy strained his ears to listen.

"Bellamy? I can smell you! Where are you?" The female voice was heard again and this time Bellamy recognized it.

It was Abigail's voice. "Abigail! Over here!" He called out with wide eyes. Bellamy started to limp in the direction he'd heard Abigail's voice come from. A few seconds later, Bellamy caught sight of Abigail through the falling snow. "Abigail!"

"Bellamy!" Abigail called out to him as soon as she'd spotted him. They ran towards each other...well, Bellamy limped.

Finally, they were close enough to see each other clearly despite the falling snow whirling around them. "Abigail, you're alive!" A crooked grin formed on Bellamy's face. He was so happy to see her. He had this inexplicable urge to hug her, but held himself back. He didn't want to freak Abigail out.

Abigail smiled softly at Bellamy in return. "The Philosopher's Stone saved me."

"That's great." Bellamy hobbled closer. "I was really worried about you."

Abigail looked down at Bellamy's legs upon noticing his limp. She frowned. "You're hurt. What happened? Did Astonia-"

"No," Bellamy quickly interjected. "I sprained my ankle while running through the snow."

"Fool." Abigail's chiding voice held a note of fondness to it. She reached her hand out to Bellamy. "Come on, let's go home." Bellamy reached his hand out-

But a shot rang through the air at that moment.

Using her superhuman reflexes, Abigail tilted her head to the side to avoid the shot. The bullet cut some of her hair off, and Bellamy watched as a thick lock of white hair floated down to the snowy ground. Abigail frowned darkly. "My hair."

Abigail looked past Bellamy and spotted Astonia, shotgun raised. The Huntress had one more shot before she'd need to reload. Bellamy turned to regard Astonia next, and eyed her warily.

Astonia pointed her shotgun at Abigail. "I can't believe you're still alive. As I recall I shot you right in the heart. Whatever." She lifted her shoulders in a shrug. "If at first you don't succeed, try, try again! I'm going to make a coat out of you, Yeti Girl!" The wind was causing Astonia's gold and black coat to billow out behind her dramatically and lent to Astonia's already intimidating appearance.

"Astonia, no!" Bellamy shouted.

Astonia lowered her gun's position slightly, aiming for Abigail's heart once again, and fired.

Abigail bent her knees and leapt high into the air, avoiding the shot. She landed with a hard thud in the snow, causing snow to fly up into the air all around her. The yeti let out an enraged roar, and beat her chest with her fists before charging towards Astonia with menacing intent.

Astonia's brown eyes flared in fear. "Uh oh." The Huntress tried to reload her shotgun as quickly as possible, but the yeti was

fast, and reached Astonia before she could finish loading her shotgun.

As quick as lightning, Abigail reached out and snatched Astonia's gun from her hands. The yeti smiled wickedly, showing her pointed fangs before using her bare hands to crush Astonia's gun into a metal ball. Abigail tossed the useless ball of metal over her shoulder in a careless gesture.

Astonia's eyes were wide like saucers as she saw what Abigail had managed to do with her bare hands. The yeti girl was strong. The Huntress knew she couldn't underestimate her opponent any longer. She'd tried to kill this yeti girl twice now, and twice she'd managed to come away unscathed.

Abigail closed the distance between her and Astonia, and opened her mouth to roar loudly right in Astonia's face. "Rawr!"

Even though a glob of spit hit her cheek and Astonia's first reaction was to attack the yeti girl she put her hands up before her in a surrendering gesture. She could always get revenge for that insult later - when she had more guns and bullets. "I...surrender?"

Abigail snorted at the cowardly display. "Of course you do." She narrowed her silver eyes at the Huntress threateningly. "Stay away from Bellamy, you crazy bitch."

Having said her piece, the yeti turned around, stomped over to Bellamy, and swooped the bookworm up into her furry arms. "Whoa, Abigail! What are you doing?" he protested.

Abigail just smirked down at him as she held him bridal-style. "You're injured. We'll get back home faster this way," the yeti declared before taking off into the forest at a rapid pace.

"I'm not some damsel in distress!" Bellamy's objection echoed through the surrounding pine trees.

As soon as the odd duo was out of sight, Astonia sank to her knees in the snow, her trembling legs giving out beneath her. She'd been...afraid. "Dammit!" That yeti girl was strong. Astonia realized that she probably couldn't defeat the yeti on her own. Especially, since Astonia had spied Abigail's stone servants in the enchanted mirror. This meant that the Huntress was outmatched *and* outnumbered.

Astonia nibbled on her thumbnail for a moment as she thought about what to do next. She'd need backup if she were to get her beloved Bellamy back. "That's right. Reinforcements." A sharp gleam came to Astonia's intelligent brown eyes. "Of course. There's always safety in numbers. I can't give up. Bellamy belongs to *me*!"

The Huntress pushed herself up off the snow and dusted herself off. She had a plan. Astonia returned to her cabin right away, and approached the nurses who were still milling about on her front lawn. After using the enchanted mirror to show the nurses the yeti, who was whisking Bellamy away to her 'evil lair', Astonia was easily able to recruit their help in order to 'rescue' Bellamy.

A cunning smile curled Astonia's lips once she'd gotten their agreement to help. That had almost been too easy. Astonia decided to change into something that would be a little more practical to face the yeti in, and dressed in her red leather catsuit, matching boots, and long black mink coat.

Astonia had one other place she had to visit in order to get even more reinforcements and so left the cabin. Louise was right behind her, acting worried and concerned as she wrung her hands together. "Astonia, where are you going?" Louise demanded.

"The *Polar Bear Pub*," Astonia replied nonchalantly.

Louise instantly became suspicious and narrowed her eyes at the Huntress. "Why?"

Astonia whirled around then and faced Louise, glaring dangerously at her best friend. "You're either with me or against me, Louise! What's it going to be?" She placed her hands on her hips.

Louise knew that whatever Astonia was up to that someone had to at least keep an eye on her and make sure that she didn't cross any lines. She let out a defeated sigh. "I'm your best friend, remember?"

Astonia grinned wolfishly in response, and once she'd mounted her snowmobile she offered her hand to Louise to help the chubby girl get on behind her. Astonia turned on the engine and immediately headed for the pub.

As soon as Astonia parked the snowmobile in front of the pub, she turned the engine off and the two girls dismounted. When they entered the pub all eyes were on them in seconds. Astonia was used to being the center of attention, so this didn't bother her in the slightest.

Louise was less used to this much attention though, and hid behind Astonia shyly. Because of the fierce snowstorm *all* of the Hunters happened to be there. No one could hunt in weather like this after all. Astonia had been counting on this, of course, and looked pleased.

The Huntress straightened her back, raised her chin, and spoke loudly to make sure that she had everyone's attention. "Greetings, fellow Hunters!"

All the Hunters smiled, waved, and greeted Astonia with equal enthusiasm. "Hey, Astonia." "Sup, Astonia?" "What's going on, Astonia?"

"I'm here because I need everyone's help," Astonia announced. "The legend of the yeti is…real. And she has captured one of our beloved townspeople!"

Low, excited murmurs rose up amongst the Hunters as they began to talk among themselves. A few people laughed, and the laughter was becoming contagious.

But then Astonia's father, Gaston, stood up from where he'd been seated at one of the long pine tables. "Do you have any proof, daughter?"

Astonia smiled devilishly. "Of course I do, Dad." She whipped out the enchanted mirror and whispered to it. "Show me the yeti girl." The silvery surface of the mirror glowed and shifted until the surface stilled to reveal the image of Abigail carrying Bellamy across the frozen lake in a princess-carry hold. "Here she is…the yeti girl!" Astonia pointed the mirror towards her father to show him the image first.

Gaston glanced at the mirror's surface and his eyebrows shot up to his hairline when he saw the yeti and Bellamy. A pleased smile curled his thin lips. "How…intriguing. Show the others, daughter mine."

Astonia obediently showed the image of the yeti to the other Hunters by facing the silvery surface of the mirror in their direction. The Hunters had varying reactions to spotting the image of the yeti in the mirror from gasps of horror to fearful widening eyes and dropping jaws.

"Hey, isn't that Bellamy DeWinter?" Oscar asked with a frown on his face.

Astonia nodded. "Yes. The creature has kidnapped Bellamy DeWinter! God only knows what she intends to do to him. Eat him. Or perhaps even *mate* with him!"

Oscar shuddered in disgust. "Gross, man."

"We cannot allow this creature to remain alive!" Astonia said adamantly, enjoying the looks of sheer horror that were playing on everyone's faces at this point. "She's bewitched Bellamy into thinking that he's in love with her. There's no telling how many young, handsome men the yeti girl will kidnap to slake her lust!"

Swept along by Astonia's pace the crowd began to join in with their own loud exclamations. "Yeah! Our sons won't be safe from the *lustful* yeti girl!" "She's an abomination that should be destroyed!" "She's too dangerous to be left alive!" "She's a monster!" "A beast!" "We must kill the beast!" "

A pleased, wicked smile curled Astonia's red lips as all the Hunters began to chant 'Kill the yeti!' over and over again. She had complete control over this crowd, no, *mob*.

There was a matching sinister grin on Gaston's face. His daughter's merciless, manipulative behavior was making him proud. "That's my girl," he muttered to himself.

Louise was looking around at the chanting mob in mounting alarm. "Oh no." Astonia had gotten everyone to follow her lead so easily. She was charismatic like that. There was no stopping them now. Anything she could say would only fall on deaf ears. "I'm sorry, Belle. There's nothing I can do." She watched as the Hunters started grabbing their guns, shotguns and rifles as they prepared for the hunt to come. Louise rubbed her arms where goosebumps had broken out over her flesh. *Astonia never misses her mark.*

***

By this time, Abigail and Bellamy had reached the front door to the mansion. Jett opened the door for them as soon as he heard their knock, and the yeti carried Bellamy into the living room where she deposited him on the jade armchair sitting in front of the fireplace.

Abigail clucked her tongue at what he was wearing - his *Iron Man* T-shirt, faded jeans and sneakers. "Why don't you *ever* have a winter coat? You do realize that you live in Alaska and *not* Hawaii." The yeti's gray eyes narrowed as she took in the T-shirt that Bellamy was wearing since it was awfully familiar. "That T-shirt…?"

Bellamy shivered and rubbed at his arms where goosebumps had formed from the cold. "I know, right? I keep getting kidnapped by crazy girls before I have the time to put on a coat." His tone was lighthearted, but there was a slightly bitter edge to it that caused Abigail to feel guilty.

Abigail plopped down onto the armchair across from him and sighed heavily. "Bellamy, you and your mother are no longer my prisoners here. Feel free to leave whenever you wish." She began to fiddle with her hands nervously as she awaited his response.

A flash of surprise crossed Bellamy's blue gaze. Abigail…was freeing him? "Abigail…?" He smiled crookedly at the yeti girl. "Well, sorry, but you won't be able to get rid of me that easily. I still need to help you find a way to break the curse. I made you a promise, remember? And it's one that I intend to keep. Besides, I like it here. And I like being here with…everyone." *And I like being here with you.* He added the last silently to himself.

Abigail looked up from her hands and gave Bellamy a searching look. She was strangely touched by his soothing words. She could hardly believe that after everything she'd put him through that he was still willing to help her try to find a way to break the curse. She'd been nothing but selfish this entire time. "Bellamy, there's something I need to tell you-"

"Bellamy!" came an excited, girlish squeal. Kristal had entered the living room and ran over to give Bellamy a hug.

Bellamy patted Kristal's hard head affectionately. "Hey there, kiddo."

Kristal sniffled. "We were all so worried about you when you got kidnapped by that crazy, fur coat girl! Are you okay?" She gave Bellamy a concerned, scrutinizing look.

Bellamy was sure that if Kristal wasn't made out of quartz that her eyes probably would have been teary. He felt a little bubble of warmth form inside of his chest at her obvious concern. He was really beginning to see Abigail and her servants as…a kind of second family. He finally felt like he'd found a place where he fit in. "Yeah, I'm okay. Abigail saved me." There was a twinkle in his blue eyes as he said the last part.

Kristal beamed up at him. "Of course she did!" The yeti's cheeks were beginning to take on a magenta hue. "Anyways, I came to tell you both that the storm has finally stopped." An impish expression formed on the little girl's face. "And you all know what that means, right?" She gave them an expectant look.

"Uh...?" Bellamy lifted his shoulders in a helpless shrug.

"It's time to build a snowman!" Kristal declared, and then rolled her eyes at Bellamy. "Duh."

The corner of Bellamy's mouth twitched in amusement, and he shot Abigail a questioning look. She nodded in acquiescence and smiled slightly. "Alright then, *Anna*," Bellamy joked as he thought about how similar Kristal was acting to Elsa's sister in the movie *Frozen*. "Let's go build a snowman!" Bellamy was already headed for the front door with Kristal tagging along behind him when Abigail cleared her throat loudly to get their attention.

"Ahem. Aren't you forgetting something, Belle?" Abigail asked, raising an eyebrow at him and tapping her foot upon the floor repeatedly. Bellamy gave Abigail a questioning look. "Oh my God, what's wrong with you? Hurry up and put on a winter coat before you turn into an ice sculpture out there!"

Bellamy looked down at himself and realized sheepishly that indeed he was once again underdressed for going outside. After Bellamy had finally put on a winter coat he swooped Kristal up into his arms and placed her on his shoulders.

"Whee!" Kristal squealed excitedly and wrapped her arms around Bellamy's neck so that she wouldn't fall off, while Bellamy placed his hands on the girl's legs to keep her steady.

Abigail frowned at the two as she followed after them. They were being incredibly reckless. "Bellamy, be careful with her. She's made out of quartz, you know. If she were to fall-"

"I would *never* let her fall," Bellamy quickly interjected. "Don't worry, monkey face. Ready, Kristal?"

"Giddy-up, horsey!" the little girl ordered.

The trio exited the mansion, and headed for the front gardens. The storm had cleared revealing clear blue skies overhead with only a few scattered white clouds. The gardens were covered a thick blanket of soft, powdery snow that was sparkling from the sun's rays. It was a dazzling sight.

Kristal looked up, spotted a cloud that resembled a yeti, and pointed up at it. "Look, it's Abigail!"

Bellamy followed Kristal's line of sight and spotted the cloud that did indeed look like a yeti. Although, the cloud yeti was a little more furry and ferocious looking. "Hey, you're right. It looks just like her-ow!" The bookworm turned to see Abigail standing next to him. She'd just pinched his arm. Bellamy gave Abigail a chagrined look before setting Kristal down on the snow. As soon as the girl's tiny feet touched the ground she ran off and stopped by a large pile of snow, which she began to pat with her hands.

A thoughtful frown formed on Bellamy's face as he watched Kristal's actions. "Doesn't she feel cold? Maybe we should have put some mittens on her."

"She doesn't *feel* anything," Abigail revealed in a sad tone. "And as the curse progresses she'll become more and more like a real statue - cold, lifeless, unmoving, unfeeling. She'll eventually lose the ability to talk too." Abigail shook her head of such dour thoughts. "Hey, let me help you, Kristal!" Abigail walked over to Kristal and began to help the little girl to build a snowman.

As Bellamy watched Abigail and Kristal building a snowman together his heart clenched painfully inside of his chest. And when Abigail giggled and smiled brightly, that's when he realized something - *I love her.*

"Hey, Bellamy, get your lazy butt over here and help us!" Abigail called out to him.

It was funny - even though Abigail still had blue skin and most of her body was covered by white fur, she didn't look like a monster to Bellamy anymore. She just looked like…Abigail. Bellamy flashed her a grin. "Coming!"

For the next couple of hours, Bellamy helped the girls to build several snowmen and snowwomen. "So, anyone we know?" Bellamy asked as he stood back and admired their creations.

Kristal giggled and gave Bellamy a disbelieving look. She began to point to the different snowmen and snowwomen. "That one is Abigail, that one is you, that one is me, and that one is Daddy."

The snowman representing Jett was holding hands with the child snowgirl that represented Kristal. The snowman representing

Bellamy was holding hands with the snowwoman representing Abigail.

Bellamy looked at the two snowpeople that were holding hands and blushed. "Why are Abigail and I holding hands?"

Kristal's eyes widened and she just giggled knowingly. "That's obvious, silly. That's because you and Abigail are-"

The sound of multiple snowmobiles with their loudly rumbling engines, and sleds pulled by teams of barking dogs approaching Abigail's estate reached their ears as that moment.

Bellamy's carefree expression instantly turned concerned. "What the hell?"

The hair on the back of Abigail's neck was standing on end in warning. "I'll go take a look." The yeti ran over to a tall pine tree and began to climb it using her claws. In less than a minute she was already fifty feet up. She looked in the direction the cacophony of sound was coming from and gazed at the frozen lake.

That's when she saw them breaking through the edge of the forest, and start to cross the frozen lake. Her eyes narrowed warily. There were several snowmobiles and dogsleds. The people riding them were wearing gray, blue and white winter camouflage and had rifles and shotguns slung over their shoulders by brown leather straps. *Hunters.*

Abigail's lip curled back in an angry snarl. A flash of red captured her attention and she spotted Astonia, riding a snowmobile, and leading the group of Hunters. *Astonia, that bitch!* Of course *she* would be leading them. Why was Abigail *not* surprised? What did surprise her was that a chubby girl who didn't look like a Hunter was seated behind Astonia on the snowmobile. Abigail fleetingly wondered why the girl had come here.

Abigail let out a heavy sigh that was partly resigned, partly angry. She'd known this day would come eventually. Known that when the humans living in Yeti Town discovered that she was real and not just a legend that she'd be hunted down and killed just like an animal. This was inevitable.

In that moment, Abigail found that she was less worried about herself, and more worried about the fate of her servants. She knew deep in her bones they would fight to protect her. And stone wasn't exactly bulletproof. If any of her servants took too many hits - they would shatter. *Shit.*

Standing at the base of the tree, Bellamy called up to Abigail. "What do you see?"

"Intruders!" Abigail shouted down before climbing back down the tree, her expression grim. The yeti landed on the snowy ground with a thud, snow flying up into the air. "It's Astonia, and she's brought *friends*. Talk about an evil ex, Belle."

Bellamy swore. "Shit. Hunters. What do we do?"

Abigail arched a white eyebrow at Belle. "I think you mean what will *I* do. I will fight. But you will not. They have guns, Bellamy, and you're *not* bulletproof."

Bellamy angrily narrowed his eyes at the yeti. "Neither are you. And if you're going to fight then…I'm going to be at your side fighting too. This place has become my home. And I want to fight to protect it alongside you and the others."

At first, Abigail was shocked by Bellamy's intent to fight by her side, but then she realized she shouldn't have been so surprised. Bellamy DeWinter was a *good* person. He'd shown her this time and time again. And perhaps it was this goodness that had rubbed off on her.

She was surprised at herself for even caring about her servants when there had once been a time when she'd probably have used them as shields. Yep, she'd been that selfish. Now…she was different. Something had fundamentally changed inside of her. Bellamy DeWinter had brought out the best in her. "Okay." Abigail turned to Kristal. "Kristal, I want you to go back inside the mansion where it's safe."

Kristal hesitated and a pout formed on her cute face. "But I want to stay and help!"

Bellamy crouched in front of Kristal and patted her head. "You're really brave, kiddo. But you should really leave this to us grownups."

Kristal frowned. "You're not that much older than me, you know? But, okay. I'll go tell Daddy what's going on." She turned and ran off, heading for the mansion.

Bellamy and Abigail watched as Kristal reached the front door and entered the mansion. A few minutes later, the door was opening again, and Jett stepped out followed by the rest of the household staff. Their duty was to protect the Master of the House a.k.a Abigail Snow.

Abigail had learned to expect their loyalty, but she no longer took it for granted. She was pleased to see them, and felt comforted knowing that they had her back. At the same time, she was worried about them. Their fate was still in her hands. She wasn't quite sure if she could handle that responsibility, or if she deserved to have it.

Jett reached Abigail and Bellamy first. "I hear we're about to be invaded. What are your orders, Milady? Should we meet them here, using the outer wall for protection, or go out to face them on the lake?"

Abigail thought about it for a moment. It would be dangerous, but perhaps she could use the lake to their advantage. If her stone servants fell into the icy lake they would survive. All they would need to do is walk back to shore and emerge from the water. They were completely unaffected by the cold and cold water. Maybe if the frozen lake started to crack the intruders would get scared off and make their retreat. The only one she had to make sure didn't fall into the lake was Bellamy.

Abigail turned to face the gathered household staff, which consisted of maid, butler, and cook statues made of lapis lazuli, turquoise, jade, black onyx, red jasper, tiger's eye, quartz and other semi-precious stones. This was her army. These were her servants. These were her...*friends*.

"Everyone, I thank you for your loyalty, and your bravery," Abigail began, chin raised proudly. "We shall go and face these intruders on the frozen lake. Let us strike fear into their hearts by making them fight on such a precarious battleground!"

"Yes, Milady!" all the servants called back in agreement. With Abigail leading the way her army headed out of the estate and towards the lake.

When Astonia spotted Abigail, Bellamy, and the stone servants exiting the tree line at the lake's shore she raised her hand to stop the Hunters' forward advance. The dogsleds and snowmobiles obediently came to an abrupt halt.

Abigail's group continued its advance and started to walk over the iced-over lake while slowly and cautiously approaching Astonia's army. Once Abigail's group was only a few yards away from the Hunters, Abigail raised her hand to stop their advance. Both armies glared at each other as they waited to receive orders from their leaders.

Astonia turned the engine of her snowmobile back on and drove forward a couple of yards so that she could address the yeti within earshot. "Abigail! Release Bellamy at once. Or prepare to face the consequences of your actions!"

Abigail growled low in her throat in response.

"Astonia!" Bellamy interrupted the girls before a catfight could erupt. "Go home! Stop being a crazy stalker!"

Astonia flushed in embarrassment and sputtered indignantly. A few Hunters laughed at Bellamy's words. She quickly recovered, however. "You see, everyone, the yeti girl has *bewitched* him!"

Most of the Hunters nodded in agreement at Astonia's claim since it made sense, but Oscar and Crispin didn't look entirely convinced.

"You leave me with no choice," Astonia started in a regretful tone. "I must kill you, Abigail."

Abigail raised a furry, white eyebrow at Astonia. "You can try," she said dryly.

"Leave the yeti girl to me!" Astonia yelled out to her army. "She is *my* prey! Everyone else is to handle the stone servants!"

"Yes, Astonia!" the Hunters yelled their assent, raising their weapons in the air.

Louise noticed that everyone had agreed to follow Astonia's order - all except for Gaston. He'd remained silent and there was a calculating glint in his eyes. A glint that Louise had seen before and one she didn't like one bit. He'd had that same glint in his eyes the same day he'd told Astonia that she needed to kill and stuff her pet rabbit.

"Charge!" Astonia ordered, waving her hand forward.

"Attack!" Abigail called out in response.

The two armies charged towards each other and crashed together like two ocean waves. The sound of gunshots and the sound of bullets hitting stone with a clinking sound soon filled the air.

Abigail loped towards Astonia while the Huntress drove towards the yeti, raised her shotgun, aimed, and fired once she had a good shot. The yeti surprised Astonia by lithely dodging the attack. The yeti was at home on the slippery ice. This was her element.

When Abigail was close enough she leapt up through the air towards Astonia. Astonia raised her shotgun again, but was unable to fire in time before the yeti rammed into her. Astonia was knocked off her snowmobile and crashed into the ice with the yeti still on top of her.

Louise let out a squeak of alarm, but she'd somehow managed to stay on the snowmobile even while Astonia had been knocked off. She prudently decided to put some distance between herself and the yeti that Astonia was still fighting fiercely. Louise was pretty sure Astonia could handle herself, but she would keep a close watch on her friend in case she did need Louise's help. Louise's eyes flared as she watched her friend and the yeti rolling across the ice as they wrestled each other, and fought for possession of the shotgun.

***

When the two armies had charged towards each other, Bellamy had charged right along with the stone servants. But much to his chagrin, the Hunters completely ignored Bellamy and concentrated on attacking the stone servants. That's when Bellamy realized that he was basically considered a 'hostage' in this strange situation.

Bellamy let out an irritated huff and scanned the battlefield for any sign of Abigail. He spotted her flying through the air and watched wide-eyed as she slammed into Astonia, knocking the Huntress off the snowmobile. Bellamy winced when Astonia's back hit the ice hard and then the two girls began to roll across the ice as they fought for possession of Astonia's shotgun.

Bellamy let out a whistle. Abigail was tough. But he was still nervous about how well a yeti could do against a gun. And Astonia was an expert markswoman. He started to make his way towards the two girls when Oscar suddenly stood in his path with a stern expression on his face. "Stop! Don't move, Bellamy!"

Bellamy arched an eyebrow at the young Hunter when he actually raised his shotgun and pointed it at Bellamy. He put his hands up before him in a surrendering gesture. "Really? Are you *really* going to shoot me, Oscar?" When Oscar didn't back down right away Bellamy continued, "Look, if this is still about Astonia...I'm really sorry, man. I swear, I don't even *like* her."

Oscar let out a heavy sigh at Bellamy's admittance, and lowered his gun. "Look, I know alright. There's a lot of strange shit going on here. But you need to stay out of *this*." Oscar waved his hand at the frozen lake that had become an intense battlefield.

Bellamy glanced around for a second and his blue eyes flared. It was insane. Hunters had dismounted from their dogsleds and snowmobiles, and were firing their guns at Abigail's stone servants. Bullets were flying through the air and Bellamy flinched each time a bullet hit one of Abigail's servants, expecting he or she to shatter to dust.

But the stone servants were surprisingly resilient and just continued to stride forward and attack the Hunters, grabbing the guns right out of their hands, confiscating weapons, picking up Hunters by the front of their jackets and then tossing them across the slippery ice.

The Hunters cried out as they went skidding and sliding across the ice. The stone servants raised their confiscated guns and aimed at a section of the ice that pretty much separated the two armies. Consecutive shots were fired. The bullets hit the ice, causing it to crack and then break away until there was an icy river between the Hunters and the stone statues with large chunks of ice floating in it. The Hunters stared in disbelief at the newly formed river, and were too afraid to risk crossing it.

Oscar frowned at this startling development, and turned his attention back to Bellamy. "You're under the yeti's spell, man. We're trying to save you!"

"I only need saving from you trigger-happy bastards," Bellamy countered. "The yeti - Abigail - *never* hurt me."

"I find that hard to believe." Oscar gave Bellamy a skeptical look. "She's a *monster*."

Bellamy's exasperated expression turned disappointed. "Are you really going to judge Abigail by the color of her skin?" Oscar flinched guiltily. "So what if her skin is blue. She's a *good* person!"

"I want to believe you, but…it's hard," Oscar admitted softly.

"Actions speak louder than words. Just watch," Bellamy turned his attention back to where the yeti and the Huntress were fighting. "Abigail is *no* monster. She would have killed Astonia using her superhuman strength by now if she was. You'll see."

Oscar let out a defeated sigh and followed Bellamy's line of sight. "Fine. We watch." He folded his arms over his chest with a huff.

By this time, Astonia had managed to get out from under Abigail. She jumped backwards to put some distance between herself and the yeti, raised her shotgun and fired - using her second loaded cartridge. Abigail dodged the bullet. Astonia swore. "Shit. Fine! If that's the way you want it!" The Huntress whipped out a hunting dagger and got into a fighting stance. The sun reflected off of the dagger's blade and gleamed.

Abigail released a loud roar before charging towards Astonia. When the yeti was close enough she attacked with a swipe of her claws that was quickly blocked by a dagger blade.

Claws and steel clashed in a deadly dance. Abigail dodged vicious dagger swipes and slashes while Astonia ducked razor-sharp black claws. They were pretty evenly matched, and Bellamy wasn't sure who would gain the upper hand until something unexpected happened to interrupt their fight.

A shot rang out and then the ice around Abigail and Astonia's feet started to crack and then abruptly gave way. The yeti and Huntress fell into the icy lake with a splash, and sank beneath the surface.

The ice-cold water was shocking, but Abigail wasn't injured this time around or dizzy with blood loss like the last time this had happened to her, and so began to swim back up towards the surface. She glanced down to see if Astonia was swimming back up to the surface too. Since, of course, Astonia wouldn't go down that easily.

But Abigail was surprised to see that Astonia *wasn't* swimming back up towards the surface! *What the hell?* Astonia's eyes were closed, and she was sinking fast. She'd drown at this rate. *Good riddance.* Abigail thought cruelly to herself as she glanced back towards the surface with a triumphant expression on her face, but then she glanced back down at the sinking form of Astonia. *Aw, hell!*

Abigail couldn't just let Astonia sink to her death. The crazy Huntress was only acting this way because of Bellamy's curse. She was a victim in all this, not a villain. Abigail swam down towards Astonia, and upon reaching the other girl wrapped her arm around

Astonia's waist. Then the yeti began to swim Astonia back up towards the surface.

They broke through the surface a minute later, and Abigail used her claws to pull herself out of opening in the frozen lake entirely before swiftly spinning around to grab Astonia's wrist, and pulling the other girl out of the water and onto the solid ice.

Astonia turned on her side and coughed up a great deal of water. When she sat up and looked around the first thing she saw was the yeti girl Abigail who'd obviously just saved her life. Astonia frowned though when she wondered who'd shot at their feet in the first place. She quickly scanned the surrounding area and noticed that her father was approaching them with purposeful steps. "Dad? Did *you* shoot the ice?" *Please, don't let it be true.* She thought to herself with a sinking feeling in the pit of her stomach.

"Yes. I did," Gaston admitted with a wide smile on his face. A smile that didn't reach his cold, brown eyes.

Astonia gave her father a hurt, incredulous look. "I...almost *drowned* because of you!"

Gaston shrugged lackadaisically. "The ends...justify the means. If I kill the yeti...I will become an immortal legend. A world renown Hunter!" He pointed his semiautomatic hunting rifle at Abigail.

"Father! How could you?" Astonia accused hotly and then realized what her father was doing. She quickly stood up on shaky legs and suddenly Louise was at her side, helping her to remain standing. Astonia shot her friend a grateful look before returning her attention to her father. "No, don't! Abigail saved my life! Didn't you just see that? She's *not* a monster! I...was wrong!"

Gaston barked out a laugh. "Ha! I don't care. As long as she *looks* like a monster everyone will believe my story - how the yeti attacked you and how I killed the yeti girl in order to protect you. Pity, that the story of the yeti killing you and then I avenging you can't happen now. It had a nice *heroic* ring to it. Farewell, yeti!" He started to pull down on the trigger.

"No!" Bellamy slammed into Gaston's side at that moment. A shot split through the air, but the bullet missed Abigail and Astonia. Bellamy and Gaston slammed into the ice hard. Bellamy reached for the shotgun, grabbed the muzzle, and began to try and pull it out of Gaston's iron grip, but to no avail.

Gaston growled furiously and wrenched the gun out of Bellamy's hands before hitting the bookworm hard across the face with the butt of the shotgun. Blood trickled down the side of Bellamy's head, and he saw stars.

Gaston stood up and glared down at Bellamy. "Don't get in my way, boy." The Hunter turned his attention elsewhere.

Bellamy worriedly followed Gaston's line of sight. "Abigail…" He was too far away to protect her this time, and his head was throbbing in pain. *Shit!*

Abruptly, Kristal appeared. She stood in front of Abigail and spread her arms at her sides. "I won't let you hurt my friend!"

Gaston's lip curled in a sneer at the sight of the little girl made out of blue quartz, and without hesitating he pulled down on the trigger of his hunting rifle - again and again. Several bullets flew through the air heading towards Kristal and Abigail. The bullets hit Kristal with a tinkling sound. Kristal successfully shielded Abigail from the bullets with her hard body. However-

Cracks began to form on Kristal's body. Abigail's eyes widened in horror as she saw the cracks forming on Kristal's back, and she quickly stood up. "No! Kristal! Get away!"

Bellamy also noticed the cracks forming on Kristal's body and a wave of dread swept over him. "Kristal!"

Kristal seemed to realize what was happening though and glanced behind her at Abigail before then meeting Bellamy's panicked gaze. "Bye, bye," Kristal said before her body shattered into hundreds of pieces of blue quartz that hit the ice and then skidded over the surface of the frozen lake.

Watching Kristal's body shatter and the pieces of blue quartz fall and hit the ice seemed to happen in slow motion to Bellamy. And yet he'd been unable to do anything to stop it. The way the sunlight glinted off of the pieces of falling quartz was beautiful and yet horrendous.

"No!" Abigail cried out, her voice cracking, and tears filled her solid silver eyes.

Gaston pulled back on the trigger again, but a clicking sound filled the air. He was out of bullets. He swore, tossed his rifle aside, and pulled out his wicked hunting dagger. "Looks like I'll have to finish her off the old fashioned way." He ran his tongue along the blade of his knife in a feral manner.

"Oh no you don't, you bastard!" Bellamy lunged at Gaston, and wrapped his hand around the wrist of the hand Gaston was holding the dagger with.

"Out of my way, boy," Gaston snarled, viciously punching Bellamy in the face with his free hand.

Bellamy staggered backwards dizzily and the side of his face throbbed in pain. Gaston continued his approach towards Abigail until Jett stepped into his path next.

Gaston raised an eyebrow at the onyx butler. "Out of my way, *Alfred*."

"You killed my daughter," Jett said lowly. The butler's eyes were narrowed hatefully and Bellamy thought that Jett had never looked more intimidating than he did in that moment. "Prepare to die." The butler approached the Hunter with swift, purposeful steps.

Gaston wasn't intimidated easily though and simply got into a fighting stance and swung the dagger at Jett. Jett caught his wrist and then began to bend Gaston's wrist back. "Shit. Let go, you son of a bitch!" Gaston snapped angrily, and then screamed as Jett mercilessly broke his wrist.

Jett's hand shot out and wrapped around Gaston's throat. The butler lifted Gaston up off the ice and then carried him over to the opening the Hunter had shot into the ice earlier. Gaston saw where Jett was taking him and struggled in Jett's iron grip, raking his nails over Jett's stone hands futilely. Jett held Gaston out over the pool of icy water so that his feet were dangling over the water's surface.

"No, don't!" Gaston choked out. "Let me go!"

Jett smirked coldly. "As you wish, Sir." He let go of Gaston who fell into the icy lake with a splash. Gaston sank below the surface and did not resurface.

Abigail sank to her knees next to the pieces of blue quartz that used to be Kristal. Tears streamed down her face as she cried openly, and Bellamy watched as her tears turned into snowflakes.

With a heavy heart, Bellamy approached Abigail, Astonia, Louise, and Kristal's broken body. Harsh sobs wracked Abigail's body and she wrapped her arms around her torso, hugging herself. "This...is all my fault," she said in despair.

A dark cloud fell over Bellamy's face at the yeti's broken words. He knelt beside Abigail and placed a hand on her shoulder. "No. This is not your fault. But we do know whose fault all this is. The sorcerer Agathon. He is to blame for all of this. All he leaves is pain, death, and suffering in his wake."

Astonia was looking down at Abigail as if she were seeing her for the first time. "I'm sorry," she said quietly.

"Not your fault," Bellamy said adamantly. "None of this is your fault either."

Astonia's brow furrowed in confusion. "I don't understand. But thanks for saying that."

Jett approached Abigail and the yeti caught sight of him. "Oh, Jett!" Abigail launched herself into Jett's arms and sobbed loudly. "I'm so sorry! I'm so sorry!" she repeated over and over again.

A determined expression formed on Bellamy's face as he watched Abigail's emotional breakdown. Abigail's heart was breaking...and it was causing his own heart to break. "Astonia, can I speak with you for a moment? Alone." He glanced at Louise who was standing at Astonia's side, a silent support.

"Uh, sure," Astonia replied in surprise. "Wait here, Louise."

"Okay," Louise said while giving Astonia and Bellamy worried looks.

Astonia and Bellamy walked away from the others until they were out of earshot. Then Bellamy spoke in a low voice, "Do you have the enchanted mirror with you?"

Astonia blinked. "Uh, yeah."

"I need it," Bellamy said firmly.

Astonia reached into her mink coat and pulled out the mirror. She handed it to Bellamy with a sheepish look on her face. "Here. Again, I'm sorry for everything. Even if I love you...I went too far. That little girl..." Astonia shook her head as she tried to get the image of Kristal shattering to pieces out of her mind. "What do you intend to do?"

"I plan to end all of this pain and suffering," Bellamy started, as he gripped the mirror's handle tight until his knuckles turned white. "Once and for all."

There was a strange gleam in Bellamy's blue eyes that Astonia had never seen before on the gentle man's face. It looked so out of place that it made Astonia feel uneasy. This wasn't like Bellamy. Not at all. "How exactly do you intend to do that?" Her voice was laced with concern.

"By destroying the source of all this," Bellamy said without meeting Astonia's questioning gaze. "Mind if I borrow your snowmobile…and your shotgun?"

Astonia hesitated for a moment before holding her shotgun out in Bellamy's direction. "Sure. Go right ahead." Bellamy's fingers wrapped around the muzzle of the gun, but Astonia didn't let go of it right away. "This is my favorite gun. I'll be wanting it back. Understand?"

Bellamy nodded and a lopsided smile formed on his face. "Yeah. I get it." Astonia let go of the shotgun then. He turned and headed for the snowmobile.

Astonia watched him walk away from her and found herself calling out, "Uh, Bellamy?"

"Yeah?" Bellamy glanced over his shoulder at her.

"Good luck," Astonia called.

"Thanks. I'm probably going to need it," Bellamy said grimly as he mounted the snowmobile, turned on the engine, and held the mirror. "Show me the sorcerer Agathon." The mirror's silvery surface glowed, shifted, and stilled to reveal a gigantic oak tree deep in the forest. Bellamy frowned when he noted that the oak tree was the same one from the dream he'd had about Abigail.

Sorcerer Agathon…I'm coming for you. Bellamy drove off into the forest. He did not look back.

To be continued in…Chapter 9:

Chapter 9:

Bellamy drove through the forest on the borrowed snowmobile at top speed - zigzagging through the pine trees. The snowmobile smoothly glided over the snow. Armed with Astonia's double-barrel shotgun and wicked hunting knife, he planned to confront and *kill* the sorcerer Agathon in order to not only break his own curse (and hold over Astonia's heart) but Abigail's curse as well.

If he managed to defeat Agathon, Abigail would get her old body back. And Abigail's servants would turn from stone back into flesh and blood.

Kill.

Bellamy was about to try and actually *murder* someone. The unsettling thought caused his stomach to tie itself up into knots. He felt nauseous and bile rose up in his throat that he was forced to swallow down. Could he really do this? Could he *really* end the life of another human being?

Flashes of everything that had happened zipped through his mind - the dream vision he'd seen of Abigail's past, the death of her mother, the disappearance of her father, Agathon offering Abigail the Philosopher's Stone in exchange for shelter from the rain, and then turning her into a monster and her servants into stone statues when she'd refused. Living statues like Kristal.

When the image of Kristal shattering into a hundred pieces filled his mind, Bellamy clenched his hands more tightly around the handlebars until his knuckles turned white. Images of his mother's past flew through his mind next - her encounter with the sorcerer Agathon, the granting of her wish, and how Raul DeWinter had fallen in love with Doris.

Raul. Bellamy's father who'd died a brave hero, and had turned out to be a man who'd loved the mother of his child. Bellamy recalled his mother's sad, tear-stained face, and the image shifted into Abigail's tear-stained face. Jett had been unable to cry at the loss of his own daughter because tragically a stone statue didn't have that ability.

It was all just too *unfair*.

A grim expression settled over Bellamy's face. Yeah...yeah he could kill Agathon.

Bellamy knew in his heart that Abigail would have come with him if she'd known what he planned to do, and having a powerful yeti on your side when you're going up against a powerful sorcerer would have been a good thing. But...Abigail had suffered enough. *His* hands would be stained with blood. He'd be a *murderer*. He didn't want Abigail's hands to be stained with blood too. He wanted to spare this from her. He wanted to protect her. Save her. He...loved her.

Bellamy looked down at the mirror's surface, which was showing the path he had to take to arrive at the sorcerer Agathon's evil lair, er, home.

A wolf's howl echoed through the forest. This howl was followed by several other howls as if the wolves were responding to the call of the first. Bellamy glared at the trees wondering when the wolves had spotted him.

From out of the trees a pack of wolves emerged and began to chase after Bellamy. *Shit!* Bellamy turned around, aimed his shotgun at the wolf that was closest to the snowmobile, and fired. The bullet hit the wolf that yelped in pain and hit the snow.

Bellamy was surprised he'd even managed to hit the wolf. That had been his first time using a shotgun. Maybe since his father Raul had been a Hunter...it was in his blood. A wry smile formed on Bellamy's face at the thought. It was like the ghost of his father was protecting him.

From Bellamy's right a wolf leapt at him from a small outcropping of rock that had put the wolf positioned above the trail. Bellamy turned, aimed the shotgun in its direction, and fired. The bullet hit the wolf's chest, and it fell to the snowy ground.

With trembling, chilled fingers, Bellamy hurriedly reloaded the shotgun with two more cartridges. With two of their own dead the wolf pack decided to fall back for the time being. Bellamy let out a sigh of relief as he watched them go, but knew he wasn't out of the woods just yet.

Bellamy was now convinced that the unnatural appearance of all these predators close to Yeti Town was definitely connected to the sorcerer Agathon.

And he was right.

A loud roar reverberated through the trees and then a lynx appeared on the path behind him. "Great, just great." Bellamy picked up speed, hoping to put distance between himself and the lynx. But she was a fast, sleek, feline creature, and was closing the distance between them pretty quickly. It was unnerving to watch.

Bellamy turned, aimed his gun at the lynx, and fired. The shot rang out and the lynx gracefully dodged the shot. Bellamy's eyes widened at its display of agility. He was impressed and also worried. He only had one shot left before he'd have to reload. Why didn't Astonia wield modern hunting rifles like most of the other Hunters, Bellamy wondered irately. He aimed his gun at the charging lioness again.

However, a pine tree abruptly appeared in front of him, and he was forced to keep his eyes on the path ahead unless he wanted to end up flattened into a pancake. By the time he turned back around to aim at the lynx again he discovered that the creature had pounced and was flying through the air towards him, its maw wide open, teeth gleaming, and claws extended.

"Oh shit!" Bellamy swore and tried to bring up the shotgun, but knew he wouldn't make it in time. He was *so* dead.

At that moment an enormous, white blur rammed into the lynx from the right. Bellamy watched in a mixture of awe and horror as a polar bear attacked the lynx that savagely fought back. The two creatures rolled across the snow in a flurry of snapping maws and raking claws.

"I never thought I'd be glad I was such a popular guy with the ladies!" Bellamy remarked with a wry smirk as he watched the female polar bear pinning the lynx down on the ground. He returned his attention to the path in front of him and a few minutes later he was exiting the forest into a clearing where an ancient oak tree stood.

The tree was the same one from Bellamy's erotic dream with its stunning canopy of yellow, red and orange leaves. Although Bellamy hadn't noticed in the dream that on the tree's trunk was a door that had been painted a dark green color and had a bronze doorknob.

Bellamy stopped the snowmobile and turned the engine off. If he was lucky the sorcerer hadn't heard the snowmobile's engine. There was no reason to unnecessarily alert Agathon to his presence and he decided to go the rest of the way to the tree house on foot.

Just as Bellamy was dismounting the hair on the back of his neck stood on end. He rubbed his neck anxiously and narrowed his eyes at the surrounding trees. He was being watched. Several pairs of gleaming eyes were staring at Bellamy through the trees and foliage, and he gulped. He was completely surrounded by hidden predators. If they decided to come out and attack Bellamy - he'd be ripped to shreds in seconds.

Bellamy waited and held his breath for a few seconds, but the creatures remained hidden in the trees. They were keeping their distance. He wondered if they were instinctively afraid of the sorcerer Agathon and his magic, and felt a little stupid about his own lack of fear. He should probably be terrified about who he was about to try and face.

Well, Bellamy was scared, but he was feeling strangely numb about what he intended to do. Like all this was a dream or something. He loaded the shotgun with two cartridges and noted that his hands were trembling. Well, his body was afraid.

He took a deep breath before he began to cautiously approach the tree house. Upon reaching the door he grabbed the doorknob, turned it and opened the door. He was surprised that the door was unlocked. But Bellamy supposed there probably wasn't much that a powerful sorcerer had to be afraid of.

As silently and stealthily as possible Bellamy made his way inside. The dwelling was more spacious on the inside than it appeared to be on the outside. Bellamy deduced it had to be some kind of magic spell like the one that made Hermione Granger's handbag expand in *Harry Potter*.

Bunches of dried herbs and flowers hung from the ceiling filling the house with a pleasant herby smell. The interior of the tree house was strangely cozy and inviting, reminding Bellamy of a 'Hobbit Hole'. But then Bellamy noticed that a few dead blackbirds were hanging from the ceiling as well, and shuddered. So much for *inviting*.

The sorcerer had a long, wooden workbench that was covered with a modern chemistry set, beakers, test tubes, and a test tube holder. He was reminded of Abigail's laboratory. But then he spotted a glittering pile of precious stones: rubies, sapphires, diamonds and emeralds. *Whoa.* Sorcerer Agathon may have been an evil bastard, but he was definitely loaded. There was also a series of scales used for weighing stones or gold sitting on the workbench.

One of the things Bellamy remembered reading about the Philosopher's Stone was that it had the ability to turn base metals into gold. Considering there was a large pile of gold nuggets on Agathon's workbench Bellamy assumed that the sorcerer must have known how to use the stone to produce such results when he'd been in possession of it.

Bellamy's attention was then drawn to the cloaked figure that was standing in front of a stone fireplace while stirring the purple-colored, bubbling contents of a large black cauldron that hung over the hearth. It was the sorcerer Agathon.

The sorcerer was wearing his usual dark blue, velvet, hooded cloak embroidered with the pattern of golden stars. Bellamy could hardly believe his luck - the sorcerer actually had his back turned to him. He raised Astonia's shotgun and pointed it at Agathon's back. But then, he hesitated. This…seemed too easy.

And shooting someone in the back was incredibly cowardly, but…

Bellamy had the feeling he only had one shot at this since he was going up against a powerful sorcerer. He grit his teeth in determination, pulled down on the trigger, and took the shot. He fired his second shot right afterwards for good measure. He had a gut feeling that just one bullet wouldn't be enough to kill the sorcerer.

The two bullets whizzed through the air towards Agathon, but instead of hitting him the bullets appeared to hit some kind of invisible energy shield which flickered to existence briefly with a blue-tinged light. The sorcerer spun around to face Bellamy, a livid expression on his handsome face.

Oh crap. Bellamy realized he was *so* screwed. The shotgun fell from his limp fingers and hit the floor with a clatter.

"How rude." Agathon's lip curled back into a disgusted sneer. "You come into *my* home uninvited, and try to shoot me in the back? You possess a startling lack of manners. Who are you and why have you come here, boy?"

Bellamy raised his chin, even though he was terrified by the sorcerer's intimidating aura. "Perhaps, you'll remember the names of the people you cursed. I am the son of Doris DeWinter and Raul DeWinter!"

His eyes flashed with recognition and Agathon's eyebrows rose, revealing his surprise. "Ah, you are the *cursed* child?"

"Nope. That's Harry Potter's son," Bellamy objected with a mocking smirk. "My name is Bellamy. Some of my friends call me 'Belle'. But since you're *not* my friend you'd better just call me Bellamy. I'm here to avenge what you did to my mother and father!" Bellamy whipped out Astonia's hunting dagger and got into a fighting stance. Or at least, he hoped that he looked like he knew what he was doing when he chose his current stance.

Agathon looked amused, and a dark chuckle slipped past his lips. "Ah, you're here for revenge. I see. But, you cannot kill me. You're throwing your life away, boy!"

There was a steely, determined expression on Bellamy's face though. "Even so, I have to try." Bellamy let out a yell as he charged towards Agathon. In an overhead downward slash he brought the hunting dagger down on Agathon in a two-handed grip. "This is for Abigail!"

But instead of splitting Agathon's skull open the dagger impacted against an energy shield and the steel blade shattered. Jagged pieces of sharp metal went whizzing dangerously through the air and one piece sliced into the side of Bellamy's face.

At the mention of Abigail Agathon's blue eyes widened slightly, and sparkled with interest. Agathon reached out, wrapped his hand around Bellamy's throat, and lifted the young man up off the floor. "Abigail? Do you mean Abigail Snow?"

Bellamy raised his hands and tried to pry Agathon's hand off of his throat while giving the sorcerer a hateful glare. "Yes," he spat.

Agathon grew intrigued. "How do you know Abigail? She should still be a yeti. I haven't sensed that she's broken the curse."

"Yeah, she's still a yeti," Bellamy confirmed nonchalantly. "So?"

Agathon's eyes narrowed suspiciously at the bookworm. "If she's still a hideous monster then why are you here trying to kill me for her sake?"

"That's none of your damned business, Lockhart!" Bellamy snapped.

"Oh, but it *is* my business because I am the one who set all of this in motion," the sorcerer snarled in Bellamy's face as he searchingly gazed into Bellamy's eyes. "I wonder if the selfish, narcissistic Abigail would come to rescue you, from me? That would surprise me greatly because in the end Abigail only cares about *herself*!"

Bellamy noticed the crazed glint in the sorcerer's eyes, and gave Agathon a pitying look. "Why are you even doing this?"

"I have no need to explain myself to you, boy," Agathon snapped as he increased the pressure around Bellamy's throat so that he began to see black spots in front of his vision. "Now, let's get you comfortable while we wait for Abigail to arrive. If Abigail doesn't show up by sunset to rescue you then…you shall die." A sinister smile spread across the sorcerer's face.

Bellamy's eyes flared in alarm, and he renewed his struggles with extra vigor, but the pain in his throat was too much and he sank into unconsciousness.

***

It took almost an entire hour for Abigail, Astonia, Louise, and her stone servants to gather up all of the broken pieces of Kristal's body and place them into burlap sack. Abigail was so lost in her grief over Kristal's death that she barely noticed that Astonia was helping them.

Once Abigail put the last piece inside the bag she tied it closed, stood up, and handed the bag to Jett. Jett nodded at her in silent thanks. Abigail glanced around looking for Bellamy, and it was only then that she noticed his absence. "Where's Bellamy?" Her lips dipped into a frown.

Everyone shrugged as they glanced around for any sight of the bookworm. But when Abigail's gaze landed on Astonia - the

Huntress immediately looked incredibly guilty. The yeti narrowed her silver eyes at the lovesick woman. "Astonia, where's Belle?"

Astonia lifted her shoulders in a careless shrug. "He…left."

"Left?" Abigail blinked. "Left where…?"

"I don't know, okay?" Astonia huffed before flipping her long black hair over her shoulder. "All he said is that he was going to go and end this. He took the enchanted mirror with him, and he also borrowed my shotgun and my hunting dagger."

An alarmed look fell over Abigail's face. Bellamy…he couldn't have. Had he gone to face the sorcerer Agathon all on his own? Her frown deepened at the outrageous thought. What the hell? He was no match for a *sorcerer*!

And had Bellamy really left with the intention of *killing* Agathon? That didn't seem like the kindhearted Bellamy at all. Kristal's unexpected death…must have been the last straw that broke the camel's back. Obviously, Bellamy could no longer bear watching his loved ones suffer at the hands of Agathon's curse.

And Bellamy must have known Abigail would have wanted to go with him. But he'd wanted to spare her from getting her hands dirty.

Abigail nibbled on her claw as she thought about Bellamy's intentions. The very idea of Bellamy facing off against the sorcerer Agathon all on his own caused a chill to crawl up Abigail's spine. *He'll be killed.* She had to go and save him because…

Life without Bellamy wasn't worth living.

She loved him.

"Whatever it takes, I'll get him back somehow," Abigail said aloud with a determined expression on her face.

"But you don't even know where he went," Astonia started to object. "How will you be able to find him without the magic mirror?"

Abigail removed the chain that held the Philosopher's Stone from around her neck, and held it so that it dangled from her hand in front of her. "With this. When the sorcerer Agathon turned me into a yeti he turned me into a magical creature of legend. That's why I can do *this*." Abigail closed her eyes and concentrated, visualizing Bellamy in her mind. The Aurora Borealis quartz began to spin and then it swung out and held its position while pointed in a certain direction.

Abigail's silver eyes snapped open and she glanced down at the stone. "Bellamy...is that way." She smirked.

"Wow." Astonia looked impressed. "Well, good luck, yeti girl. Go get your man!" She tossed Abigail a wink.

A flash of surprise crossed Abigail's face and her cheeks burned. "He's not mine!"

"Uh huh. Sure." Astonia didn't sound at all convinced. The two girls started laughing then. Once they managed to get their laughing under control Astonia spoke, "Do you know how to ride a snowmobile?"

***

Astonia ordered one of the Hunters to lend Abigail their snowmobile and as soon as she'd mounted it, Abigail took off into the forest. She drove as fast as she could, zigzagging through the trees. The closer she got to her destination the more predators she saw out of the corner of her eyes, watching her warily through the trees as she passed through their forest. She wondered if the animals could sense how angry she was, and if that was what was keeping them at a distance.

One wolf had gotten a little too close to the snowmobile and Abigail turned her head, opened her mouth and roared loudly in its face, causing it to yelp in fear and immediately run off with its tail between its legs. Any animal that got too close to the snowmobile was given similar treatment.

When Abigail finally broke through the edge of the forest and entered the clearing where the large oak tree stood, the first thing she noticed was the abandoned snowmobile that must have been the one Bellamy had borrowed from Astonia.

Abigail pulled her snowmobile right beside the other one, turned the engine off, and dismounted. She began to head towards the gigantic oak tree, and blinked when she noted that it was the same tree from the dream she'd had about Bellamy. Her...*erotic* dream about Bellamy.

The reminder of that dream caused her cheeks to flame and take on a magenta hue. She hoped Bellamy was alright. Because if he weren't - there would be hell to pay.

Abigail tried to approach the front door of the tree house as silently as possible, but the snow crunched loudly beneath her heavy footfalls causing her to wince. Once she'd reached the front door she discovered that it was already slightly ajar and simply pushed it open.

Because the sorcerer Agathon was expecting company this time around he was currently seated on a lush armchair upholstered with dark blue and gold silk that was facing the front door. His pose was relaxed, and he held a glass of brandy in his right hand, which he was swirling slowly. A bemused smile curled his thin lips as Abigail opened the door and stepped inside his home.

"Well, well, well, you actually came to rescue him." Agathon's golden eyebrows rose to his hairline. "Color me surprised. I didn't expect you to actually come, Abigail. But it's a good thing for him that you did. I planned to kill him at sunset!" The sorcerer chuckled darkly.

"Agathon," Abigail said through gritted teeth. "Where's-?" She glanced to the side and that's when she spotted Bellamy who was currently shirtless and chained to the wall. Thick shackles were around his wrists that were attached to long chains that were secured to the wall so that Bellamy's arms were raised above his head, and spread.

Abigail sucked in a surprised breath at the unsettling sight. The last time she'd seen Bellamy he hadn't been in very good shape after his fight against Gaston. There had been blood and bruises on his face. Now Bellamy's injuries were even worse. Ugly bruises were forming around his neck, and angry, red welts covered Bellamy's bare chest. Had Bellamy been whipped? *What the fu-?*

"What did you do to him?" Abigail growled, bearing her fangs at the sorcerer.

"The boy needed to be disciplined," Agathon drawled. "I couldn't let him off so easily for having tried to shoot me in the back. Like a coward."

Bellamy looked up at Abigail, and smiled weakly. "Hey, Abigail." But then his expression turned concerned. "Abigail, you have to get out of here. Agathon is too powerful."

Abigail wasn't really listening to the words that were coming out of Bellamy's mouth; however, her silvery eyes were pinned to his injuries. She began to tremble from the rage she was feeling. "You *hurt* him. You hurt *my* Bellamy!" The yeti spun to face the sorcerer, a fierce gleam in her eyes. She let out a load roar and beat her chest before charging towards Agathon with murderous intent.

Agathon just chuckled at her. "How foolish." Abigail reached Agathon and punched. Her fist collided against Agathon's magical shield, and Abigail made a growling sound of frustration. Abigail raised her fists and began to beat against the shield again and again.

Agathon arched an eyebrow at her futile attacks. "That won't work. The shield is magical. Only *magic* can break it." His tone was condescending.

Abigail smiled, revealing her fangs, roared, and continued to pound her fists against the energy shield with renewed energy.

That's when the strangest thing happened.

Cracks began to form on Agathon's energy shield and began to spread. A befuddled expression formed on the sorcerer's face as he watched what was happening. "This…can't be possible."

"Oh, it's possible!" Abigail countered. "You turned me into a *magical* creature, Agathon. I possess magic!" Seconds later, Agathon's magical shield shattered, and there was nothing standing between the yeti and the sorcerer.

Abigail smiled sharply, revealing her fangs again, before she reached out and grabbed Agathon's leg. She lifted the sorcerer up off the floor and smashed him down on the floor repeatedly.

Bellamy cringed, having sympathy pains as he watched the sorcerer getting slammed into the floor. "*Ohhh*, Hulk Smash. That's gotta hurt." He smirked.

Agathon groaned from his prone position on the floor at Bellamy's feet. Abigail snorted and let go of Agathon. Agathon turned his head and spat out a tooth. He pushed himself up off the floor and stood on shaky legs. The sorcerer had never been angrier in all his long life. He'd never been so humiliated.

"It's *over*, Agathon," Abigail stated firmly. "Now, use your magic to break the curse on both of us!"

Agathon smiled, showing his bloody teeth. "You actually think that I would break the curse after the way you just treated *me* - the Great Sorcerer Agathon! Think again." Agathon glanced at Bellamy and a positively evil idea came to mind. "I can tell you're fond of him, Abigail. But love can be a destructive force.

Especially, in that monstrous form of yours. I wonder how your inner yeti will react to falling *obsessively* in love with Bellamy?"

Abigail's brow furrowed in confusion. "What the hell are you talking about, Agathon?"

Bellamy began to panic as he began to realize just what Agathon had in mind. *Oh shit.* He began to struggle against his restraints. "Don't do it, Agathon!" A look of horror had settled over Bellamy's face.

"It's a shame you'll never get to find out how he feels about you," Agathon cackled before grabbing Bellamy's glasses and yanking them off his face. He threw them to the floor and stomped on them with his boot with a resounding *crack*.

Bellamy couldn't help it - he shot Abigail an alarmed look.

Abigail looked at Bellamy and their eyes met. Without his glasses on Abigail could see that Bellamy's eyes were a perfect sky-blue color and he was also incredibly handsome.

"Um, hello, Earth to Abigail," Bellamy said when Abigail just remained staring at him for several seconds while remaining perfectly still. "Please don't tell me you've fallen madly in love with me? I don't think I could survive mating with a yeti." He shuddered at the visual image that produced in his mind.

Abigail snapped out of her stupor, and blushed at Bellamy's perverted words. "W-What? Why would I be in love with a nerd like you! Pu-lease." She waved her hand dismissively through the air.

Agathon looked stumped. "Huh. This…usually works. How is the curse not activating?"

Bellamy shrugged carelessly. "Hell if I know. Performance issues…it happens. There's no need to beat yourself up about it, Agathon."

"Um, there's a confession I need to make," Abigail announced with a slightly guilty look on her face.

"Oh, do tell," Bellamy prompted.

"I've already seen you without your glasses, Bellamy," Abigail revealed.

"Huh? When?" Bellamy blinked.

"After you collapsed from your fever when you'd first arrived at my mansion and I took care of you," Abigail began to explain. "Your glasses were kinda in the way so I took them off for a moment to set the cool towel on your forehead. There have been other times too…"

"Huh?" Bellamy gaped at the yeti with his jaw hanging slightly open out of his shock. "So the curse never worked on you…from the very beginning? Weird."

"Don't get me wrong," Abigail started. "You *are* handsome, but it's not like I'm going to go crazy in heat or anything."

"Good to know." Bellamy nodded to himself as a wave of relief swept over him.

Agathon was growing more and more pissed off as he listened to this silly exchange. "Bravo, Abigail. *You* won't kill Bellamy with your obsessive love. I suppose I'll just have to kill him myself as punishment for the horrible, disrespectful way you've both treated me! But first," Agathon said as he reached out with lightning fast movements and grabbed the Philosopher's Stone before ripping it off the chain hanging from around Abigail's neck. "I'll be needing *this*." Stone in hand, Agathon summoned his staff and placed the stone on its apex. Agathon pointed the scepter at Bellamy and smiled cruelly. "Say goodbye to your only friend, Abigail!" The Aurora Borealis quartz stone began to glow brighter and brighter as it pulsed with magical energy.

"No!" Abigail shouted. The yeti used her superhuman speed to place herself between Bellamy and Agathon, and stretched her arms out at her sides. "I won't let you!"

A magical blast flew out of Agathon's scepter and towards Bellamy. But it hit Abigail right in the chest instead. Bellamy watched Abigail take the hit in horror, his eyes wide. "Abigail, no! Shit."

Agathon gaped at the yeti in shock. "Why did you do that?"

A soft, sad smile formed on Abigail's blue lips. "Because…I lied. I actually *do* love him." As the yeti said these words her body began to turn into blue quartz.

Bellamy painfully dislocated his thumbs so he could get out of the shackles that were around his wrists, and finally managed to pull his hands through the bloody shackles. Bellamy moved around Abigail so that he was facing her. He watched her quickly turning to blue quartz in horror. "Abigail, no…no! Fight it, Abigail! You have magic too, don't you? Shit! I can't lose you, Abigail. Not like this!" He gripped her shoulders which had become cold and hard to the touch.

Abigail tried to speak, but her lips could no longer move.

It only took seconds for Abigail to completely turn into a statue made of blue quartz. "No!" Bellamy cried.

"Serves her right," Agathon snorted. "Foolish girl."

Bellamy ignored the sorcerer, reached out, and stroked his hand down Abigail's stone hair affectionately. "I never got to tell you...I love you too, monkey face." He leaned forward and pressed his lips against Abigail's tenderly. He felt his eyes burn when he felt how cold and hard her lips were beneath his. How...lifeless.

If this were a fairytale then his kiss would be like magical or some shit, and the curse would be broken, and Abigail would come back to life.

But the minutes ticked past mercilessly and nothing happened.

Abigail remained stone.

Bellamy pulled back and kept her face cupped in his hands. He pressed his forehead against hers. A choked sob slipped past his lips, and a single tear leaked out of Bellamy's eyes. The tear trailed down his cheek, fell, and landed on the very tip of Abigail's nose.

Bellamy sank to his knees as a wave of hopelessness crashed over him. "Why?" he demanded brokenly as he looked up at the sorcerer Agathon with a haggard, defeated expression on his face.

Agathon stared down at the broken young man and figured he'd been punished enough. "I suppose I owe you that much. I fell in love once, and it was with Abigail's mother, Holly Snow. She was already married, at the time. I'd been in a battle against another sorcerer. We'd fought over possession of the Philosopher's Stone, and I was gravely injured. I arrived at Snow Mansion seeking shelter, protection, and medical assistance.

"It was Holly who answered the door, and she decided to let me in and even cared for me herself despite having servants who could have handled the task. She saved my life, and I fell in love with her. It wasn't very hard. She was so very beautiful and kind. However, I was unnerved to discover that Holly was sickly, dying.

"I immediately tried to discover a way to save her. I thought that I could guide her husband, Aspen, in the right direction, and provided him with books on alchemy. I intended to have him eventually use the Philosopher's Stone to save her life. I didn't expect Aspen to become skilled enough to create his own artificial Philosopher's Stones, nor did I expect him to create a potion, which mimicked the elixir of life and give it to Holly.

"The elixir was a failure and turned Holly into stone. I tried to use the power of the Philosopher's Stone to turn her back to normal, but I failed. My love for her was unrequited so it wasn't powerful enough to restore her to her former state. Aspen probably could have used the Philosopher's Stone to awaken her, but I was a jealous man.

"*I* wanted to be the one to save her, and by the time I realized my foolishness it was already too late because Aspen drank the same failed elixir and joined Holly. Abigail became the owner of the estate. Not long after, I tested Abigail to see whether or not she was capable of a love pure and selfless enough that could activate the power of the Philosopher's Stone to save her parents.

"Unfortunately, Abigail failed my test, and in my anger and disappointment I cursed her. The only way to break the curse would be for Abigail to sincerely fall in love with someone, and for that person to love her in return." Agathon waved his hand in Abigail's direction. "Apparently, her love for you wasn't sincere, Bellamy. Or maybe it's *your* love that isn't sincere."

"Fuck you," Bellamy snapped hotly. He pushed himself up off the floor and faced Agathon. "I don't think you know anything about true love, Agathon. Because I *know* Abigail meant what she said, and I meant what I said. I love Abigail…*in whatever form she takes*."

At that moment, the blue quartz statue of Abigail began to glow brightly. The blinding light caused Bellamy and Agathon to both shield their eyes. This was followed by a shattering sound, as the statue broke apart. "Abigail, no!" Bellamy shouted as he squinted into the light. He watched pieces of quartz fall and hit the floor, and the image of Kristal's body shattering flashed through his mind.

But when the light finally died down, there wasn't just a pile of broken blue quartz pieces at Bellamy's feet. A glowing female figure was standing before him where the statue had been only seconds before. *What the hell?*

When the glow dimmed the woman was revealed to be completely naked. She was absolutely stunning. The girl was tall, willowy with nice curves, pale skin, and long white hair. Did Bellamy already mention that she was naked? When the woman opened her eyes it was to reveal gray eyes framed by long, dark lashes.

Bellamy took a step forward towards the woman and stared into her eyes searchingly. He saw recognition and other emotions swirling in her gray gaze. "Abigail?" Bellamy questioned softly.

Abigail's lips quirked into a wry smile. "No shit, Belle."

A grin split across Bellamy's face, and he beamed at her. He was so fucking happy. "You're...you again. I mean, you were always you, but now you're like hot. Supermodel hot. Does that sound superficial? Because really, babe, you are rockin that new body of yours."

A pink tinge rose to Abigail's pale cheeks.

Bellamy caught sight of his discarded winter coat on the floor and quickly picked it up before handing it to Abigail. "You'd better put this on. You're way too distracting...like that. Plus, Agathon is totally checking you out right now and it's creepy as fuck."

Agathon startled at his name and his brow furrowed. He looked stumped. "But...how is this possible?"

"You said it yourself, pal. The power of true love and all that jazz. Abigail and I *love* each other, and it's *sincere*." Bellamy gave Abigail a fond look before turning his attention to the sorcerer once more. "On that note, we don't really need *you* anymore, do we? Not now when we have the power of true love on our side."

"What are you-?" Agathon started.

Before the sorcerer could properly react, Bellamy yanked the staff out of Agathon's hands and looked at Abigail who'd finished putting on the coat. "Let's do this, together, babe."

"Right." Abigail placed her hand on the staff along with Bellamy. Together they pointed the scepter at Agathon.

Agathon looked scandalized before his expression turned incredulous of their actions. "No! What are you doing?" He started to stalk towards them.

Bellamy smirked. "Saving the world, maybe? Well, at least Yeti Town. We're going to give you a little taste of your own medicine, Agathon. And your curse won't break unless someone decides to love you. Now, babe!"

Bellamy and Abigail concentrated and sent a rainbow colored blast of magical energy flying into Agathon's chest.

"You can't do this to me!" Agathon objected as he tried to approach them even as the blast of energy was hitting his chest. "I am the Great Sorcerer Agathon!" He cried, reaching out to grab the staff, his cloak billowing out behind him dramatically. Agathon started to turn into gleaming, white marble. "No!" He cried and in seconds he'd been completely turned to stone.

Bellamy walked around the white marble statue that was now the sorcerer Agathon and inspected it curiously. "Well, he's no Michelangelo's David, but...some lonely, nerdy chick who likes romance novels may end up falling in love with him even though he's a statue. What do you think, babe?" He turned to give Abigail a questioning look.

"So it's 'babe' now?" Abigail arched an amused eyebrow at Bellamy. "What happened to 'monkey face'?"

Bellamy pouted. "Well, I thought that would be pretty obvious."

"But I *like* the nickname 'monkey face'," Abigail whined petulantly.

"Monkey face it is then." Bellamy pulled Abigail close and kissed her with tender, adoring passion. A few minutes later they pulled back from each other, breathless. "We should probably head back to the estate. I bet that with the Philosopher's Stone, and the power of our true love we can turn all of your servants back to normal." There was a twinkle in Bellamy's blue eyes.

His eyes were so...blue. Abigail was having a hard time getting used to being able to see Bellamy's eyes so clearly now that he wasn't wearing those awful, nerdy glasses. "All...except for Kristal," Abigail said sadly as she suddenly remembered the poor girl's fate.

"Yeah," Bellamy agreed in an equally somber tone.

Abigail nibbled her lower lip. "I do hope we'll be able to save the others though."

"Well, there's only one way to find out." Bellamy held his hand out to Abigail. "Shall we?"

Bellamy and the now human Abigail hopped onto one of the snowmobiles, and drove back to Abigail's estate. By the time they were crossing the frozen lake no one was there. Bellamy deduced that everyone must have already returned to the mansion.

With slightly heavy hearts, Bellamy and Abigail walked up the steps to the front door and knocked. Jett opened the door for them and gawked at Abigail - human once more. "Milady, you've returned!"

"Yes. So I have, Jett," Abigail said somberly.

Jett just smiled though. "There's something Astonia would like to show you, Milady."

Abigail gave her butler a questioning look. "Astonia? She's still here?"

"Right this way, Milady." Jett led them into the ballroom where for some reason the entire household staff had been gathered. They were all standing around in a circle and obviously blocking *something* or perhaps *someone* from view.

Abigail instantly grew nervous by their strange behavior. "What is it?" The crowd of servants began to part for Abigail and Bellamy to reveal a very smug looking Astonia.

"Hey, guys, you won't believe what I decided to do." The Huntress tossed a small plastic tube into the air and caught it. "Take a look at this." Astonia stepped aside to reveal-

"Kristal!" Abigail burst out in a mixture of shock and surprise. "But...how?"

"Super Glue," Astonia explained in a haughty tone. She was obviously quite pleased with herself. "And let me tell you, it wasn't easy. Everyone helped. As soon as we placed the very last piece all the cracks disappeared. She hasn't moved or talked yet though. So the rest is up to you two, I guess. At least there's hope. Good luck."

Abigail looked at Bellamy questioningly. Bellamy nodded at her. Standing directly in front of Kristal, Abigail and Bellamy placed their hands on the sorcerer's staff together and pointed the Aurora Borealis quartz at Kristal.

The duo concentrated on their love for each other, and for Kristal, as well as their wish for her to return to normal. A rainbow colored light shot out of the stone and hit Kristal's body. The blue quartz statue glowed brightly before it exploded, to reveal-

Kristal whole and human once more, and dressed in the frilly pink dress she'd had on the day she'd been turned into a statue. Kristal blinked wide brown eyes open, and then looked down at her peachy colored hands in astonishment, opening and closing her hands into fists. "Oh my God, I'm human again!" Everyone that was able to have tears in their eyes had them there as they watched the scene unfold.

"Kristal!" Abigail went over to hug the girl fiercely.

"My daughter!" Jett exclaimed as he joined in on the hug.

"Ow, *Dad*," Kristal complained in a whining tone. "You're crushing us!" She started to giggle.

Jett pulled back, immediately apologetic. "I'm sorry, Kristal." Kristal grew teary eyed, and sniffled as she gazed upon her father and Abigail seemed to know why.

"Let's turn your dad back to normal next," Abigail suggested as she reached out to pat the girl's head in a soothing gesture.

Kristal nodded.

Right after that Bellamy and Abigail turned Jett from a stone statue back into a human once more. As soon as Jett was back to normal he embraced his daughter, and then gave Bellamy a fist bump.

Bellamy and Abigail used the power of the Philosopher's Stone to turn all the servants back into their human forms next until there were only two statues remaining inside of the mansion - the statues of Abigail's mother and father, Holly and Aspen Snow.

"I don't think I can do this," Abigail objected as Bellamy guided her towards the foyer with his arm wrapped around her shoulders for support. "What if it doesn't work?" She started to wring her hands together nervously. "What if they're really just statues?" Abigail's breathing was beginning to become a bit irregular as she began to panic.

Bellamy squeezed her shoulder in a comforting gesture. "Hey, relax. I'm right here with you, monkey face. And no matter the outcome…we all love you."

Abigail took a deep breath then to steel her nerves, and let it out slowly. "Alright, I can do this. Let's do this. Together." The couple placed their hands on the staff and pointed it at the two statues. They concentrated on their love for each other, and Abigail concentrated on her love for her mother and for her father who she'd recently forgiven. After all, Aspen had also been a victim of the bitter and jealous sorcerer Agathon.

A huge blast of rainbow colored light hit the two statues at the same time and engulfed them. The statues began to glow brightly and then they shattered. Abigail squinted through the light and stone dust cloud that slowly began to clear. "Mom? Dad?"

"Abigail?" "Abbey?"

Abigail's eyes widened at the sound of her parents' voices, and tears sprang to her gray eyes. She covered her mouth with her hand, and just stared as her mother and father appeared clearly.

Placing a hand on the small of her back, Bellamy pushed Abigail towards her parents. The heiress stumbled forward. "Mom? Dad?"

Her parents nodded. They both had bittersweet smiles on their faces, and tears in their own eyes. "Mom! Dad!" Abigail rushed over to them and embraced them fiercely.

Bellamy wiped a tear from his eye as he watched their little family reunion. He decided to go join them with a loud, "Group hug!"

"Uh, who is he?" Aspen questioned in an amused tone.

"Mom, Dad, I would like you to meet my boyfriend Bellamy DeWinter," Abigail introduced with a proud note to her voice.

Bellamy was immediately incensed. "*Boyfriend*? After everything that's happened I thought you'd at least introduce me as your fiancé. After all, it was the power of my love for you that helped to turn your parents back to normal, monkey face. You couldn't have broken the curse without my help."

Holly's brow furrowed in confusion. "What curse?"

"To make a long story short your daughter was turned into a yeti by an evil sorcerer named Agathon. Only true love could break the curse, and luckily I fell in love with your daughter even though she was a hideous monster. Wait, that came out wrong. *Cute* monster." Holly raised an eyebrow at Bellamy and he instantly began to backpedal. "Not that I'm into furries or anything. Because that'd be weird. Yeah, I'm just going to shut up now." Bellamy rubbed the back of his neck awkwardly.

"Well, he's certainly…interesting," Holly said with a small smile.

Abigail and her parents laughed. "It sounds like one hell of a story you need to tell us, Abbey," Aspen said, and slipped his arm around Holly's waist protectively.

Abigail was pleased to note that her father no longer had that crazed gleam in his eyes. This was probably due to her mother's presence at his side.

"Let's discuss it over tea, shall we?" Holly suggested.

"I'm still invited to that tea, right?" Bellamy asked tentatively. "I haven't like completely weirded you guys out yet?"

Abigail shook her head ruefully at her fiancé. "I'm in love with a total nerd." She sighed.

"Love you too, monkey face," Bellamy quipped, his blue eyes sparkling with love and mirth as he gazed at Abigail. And dang she was so frickin hot now. That wasn't superficial, right? Because *daaaang*. He was looking forward to making certain erotic dreams a reality. He'd definitely make sure he had his 'happy ending'. Wink, wink. Nudge, nudge.

Bellamy flushed at his lewd thoughts and quickly amended in his mind, *I mean, I'll make sure we live happily ever after.* And on that note, he pulled Abigail into his arms and kissed her with great passion.

THE END

Author's Note: The Handsome and the Yeti audiobook is coming soon! Also, keep an eye out for the next installment in the "Genderbent Fairytales Collection" where all the classic fairytales will be genderbent! More coming soon!

Questions? Feedback?

http://www.facebook.com/authorkurokonekokamen

Twitter @KurokonekoKamen

Check out the Handsome and the Yeti Facebook page:

http://www.facebook.com/handsomeandtheyeti

Please visit the cover artist's webpages:

http://keelerleah.deviantart.com

http://www.facebook.com/keelerleah

Visit KuroKoneko Kamen's artist page:

http://kurokoneko-kamen.deviantart.com

Please support the author by leaving her a review

Thank you!

Printed in Great Britain
by Amazon